Honey for the Bears

BOOKS BY ANTHONY BURGESS

IN NORTON PAPERBACK

A Clockwork Orange
The Wanting Seed
Honey for the Bears
The Doctor Is Sick
The Eve of Saint Venus
The Long Day Wanes
Nothing Like the Sun
Re Joyce
Tremor of Intent

ANTHONY BURGESS

Honey for the Bears

W · W · NORTON & COMPANY
New York · London

Library of Congress Cataloguing in Publication Data
Burgess, Anthony. 1917–
  Honey for the bears.
  I. Title.
PZ4.B953Ho 1978 [PR6052.U638] 823'.9'14 78-15620

ISBN 0-393-31441-3

W. W. Norton & Company, Inc.
500 Fifth Avenue, New York, N.Y. 10110
www.wwnorton.com

W. W. Norton & Company Ltd.
Castle House, 75/76 Wells Street, London W1T 3QT

PRINTED IN THE UNITED STATES OF AMERICA

2 3 4 5 6 7 8 9 0

To

Maurice Edelman

В Петербурге мы сойдёмся
снова,
Словно солнце мы похоро-
нили в нём.

O. Mandel'shtam

*(We shall meet again in Petersburg, as
though there we had buried the sun.)*

Part One

One

'AND what,' asked (loudly because of the music) this patrician parrot of a Tiresias from its wheelchair, skirt or trousers hidden by tartan rugs, 'might be your purpose in going to St Petersburg?'

'Tourism,' lied Paul Hussey. The music, after its climax of shocking brass, settled to vapid rocking waltzing fluting. A most clerkly man behind the wheelchair, with eyes that the music seemed to make water, got in quickly with:

'It's the same with homosexuals. People always expect them to be at it all the time. Well, it stands to reason they can't. I don't see how they can be homosexual when they're asleep or in the W. It's the same with Communism.'

'That will do very well, Madox,' said his master or mistress indulgently. The face was trenched and riven, as by a killing life of metaphysical debauchery. That was it, decided Paul: a head that philosophy had unsexed, some final Shavian achievement. He had seen a head like it on television newsreels: an old proud eagle squatting in Whitehall among students, banning the Bomb. But these oyster-coloured eyes surveyed with disdain the scruffy redbrick layabouts who nearly filled the Cultural Saloon, the nose twitched at them.

'If you'll allow me, Doctor,' said Madox. The issue

7

of sex was still in doubt. 'Not everything you do has to be political,' Madox insisted. 'Like those diplomats that went over that time. For all anybody knows they might have gone over because of their stomachs. In Russia,' he told Paul, 'nobody gets indigestion. Everything cooked in the best butter. A worker's country,' he explained.

'That will be quite enough, Madox,' said the ancient creature. It drew out from under the rugs an arthritic hand that flashed gold and stones in the Baltic light, stiff and brittle as an antlered ringstand, an unlighted cigarette trembling between two tines.

Madox flicked a lighter aflame. At once the music lashed into some final bars of Soviet triumph, marching and kissing in Red Square, though buried deep beneath the cheap brash crashes was an ineffable Slavonic sadness. After the last thump the record hissed and clicked off. The students (an outward-bound goodwill mission called The Little Sputniks) clapped. The delegation (homeward bound) of Soviet musicians clapped. The composer, Stepan Korovkin, a plumber-like man, clapped.

'Clapping himself,' commented the smoking ringed ancient. 'Just like some circus chimp. And the music was precisely circus music. You will *never* civilize these people.'

The handsome interpretress said, 'Comrade Korovkin will now describe his aims in writing this symphony, Number Fourteen in D, whose finale you have just heard, and how far it is officially considered that those aims have been fulfilled.'

Her English accent was impeccable, but the ancient snorted smoke at it. Comrade Korovkin stood up, beamed, and started a genial harangue like his own music. He was expert, loud and fluent, a shop steward. The ancient said to Paul:

'Even now it might not be too late. There are plenty of prematurely retired colonial administrators bored with Tunbridge Wells and Eastbourne. Believe me, they would soon lick these people into shape.'

Madox was chewing his nails.

'Shhhh. Turn it up,' whined some students.

'. . . *Domogatelstvo Sovietskyevo Chelovyeka.*' Korovkin finished his first sentence-paragraph and sat down for a breather. The interpretress said:

'Aware of my formalistic errors and grateful for the fresh enlightenment brought about by a compulsory course of self-criticism . . .' The ancient was saying:

'They are only Orientals. They have their sulks and their losing face. Believe me, I have known them since before their Lenin and Trotsky were ever heard of. They even count with bead-frames.'

'Shhhhh. Quiet. Belt up.'

'. . . Aspirations of Soviet Man. Please,' said the interpretress in a governess way, 'it is very rude to speak when somebody else is already speaking. If you do not wish to listen you should ask permission to leave the room.'

'Child,' said the old creature, handing its cigarette-end to Madox; Madox gave it one puff, as if to see if it was working, then stubbed it on a table-top. 'Child, I was here first. I was sitting peaceably here with my companion-secretary when these ill-dressed little men were brought in with their cheap jangling gramophone records. Moreover, I have been travelling this route since long before you were born. I knew St Petersburg when the Winter Palace was actually *lived in*.' The Soviet musicians were all smiling nervously; their only foreign language was musician's Italian. 'Yes,' said the ancient, 'I knew St Petersburg when it was a proud imperial city, when ball-gowns came from Paris and the gentlemen wore London-tailored morning coats.'

9

'Ah, shut it,' sneered the students. 'Drop dead.'

'Let's not have any politics,' said Madox urgently to Paul. 'I can't stand fighting. For God's sake ask a question. Something harmless.'

Paul felt a pentecostal wind blow through him; his cheeks tingled; he stood up and cried:

'How about Opiskin?' There was a shock of silence. 'Come on,' said Paul, more softly, 'tell us all about Opiskin. What we all want to know is—*what have you done with Opiskin?*' He could not for the life of him explain to himself why he had suddenly become so passionate about Opiskin. He was an antique-dealer living quietly with his wife in East Sussex, going to Russia to do someone a favour. It was not even as if he were really all that interested in Opiskin, or in music at all for that matter. He seemed to have become, for this exciting instant, a mere passive voice to be used by some numinous force supremely concerned about Opiskin. Or, of course, about freedom, whatever that was.

Opiskin, Opiskin, Opiskin. The name hissed round Paul like escaping steam. He sat down. Comrade Yefimovich got up, a bigger and more fearsome composer than Korovkin, a boiler-makers' union official perhaps. He punched the air with burly fists, bellowing. Other musicians joined in.

'Barbarism,' said Dr Tiresias. 'Can you imagine, say, Glinka behaving like that, or John Field? Those *delicious* nocturnes.'

Through the din of bellowing musicians and jeer-led students the interpretress could be heard, bravely at work, shouting a litany:

'Formalistic deviationist. Defector to Viennese serialism. Traitor to Soviet art. Misrepresenter of the Revolution. Polytonal lackey.'

Paul felt a double tap on his shoulder. Here it was,

then: irons for the rest of the voyage, inland salt after. But it was only Tatyana Ivanovna, the cabin stewardess, a sweet pudding of a girl.

'*Pozhal'sta*,' she excused herself. '*Vratch, vratch.*'

Paul, bewildered at first, then remembered. He had asked that the ship's doctor be requested to look at his wife. His wife had a rich-coloured rash on her neck. He had left her in the cabin trying to sleep away the pain while he went to the musical symposium. *Vratch* meant 'doctor'. The doctor had come. (*Vratch*: such distressing overtones of quackish fumbling.) Paul said, '*Spasiba*,' and followed Tatyana out of the saloon. Some students, male and female with arms round each other, snarled. The denunciation of Opiskin was still going on. That other doctor could be heard, loud and sexless over all:

'. . . And if this man Opiskin can get you formicating little peasants into such a lather there must quite *definitely* be a lot of good in him . . .'

Amidships, the Baltic summer blew into the administrative area. 'Москва', said a poster, and the Kremlin glowered horribly. On another, Khrushchev and little Yuri hugged each other like Dum and Dee, showing triumphant teeth to the universe. In the purser's office a Cyrillic typewriter was a-clack: tomorrow's menu. It would not take long. Breakfast: rice pudding, sliced blood sausage, red caviar. Luncheon: meat balls and macaroni. Dinner: some sorry Ukrainian peasant stew. An orange each for afters, as at some kids' treat. On yet another poster Khrushchev alone, little father, roared his head off at Manhattan's skyline.

Paul entered the cabin and found Belinda wincing in her bunk. A beautiful girl in ear-rings, her dress cheap and ill-fitting, was painting Belinda's rash. It would not be possible to do anything about making her better dressed, not now, not directly. Her brush-strokes traced a delicate hatchwork, her lips were parted, entranced, but Belinda kept going 'Ouch'. That was because she was American. There was a nice blonde girl also present, a primary-school teacher of English from Pskov; her name was Lukerya; she had been directed to lowly ship's service to improve her accent; she surfaced from the galley occasionally to interpret. She said now:

'Here is the doctor. She is painting your wife's complaint with a healing Soviet lotion. I do not believe you have such in England. It is in general use in the Soviet Union and highly recommended.'

Paul, in an agony of concentration, said, '*Dobriy dyen, tovarishch doktor. Kak vui pozhivayetye?*'

'The doctor is very well,' said Lukerya. 'It is better you ask your wife how is she. Herself, I mean. Your lady wife,' she added. The Russians seemed to take to these feudal terms.

Paul asked. Belinda said:

'All I want is penicillin. There's some bug gotten into my blood-stream. Ask why I can't have penicillin. Ouch.' Her full breasts bounced with the jolt of pain. Lukerya visibly admired the flimsy decadent nightie, then said:

'All the time she asks for penicillin. That is because it is an English medicine. But we are on a Soviet ship and it is right we use Soviet medicines.'

'It's nothing to do with that,' said Paul. 'My wife's no Anglophile.' A good word, that, for Lukerya's notebook. 'She's a wicked plutocratic American,' he smiled. He saw the silly smile in the wash-stand mirror, an antique-dealer's smile.

'Oh,' said Lukerya, 'I did not know. I had thought your wife was an English lady.' She told the doctor; the doctor, unimpressed, said something furtive in reply. Lukerya said, 'What your wife is suffering from is deficiency, a shortage of vitamins. Vitamin deficiency, perhaps you could say. Very poor nutrition.' She smiled encouragingly. 'In the Soviet Union you will eat better.' The doctor had stopped painting and was mixing something in a glass.

'Oh no,' cried Belinda and Paul together.

Belinda said, 'Well, now I've heard everything.'

Paul: 'That's impossible. We're both very well nourished. You've only to look at us to see that.' He patted his small paunch. The porthole let in sunlight on Belinda's rich honeyed plumpness. 'It stands to reason,' he said. 'We're travelling first-class, so we don't belong to the under-privileged. The workers may be under-nourished, but not we.' He heard himself saying that, marvelling.

'Oh, Paul, you idiot,' moaned Belinda.

Lukerya told all this to the doctor. The doctor handed Belinda the glass, full of a swirling white something. ('She wants you to drink,' explained Lukerya.)

'She wants to poison me, that's what it is,' cried Belinda. 'Because I'm an American. Oh, you fool.'

'That was a joke,' said Paul unhappily, 'about the workers, I mean. And my wife's been long domiciled in England. We've been married twelve years now.' He must stop these little antique-dealer's japes.

Belinda shook her head with vigour at the medicine, her lips a tight line. The doctor shrugged sulkily, then suddenly smiled, shone as with inspiration, and turned to talk eagerly to Lukerya.

But she deigned to throw, smiling, one word at Paul, 'Allergiya!'

'Allergy? Oh, nonsense,' said Paul, but the two Soviet women were at once darting round the cabin like flames, Lukerya pushing past Paul to get to the clothes-cupboard, the doctor dragging suitcases from their hiding-places—under the lower bunk, behind the floor-length drape of the tablecloth.

'We must see,' said Lukerya, 'what clothes your wife wears. There is something she wears that is not good for her skin. Of course,' and she was already ferreting among the hanging dresses, 'there may also be poor nutrition. But we must be truly scientific in our approach. We must overlook nothing. Nothing,' she said, her nose among the capitalistic scents of Belinda's clothes, the proletarian ground-smell of woman.

The doctor was fumbling at one of the suitcases. She said, '*Otkruivayetye.*'

'She means you to open up,' said Lukerya. ('Open up.' The hammering on the door in the winter night, the brutal boots, the cropped heads, the fists. Had that happened to Opiskin?)

'I'm not sure where the keys are,' said Paul. 'Look, I object to this, I object strongly. Damn it, you're not customs officials——'

'We've had it,' said Belinda. 'It's all a trick. I don't believe she's a doctor at all, not with those ear-rings. They both belong to the secret police. I *knew* we'd be found out. Oh hell, why did I let myself be persuaded? Ouch.' She writhed as the rash, or the paint on it, stabbed her.

'The best way to allay suspicion,' said Paul, so rapidly that he was sure Lukerya would not understand, 'is to hide nothing. Call this a rehearsal for tomorrow. If they find us out, it'll be just too bad. But they can't kill us.' He took a key-ring from his back pocket and opened up the suitcase, a blue old shabby one. Lukerya came to look. Ten dozen drilon dresses, half the total consignment—daffodil, midnight, cinnamon, primrose, rose-blush, blood, peach, orange. The two women shed their Sovietness and gaped.

'These,' said Lukerya, 'belong all to your lady wife?'

'All,' he said. 'She likes to change her dresses often, you see. She sweats rather a lot. But I don't think she'd really miss a couple of them. Would you, dear?' he said threateningly to Belinda. She writhed and ouched. 'Here,' he said to the doctor. 'A present from a grateful patient.' He thrust one of the chemical dresses, seamless, classical, crimson, into her arms. She did not reject it. 'And for you,' giving Lukerya a sheath of royal purple. 'For being so kind and helpful.'

'In the Soviet Union,' said Lukerya, 'we do not have such things yet. But soon we shall have them. The important things first,' she said, handling the dress with reverence. 'Medical services and free bread and the conquest of space,' she said doubtfully. 'And then later better things than these. Though this,' she said, shaking herself out of the official dream, 'is very nice.' The doctor said something rapid and eager to her. 'She wishes to say thank you,' said Lukerya. 'This kindness,' she smiled, 'has made her, in respect of you at least, very Anglophile.'

Two

'I HAVE a presentiment,' said Belinda, still in her bunk. 'I've had it all along and I have it more than ever now. I'm sorry we came. We should never have agreed to do it. I'm sure something *terrible* is going to happen.'

She was very American in her pronunciation of 'terrible'. It was as though her notion of what was terrible had not substantially changed since her girl-hood in Amherst, Mass. For, except for the back-placed voice, the retracted phonemes, the dark L, the occasional and charming Elizabethan locution, she had become as British in speech as any Broadway *grande dame*. But 'Ouch' she went now. Pain didn't change much, either.

'But,' said Paul, 'I thought you were overjoyed at the idea of doing something for Sandra. Your friend and the widow of *my* friend. As simple as that.'

'Are you quite sure,' said Belinda, 'that no mail came aboard at Helsinki or Helsingfors or whatever they call the darned place?'

'Not for us,' said Paul. 'But it's only four days out from Tilbury.'

'She might have sent a card,' said Belinda. 'She said she'd be in touch. After all we agreed to do for her.'

Paul shook his head, uncomprehending. He was sitting by the bunk on the sole cabin chair, and on his knee was one of the few readable books in English that the ship's library possessed. (Oh God, those Londons and Cronins.) He had been reading it aloud to Belinda, but she seemed bored and distracted. She didn't much care for books, anyway, her father having been a professor of English literature, specialist in eighteenth-

century poetry, his school edition of *The Rape of the Lock*
ready for the press the day his daughter was born, hence
her name. Paul also was distracted. He felt something
he had not felt for months; namely, randy. Perhaps it
was the aphrodisiac throb of the engines, perhaps the
enforced indolence, most likely the many vodkas he had
drunk before lunch, now somehow woken up by the
tea-time glass of tea with lemon, the stone meringue
called a zephyr. The book was an immense Soviet novel
by T. S. Pugachev, all the characters (the hero a jig-
maker) Soviet Man or Woman and hence not characters at all. Soviet literature would kill itself because of
its inherent contradictions. Ah, subtle Marx, inheritor
of Europe's tragic dualisms. 'Tragic,' said Paul aloud,
'dualisms.'

'Tragic nothing,' said Belinda crossly. 'And Sandra
nothing, too. You can see people more clearly when
you're away from them. Sandra looking lovely in black,
as she thinks. Did you ever notice the dandruff? And
I've got a new idea about Sandra. I think Sandra
killed (ouch) Robert. I don't think it was heart failure
at all.'

Paul smiled indulgently. Fundamentally women
didn't really like one another; it always came out sooner
or later. But of course there was this rash. 'Such nonsense,' he soothed. 'You'll feel better soon, pipkin.' He
stroked her forearm, smooth and tepid as a new-laid
brown egg. The loveliness of so many women had
breakfast connotations. Sandra's hair, for instance: the
faintest tang of distant frying smoked bacon, very
choice. And this rash of Belinda's (an appetizing word,
somehow: rash, rasher, a rash for Russia), no better
despite the painting or because of the painting, had a
look of angry oatmeal.

'I've been thinking a lot about Sandra,' said Belinda,
'lying awake with this pain. I don't think it's nonsense

at all.' Because it took her mind off the rash, Paul let her have her head, smiling. She sat up, her face vivid. 'There was no post mortem or autopsy or whatever it is they have. Fit as a fiddle the night before, laughing in the pub, then—ouch.' The jab of agony fitted in well there. 'She takes him up a cup of tea in the morning, and then—ouch ouch.'

'Perhaps the pain means it's getting better, sweetest,' said Paul. 'Darkest before dawn.' Here in the Baltic summer there was no real dark. Pushkin had written beautifully about the white nights of northern Russia; Paul had tried to read Pushkin on that RAF course.

'It's when it itches,' said Belinda. 'It will all come out some day. I've been thinking a lot about that, being away from it. Everybody comforting poor little sweet weepy kitteny Sandra, late war widow (ouch), her husband with his DFC and dicky heart after ten days in a dinghy or whatever it was. Cardiac failure, and nobody thinks to examine the dregs in the tea-cup.'

'She called you in right away,' said Paul. 'You could have.'

'I never thought,' said Belinda. 'One doesn't do that sort of thing. She'd probably washed it, anyway. Very quickly. And, besides, she was supposed to be my friend.'

'Still is. Surely. What can have gone wrong?'

'She swore she'd send a postcard or something. She wrote it all down so carefully, the name of the boat and the addresses of the agencies and everything.'

'But all that's so *minor*, isn't it? It isn't as though we're going to be away all that long.'

'She's a false friend,' said Belinda. 'And also a murderess.'

Paul couldn't help smiling. Women were really such delicious creatures, and Belinda, pouting, her blue eyes wide, looked especially delicious. 'Well,' he said, 'if she

18

did murder him it wasn't for his money. That's quite certain. If he'd had any to leave we wouldn't be doing this.' Robert had done it the year before. A cinch, he'd said. Twenty dozen chemical fabric dresses bought wholesale at thirty shillings each, sold at fifteen roubles each to a certain P. V. Mizinchikov. Fifteen roubles at the unrealistic Gosbank rate was, say, six pounds. Total gross profit for Robert, say, one thousand and eighty pounds; net profit (deduct fare, subsistence, drinks and smokes) about one thousand. Mizinchikov's own profit in that country bloated with cosmonauts, starved of consumer goods—well, that was his own affair. But a thousand clear profit wasn't bad. The risks were nugatory; Russia was far more free and easy than, say, police-happy Britain. He was going to do it again this year. He'd died instead, in a bedroom full of drilon dresses. 'Poor Robert,' said Paul. 'His heart was very bad. Nobody wanted to know, getting ready for the next bloody lot. The RAF,' he said, with sudden English nastiness. 'That wasn't just something for British war films. It kept God's Own Country safe for a couple of years to sell us ersatz pig-meat.' The brief conventional anger whetted his desire.

Belinda, through long habit, let that slide over; Anglo-American bitching was really nothing but love-bites. 'Sandra could get round anybody,' she said. '*Dear* Sandra with her thweet lithp and that so cute finger in her mouth. I wouldn't be lying here suffering if it wasn't for Sandra.'

'You're far more attractive than Sandra,' said Paul breathily. 'She just isn't in your class, pipkin. You've nothing to worry about there at all, my dearest sweetest angelic pumpkin-pie.' Tumescence had become as easy as filling a fountain-pen. There the image ended. One got out of the habit. Ask any thirty-seven-year-old antique-dealer. One needed, say, a Saturday afternoon or Sunday morning to effect the necessary rehabilitation. But Saturday afternoon was a busy time—young married couples looking for door-knockers, older ones wanting warming-pans. And on Sunday morning Belinda and Sandra went to church together. Such good friends in a mere year of knowing each other, weekly church somehow sanctifying the friendship. It had been *so* nice, an old flying pal of Paul's coming to live in the same town, starting his unsuccessful radio-and-television shop in the next street. They'd had *such* good fun, harmless Saturday-night larks in one car or the other, country-pub bitter (even gin occasionally, if one or other had had a good week) and kisses and cuddles with swapped partners, the sort of thing considered only decent among people of their class, educated shopkeepers. And now Robert's war had caught up with him and he was dead and cremated; Sandra needed more than friendship.

'This rash is a mess,' snivelled Belinda. 'I think it's spreading. It isn't the pain that worries me so much. Ouch. It *looks* so terrible.' There it was again: Amherst, some Emily Dickinson girlhood nightmare. 'What are we going to do if it goes on? We're so far away from home.' ('Home' too: nasalized, columbine.) She went on snivelling. 'I'm sorry I ever came. And it's all for her.'

'It's your bit of a holiday,' said Paul firmly. His too. But they'd both been sea-sick while the ship was pointing north to Skagerrak. 'Didn't you enjoy Copenhagen?' he asked. A gritty wind in the Tivoli Gardens, the noon cold, the Carlsberg warm. 'Stockholm?' A becalmed Lutheran Sunday, a sea-gull torpid on the head of Gustavus Adolphus. But now he had her, in her bunk with a rash. 'My turkey,' he said. 'My living Thanksgiving.' But he was shy. He said, 'I think I'll take a shower.' They shared one, and a toilet, with the passengers next door, lugubrious Ukrainians given to midnight singing. Paul undressed very quickly and stood an instant, Western Sensual Man, in the porthole's eye. Two Swedish blonde kittens passed, exquisitely clean, giggling; they did not look in. 'Right,' said Paul, bolder now. 'The shower can wait till after. Make room.'

'Isn't that just typical of you? All these months, and then just when I've got this rash——'

'That's showbiz,' said Paul flippantly. 'That's the way the cookie crumbles. Move over.'

'But my rash. It hurts so.'

'I won't go near your rash. Pumpkin. Jumbo malt,' said trembling Paul. 'American beauty.' They had not so litanized Opiskin. And then he remembered why he had shouted up for Opiskin. It had something to do with Robert. But now was not the time for following up that thought.

She said, lying there passive, 'Right. You asked for it. Now then, I'll show you what I want.' She showed him.

'Oh,' he said. 'Good God.' It was something so acroamatical, so exotically tortuous a refinement, so remote from his liberal enough conception of a decently and considerately embellished (for he had taken trouble to learn; he had read the available literature) escalier to venerean ecstasy, that he took immediate fright. More, the vodka, the lemon tea, the rocky zephyr, asserted themselves in a new rôle; he didn't feel at all well. Where had she got all this from? It couldn't be from books, she didn't read books, not even the erotica that sometimes appeared in job-lots at auctions. It could hardly be from mere talk. A fish of hardly conceivable size and ugliness shot up from the whirlpool and swam into his home waters to wallow. (Ugliness? But the fish had Robert's face. No, that was wrong, that was stupid.) He said, 'Incredible.' She said:

'Oh, go away. Go on, get out. Beat it. Leave me alone.' And she rolled on to her side away from him, groaning, trying to burrow into the bulkhead.

He sat naked on the edge of the bunk, shocked, puzzled, amused, shocked, intrigued, puzzled, jealous, disgusted, abashed. And for some reason the voice of a stranger came into his mind (a customer; he'd bought an ivory back-scratcher) saying, 'A first-hand knowledge of the more efficacious modes of erotic stimulation.' He turned to Belinda, full of wonder, but she'd pulled the sheet over her head.

He patted, wondering, the warm sheeted bundle at an arbitrarily selected spot and she shrieked, muffled, 'Ouch!' Then she appeared, naked and blazing, sitting up. 'My rash, you goddamned idiot! Men are the clumsiest, most insensitive——'

The cabin-door, which Paul had forgotten to lock, swung open breezily and Yegor Ilyich stomped in. He was in charge of the first-class dining saloon but seemed to have no rank in the mercantile marine. Forbidden by the régime to be servile, he found a family relationship the only one possible with his passengers. So he could come bouncing in now without ceremony, grin with pleasure at his Uncle Pavel's total nakedness, raise a finger at Belinda's glowing torso and go 'Aha' as she disappeared under the sheet. He was babyishly handsome with a very red Stuart nether lip, his hair sleek with Brylcreem, smelling of Max Factor after-shave, his evening dinner jacket (he had one also for mornings) a well-cut Burton or John Collier. He was far too smart to be a good advertisement for Soviet Russia. As for the system, he seemed not really to understand it. He had shown Dyadya Pavel a photograph of his family round a Christmas crib; he had once performed, in the dining saloon, an obscene mime of Khrushchev, whom he called *Bolshoi Zhevot* or 'Big Belly'; he thought sputniks

22

and vostoks a waste of public money; the most notable
achievements of the West he considered to be Gordon's
Gin, Princess Margaret, drip-dry shirts, stock-car racing, Mr Harold Macmillan. He now said, 'Dinner ten
minute. You dress quick,' coming over to slap Dyadya
Pavel's bare thigh. He pulled the sheet down as far as
Belinda's shoulders and said, 'You stay here doctor say.
I bring you in cabin. What I bring? I bring red caviar,
tin crab, *oguryets* in sour cream, black bread.' While
Paul drew on his underpants, Yegor Ilyich, very much
a member of the family, opened up the clothes-cupboard and took from among the dresses a bottle of
Soviet cognac. A couple of glasses he considered his
visitor's due. He poured generous slugs for himself and
Paul, saying, 'Your wife not drink. Doctor say always,
"*Nye kurit' i nye pit'* "': not smoke not drink. Us only.' He
clinked with Paul and toasted, '*Za vashe zdorovye*.' Down
it went, all of it.

'*Za vashe zdorovye*,' responded Paul.

'Paul,' said Belinda sharply. 'I'm not having this.'

'You not have. We have,' said Yegor Ilyich with
ready wit, refilling the glasses.

'*Za vashe zdorovye*,' toasted Paul. Down it went, all
of it.

'*Za vashe zdorovye*,' responded Yegor Ilyich.

'It's the same every day,' complained Belinda. 'Just
tipping it down. Do they think we're made of money?
Ouch.'

'They do, they do,' said Paul. '*Za vashe zdorovye*.'

'*Za vashe zdorovye*.' Three-quarters of the bottle had
gone. Yegor Ilyich's red nether lip shone brilliantly. He
said, 'We finish now,' and drained the rest of the cognac
into the two tooth-glasses, examining them with serious
closeness to be sure the measures were equal.

'A goddamn liberty,' Belinda was saying. Yegor
Ilyich beamed at that, fraternally handing Paul his

portion, chucking the empty bottle into the waste-basket. He said:

'*Za vashe zdorovye*. Bloody peace to world.' He tipped it back and went, 'Aaaah.' His lower lip was a red wet fury.

'*Mir* bloody *miru*,' responded Paul. He felt an apocalyptical drunkenness climbing down by ropes from the roof to leap upon him, a team of heraldic apes.

Belinda was scolding, saying, 'Utter disgrace.'

Yegor Ilyich began to box Dyadya Pavel vigorously but gently, dancing in nimble shining pumps. Paul said:

'I'm not going to dinner. In one hour's time bring dinner in here. *Borshch*. Cold sturgeon. Pancakes with sour cream.'

Yegor Ilyich winked grossly, performed a bar or two of his mime of Khrushchev-with-little-girls, leapt up in an *entre-chat*, touched up, humming, the wings of his bow-tie in the mirror, blew a fat smack at Belinda, then danced out.

Paul turned to Belinda and said, 'Right. You're going to have it *my* way. The roast beef of Old England for you, you effete Yankee bastard.'

Three

HEIGHT thirty-five thousand. Fifteen miles off target area enemy night-fighters reported. A beam attack. Starboard engine on fire. Flak cut away a big chunk of port wing. Out of control (intercom dead, said rear gunner). Paul woke up startled to find himself naked and sweating on the red leather settee by the forward bulkhead. But they got home, Robert got home. And then he played his gramophone records (great heavy short-playing plates) lying fully clothed, his eyes glassy, on his bed: Brahms, Schubert, Schoenberg, Prokoviev, Opiskin, Holst, Bach, anonymous ancient plain-chant.

A measly utility ration of ship's lighting was coming in from outside. The cabin was dim and sinister (it must be very late). Paul squinted at his wrist-watch, his only stitch of clothing (no matter how intense and parachronic the abandon, he never took it off. Had there been abandon? He couldn't remember at all.) It was ten minutes to midnight. Good God. He looked across at the lower bunk and saw Belinda sleeping deeply, cosy in blankets, her face turned towards him. On the table was an untouched dinner: unleavened bread, red caviar, glazed hunks of sturgeon flanked by ranks of sour-creamed cucumber-wheels. Paul realized his grotesque thirst, then some knife-thrower saw that he was awake and threw dyspepsia at him. He craved something long, cold and gassy; the first-class bar closed promptly at midnight; he wiped himself down with a towel, dressed, combed his hair by touch, then left the cabin.

He need not have troubled to dress, he thought muzzily. The ship must have gone mad. Down the corridor a girl was mincing in high heels and nothing else. No, wait, she had some kind of white head-dress on. He followed her wagging bottom, hypnotized, to the end of the corridor. A fuller light broke on him there—the rococo stairhead, the wall-map with a snake of flame showing the ship's route, the bar-entrance to starboard, to port the library (at present a shrine to Major Gagarin). Paul now saw that the girl wore a pink plastic skin from neck to toe and, with shock, that the head-dress was an improvised nun's coif; round her wrist she swung rosary-beads, her other hand on her hip; she twitched and pouted. Laughter. Bewildered, Paul tried to take in the rest of the youth that stood around drinking, crowded out of the bar. It was a fancy-dress dance (of course; this was the last night of the voyage) and the motif of the costumes seemed to be anti-clerical—sheets for soutanes, blankets for monk's habits, back-to-front collars above nightshirts and dirty pyjamas. The men mostly showed bare leg, one or two wore athletic supporters, faces were burnt-corked and lipsticked clownishly. Paul, excusing himself, fought his way through (girl-angels in underwear with wings of cardboard, now much battered; more obscene nuns; an austere mother superior with habit slit to the thigh; a drunken young man with his own beard and a wire halo, stigmata on hands that held a glass and a bottle). He pushed into the bar (a card said: 'TONIGHT OPEN TILL ONE') and to the counter. There was not one first-class passenger to be seen anywhere; the steerage-travelling students had taken possession. He crushed in between a youth with a cross painted on his bare back and a friar naturally greasy and mean-looking, saying, 'Forgive me. A matter of urgency.'

The friar said, 'Piss off, Opiskin.'

26

'I beg your pardon,' said Paul. 'I didn't quite . . .'

'We was there,' said the friar, in a Staffordshire accent. 'We heard you sticking up for that bastard.'

'Look,' said Paul, 'I only want——'

'Yes?' said the barman, a large morose Mongol in shirt-sleeves. '*What* you want?'

'Budvar beer,' said Paul. 'Very cold.' The barman frowned. '*Ochin kholodno*,' Paul translated. The students laughed. Paul was given a warmish bottle.

The barman said, 'No glass,' and shrugged.

'Damn it,' said Paul, 'I'm a first-class passenger. I have certain rights. . . .'

The students laughed. The student with a cross on his back said, 'You're just not with it, dad. This is the classless society.'

'Is it?' Paul emerged breathless from a warm but life-saving swig. 'That doesn't seem to be reflected in the fare differentials.' The healing aeration was (arrrrr) at its work; he smiled nervously; there were a lot of these atheistical louts around; he would buy another bottle, but this time to take away. The Staffordshire friar-lout said:

'Them fooking bourgeois jaw-breakers.' And then, to someone behind Paul's back, 'Miss Travers, here's this pal of Opiskin's.'

Paul wiped from his cheek the wash of the two powerful plosives, then turned to see a scrawny woman in very late youth (a lecturer, presumably) who was ready for him, a mad eagerness behind her glasses. Here was real obscenity: the thin bare mottled pimpled legs, hairy on the inside, not the man's dirty shirt pied with smears of lipstick, the panel of a mock soap-powder carton slung from her neck with a string, its legend: 'LAMZBLUD, Wonder Washer, 3d off Large Pkt' —that was just pathetic and *vieux jeu*. In a Manchester accent Miss Travers said:

'So it's you, is it? Comrade Korovkin was really upset.

27

He had to lie down after dinner. He couldn't come and play the piano for the dance. He took a lot out of himself. The feeling is' (students in blasphemous dress were crowding behind her, their mouths open; she evidently had a large reputation for something) 'that that sort of thing doesn't really help to foster good relations. They are, after all, our hosts.'

'Oh,' said Paul, 'such nonsense. They're not giving anything away. I personally am paying them good sterling for a very indifferent return. Hosts, indeed.' He thirsted terribly again, so took another deep draught from his bottle. Seeing the eyes on him as he did this, he could see also that it might be taken as a provocative gesture.

There was a student with a cardboard mitre on, 'HAVE A BASH' scrawled across his chest. 'What,' he asked, 'are you doing going to Russia anyway, mate?' Paul had been asked that question once today already, though more genteelly. He wished its first asker were there now: he or she would make short work of these blotched impertinents. Paul said:

'That could be regarded as *my* business.'

'Ah,' said many.

'Ah,' said the boy-bishop, leering. 'Just what some of us thought. All shrouded in bloody mystery, eh? Sent out by some Yank organization most likely, fomenting racial hatred. His missis is a Yank,' he told everyone. 'Tries to cover it up by speaking posh, but she is. What's she on tonight then, eh?' he demanded, prodding Paul with a broom-handle crozier.

'You can leave my wife out of this,' said Paul, keeping the heat down but his grip on the bottle-neck.

'Watch it,' said a Church Father in the background. 'He's one of them given to violence. Last stab of a dying régime.'

'It's sods like you,' said the Staffordshire lout-friar,

28

'that undoes our work. We go out to teach our comrades a bit of the English language, like, and them to teach us their lingo, and booggers like you come along to arse things up. You believe in war, don't you? That's what it is. Not satisfied with one bloody Hiroshima but you must have hundreds of others. Oh yes. Well,' and he gripped Paul's lapels, twisting them through an arc like a steering-wheel, 'you won't find us lot fighting your dirty wars for you. Nothing but bloody trouble from your generation from first to last.' He did a right-hand-down, then released the lapels, dusting off his working-lad's hands after.

'To revert to Opiskin,' said Miss Travers. 'It was a perverse and wilful act to do what he did. I refer, of course,' she said in the tones of a WEA lecturer, 'to that abomination *Akulina Panfilovna*. Slyly sending the score off to Costoletta in Milan, and we all know Costoletta. Then Covent Garden puts it on. I suppose you were there, weren't you?' she accused. 'I should imagine you had tickets for the first night.'

'I don't even know what it is,' confessed Paul. 'I've absolutely no idea at all what it's all about.'

'*Akulina Panfilovna*,' said Miss Travers in clear Manchester monophthongs, 'is an opera. If, of course, you can call such a reactionary hotchpotch an opera. The heroine is a Leningrad prostitute. There are, of course, no prostitutes in Leningrad, Moscow, Kiev or any other Russian town or city.' She was into her WEA stride now; the debauched mock-clerics and pseudo-angels were adenoidally attentive. 'This Leningrad prostitute is meant to symbolize modern Russia. Oh, very clever,' she admitted, 'very clever the way this ambivalence is brought in. You don't know how to take her.' Somebody guffawed at that. 'Quiet, you,' snapped Miss Travers. 'Pay attention. The indomitable Russian spirit triumphing over all odds and all that jazz——'

29

'It sounds really interesting,' said Paul, really interested. 'I'm sorry I missed it. And,' he added, 'it sounds very orthodox.'

Miss Travers spat a bitter laugh at him. 'The setting was contemporary. Akulina Panfilovna was meant to be here and now, sneering at the collective society, the depraved individualist living her own life——'

'There you are, then,' said Paul.

'You shut it,' said the friar, 'when Miss Travers is talking.'

'Ambivalent,' repeated Miss Travers. 'Nothing satirical in the conception of the character, either musically or from the point of view of the libretto. Satire of the most vicious sort reserved for the State officials who are her customers——'

'And who wrote the libretto?' asked Paul. He must certainly watch out for this; he must ask Miss Travers to write down the name for him.

Miss Travers barked loud and hollow. 'Russapetov,' she said. 'Russapetov is now doing a clerking job in Okhotsk. That ought to cool him down.' She was most vindictive. Paul wondered why; she seemed to him to be a quite decent lower-middle-class Manchester woman on whom an education had been pasted. He asked:

'And what about Opiskin?'

'Look,' threatened the boy-bishop. 'You were on about that this afternoon. We want no more of that, see? If you want to do some mike-taking, do it with your own sort. Like the Yanks,' he sneered.

'You know all about Opiskin,' said the friar. 'Don't let on not to. Opiskin's your pal.'

'Was,' corrected Miss Travers. 'Opiskin is dead. As you very well know.'

'I didn't know,' said Paul. 'As I keep on telling you, I know nothing about it.' Certain images, terribly knotted, strangulated, began to be born. 'Honestly.'

'What you seemed to imply this afternoon,' said Miss Travers, 'was that Opiskin was killed.'

'And was he?' asked Paul. He was at once struck a dull head-blow by the student with a cross on his back. 'Hey,' said Paul, rubbing his head, 'I'm not having that, you know.' He raised his bottle threateningly. There was a clumsy little stampede away from him. A hundred grammes of beer shot down his sleeve. Everybody laughed, including the Mongol barman. '*You* can shut up for a start,' Paul snarled.

'There you are, you see,' said a squinting youth with an ill-improvised biretta. 'On to the poor bloody workers again.'

'I'm getting out of here,' said Paul sullenly. 'I think this whole thing is in very bad taste. On behalf of the first-class passengers, I hereby protest most strongly against this crudely offensive blasphemy. It lets us all down. Moreover, it indicates that you're all deplorably behind the times.'

'He has the gab-gift, I'll say that,' said a student who, mocked-up as a priest, clicked a little too cosily into the part. Others sulked and pouted at Paul's words.

'That was all right in the old days,' said Paul, 'this cheap sneering at the opium of the masses. Things, you'll find, are very different now in the Soviet Union. More liberal.'

'The less Soviet Union it,' said a cultured voice above the laughter. The speaker, in bulky brown blankets corded out of a dressing-gown, was Chaucer's Monk to the life; bald, beardless, no fore-pinèd ghost. Ah well; clericalism could be seen to contain its opposite, the one as old as the other. 'They must be set a good example.' Homosexual, thought Paul; undoubtedly. And then he said to Miss Travers:

'Music. Is that your line? Do you know the works of Opiskin, all of them?'

31

She nodded very gravely. 'I have (or rather had) to know them. I wrote an article for *Musika*. It was condemnatory, even then, but total knowledge must,' she said sententiously, bare horrid legs straddled, 'always precede total condemnation.' The students admired. 'What is it you want to know about?'

The images were untangling. Robert, newly grounded; himself, never winged. The Russian course at Fintry (all those plans for ever-closer liaison; why Fintry of all places?) and Robert's nerves going to pieces when that record was playing, something that happened in less than four minutes (a twelve-inch record, that was certain). 'A piece, as I remember,' said Paul, 'that was all jangly. All pianos and harpsichords and bells and xylophones. Would there be such a piece?' He frowned, trying to hear it in his head.

'There would indeed,' said Miss Travers promptly. 'That piece would be *Kolokol*, Opus 64. The rot already setting in, the ghastly bug of formalism biting him. He'd already been warned,' she said sternly, as though she herself had done the warning, 'but he persisted in experimenting with sonorities. He used the twelve-tone system, he tried microtonalism, even multilinear counterpoint of a highly chromatic kind. And this at a time when his native Leningrad was fighting for its life against the German Fascists. He gave the people nothing to inspire them. The seeds of that final treachery were already germinating.' One or two students clapped.

'What do you mean,' said the boy-bishop, 'saying that things is different now in the Soviet Union? Have you been let in there before?'

'Robert was there,' said Paul, 'last year. I mean, my friend was there.' Robert. That work by Opiskin that was all bells. Soon the final image would burst. A girl dressed as a fallen angel burst into the group before the bar—French knickers, black stockings, brassière, tattered cheese-cloth wings, her sweet young face pertly made up into a whore's. But her whiff of genuine angelic innocence seemed to turn sour the poor atheistic masquerade. She cried:

'Miss Travers, Mr Korovkin's up and playing the piano. Everybody's to go and dance.' Miss Travers said:

'*Comrade* Korovkin, dear,' and put her blunt fingertips on the girl's delectable shoulders. 'Well, well, so he's better, is he?' She gave Paul a malevolent look.

'Look,' said the boy-bishop, jerking his crozier towards Paul, 'don't we *do* this one first? Don't we fill him in to like teach him a lesson?'

'Aw,' said the Staffordshire friar, 'leave the sod to his conscience.'

'A general confession,' said the mock-priest without satire. 'We don't all dance, you see.'

For some reason it suddenly seemed to Paul right and just that he be punished. One of the two dialectical angels within him urged that it was always as well to accept punishment when it was offered. Bank statements lied: one was always really in the red; one should pay in while one could. It might help with this vague guilt about Robert, whom these louts called Opiskin; that was all right, that would do. Paul said:

'I don't mind. So long as it doesn't show too much. One ought to look one's best entering a strange city.' And he suddenly quite liked these sweating loose-mouthed youngsters. The angelic girl, like a light, shone on them and disclosed a cowering sort of innocence; they knew not what they did. Miss Travers was different, of course; Miss Travers knew. He smiled humbly.

'I reckon,' said a student who was a sort of, in Dylan Thomas's phrase, Jack Christ, 'I reckon he's not too bad of a bloke.' Pop-singer's long locks; jazzman's curly beard; a frail cross of broom-handle and walking-stick conjoined. 'What I mean is, he's willing, and that's a great deal. What I mean is, he's in the wrong but he admits it. I reckon he ought to be let go.'

'Everybody's to dance,' said the angel-child.

All things contain their opposite. The Staffordshire friar grunted and said, 'Well, if we're to go in there to have a dance—and let's be honest about it: those records they've been putting on was all right for frog-dances and going round the bloody maypole, if they have maypoles in the Soviet Union——'

'They have May Day,' said the child, and she made it sound (the diphthongs close, very good girls' school diphthongs) clean and pretty, as in an eclogue.

'. . . But not much good for aught else. I'll be honest with you,' he said boldly to Miss Travers, 'but there's some things about the Russians that are just that little bit old-fashioned——'

'Fashion,' said Miss Travers primly, 'is a very bourgeois concept.'

The friar suddenly looked very weary. 'All right,' he said, 'we'd better have us a drink before going in.' And then students, pulling out sterling from odd places in their garments, were vying with one another to buy Paul a glass of something. He settled for cognac (the statutory hundred-gramme flask) and was soon on fire with a blowlamp (though quite sexless) love. But he knew that that too contained its opposite; if he did not get back to his bunk soon he would start brawling. Still, he suffered himself to be led in a jolly anti-religious procession to the Cultural Saloon. Dancing was going on there: priest with nun, saint with martyr, friar with monk; Comrade Korovkin, beaming, hammered 'Some of These Days' in a twenties style that had nothing of conscious antiquarian whimsy about it; putting in corny riffs, he giggled not at the joke but at

34

his daring. Paul shone benevolently on the young dancers. To the friar he said:

'I still think it's in bad taste, you know, all this sort of thing. . . .' He indicated Jack Christ dancing with his cross for partner. The friar said:

'Well, if we're going to be honest, I thought so too, really. It's a question of the way you're brought up. Us lot were Unitarians, and my old man was very strict. But once one starts the rest has to follow. Otherwise they start saying you're chicken.'

'Whose idea was it, then?'

'Oh, it was that old doctor thing in the wheelchair. The one that's always going on about St Petersburg. I reckon it's what they call a *moph*. Like the Marines in that Kipling poem.'

'Good God.'

'You can say that,' said the friar passionately, 'but I *love* Kipling. He foresaw the end of everything.'

'No,' said Paul, 'I meant the other thing.'

'Oh, that. Dared us, as you might say. Wouldn't get out of the saloon when we were having the committee meeting. Said we wouldn't have the guts to do it. And now isn't here to see that we have. It's my belief—' here he dropped his voice '—my belief that it's a very high-up Soviet agent. In disguise. Watching what's going on. A very clever people is the Russians.'

Four

'I SHOULD have liked it,' said Belinda. 'I haven't danced for ages.'

That Godless ball had proved to be no dream. 'The Captain himself,' the young Dane had said, tucking into his blood sausage at breakfast, 'broke it up at two a.m.' He'd chewed, smirking with morning health and relish. Paul had seen the Captain once or twice, P. R. Dobronravov, a man about his own age with long eyes and a complicated though shapely mouth. 'It was made clear,' the Dane had continued, 'that officially the Establishment is all for Godlessness, but certain considerations of decency must be observed.' Paul had bowed his head over the cooling rice pudding. 'It was Third Officer Koreisha,' the Dane had said, a well-informed and self-satisfied young man, a travelling expert on torpedo pigs, 'who reported the shamelessness to the bridge. Having no longer any religion, the Russians are a very moral people, you see.' Paul's other table companions had been, that morning (they seemed to change at every meal), a Polish engineer who owned no necktie, his three sons, his fat wife whom, even when eating, he devoured with his eyes. This Pole had spread the rumour that Paul kept his own wife locked in the cabin.

Belinda felt better, though the rash was still angry. It was now afternoon and both were confined, like all the other passengers, to their quarters. They were gliding into the outer roads of Leningrad; the customs and immigration men were aboard. Shut in and smoking, Paul's heart apprehensive, they awaited a visitation—the knock, the boots, the uniform, the searching

36

questions in perfect English. He had filled in the form, made his false declaration; he was entering Russia as a criminal. The Russians were a very moral people.

'And,' said very smart Belinda, 'I doubt if we'll find much gaiety in the People's Paradise. It's all chess, isn't it? Chess and canteen tea.' Tea: that was always a pejorative term with her, a true daughter of Massachusetts. 'Slopping tables,' she went on, her mouth stretched to the lipstick, 'the clack of ping-pong bats in the distance. Baked beans on toast.' There they were, the old interpenetrating opposites: baked beans came from Boston; hell was her childhood, finding images from wartime England, her introduction to dirty tired Europe in her smart Red Cross uniform. She was always smart, very American in that. She'd elected to stay in England, though, a glutton for punishment, a secretary with *Time-Life* in Bruton Street until Paul married her. She just loved old things; that's how they'd met—Paul, manager for F. Tyson, The Curio Shop, in Richmond, selling her an old copper jelly-mould. It was chiefly her bit of money (inherited from her mother) that had established P. Hussey, Objects of Antiquity and Beauty, in Winchelmarsh, East Sussex. But he loved her too, very much, and not just, though she was three years older than he, as a mother or big sister. Beauty, yes; Antiquity, no: she could look as fresh as that fallen angel of last night. If Antiquity came into it at all it was in the context of pagan goddesses. 'And then a jolly sermon at ten o'clock,' she said, still lipsticking, so that all her words were prissily spread and chewed. 'The padre on duty they used to call him.' She sheathed her lipstick and stowed it in her bag. 'The boys slurping their tea quiet as they can, because of the Word of God.'

'Oh, darling,' smiled Paul, 'you know full well that's a British YMCA, *not* the USSR.' He saw her point, though: earnestness and direction; an ideology informing everything, even the taste of baked beans. On his knee he had a paperback English *Dr Zhivago*. This was his decoy, prohibited literature: on the fly-leaf he was carefully ball-pointing the title into Cyrillic characters, so that the book might not by any means be passed over. The Customs people could confiscate this and forget about the drilon dresses.

'The See See See Pee,' said Belinda, looking out on a Baltic as merry with sun as the Mediterranean. There were small craft about, sunburnt sailors waving, smiling; hammer and sickle on red wind-mad flags ceased to be grim emblems of labour and became lingam and yoni signs. In the far distance the great northern city lined the whole horizon. 'And there again,' she said. 'I suppose they'd call that a trawler. CCCP on its bows or whatever they are.' Hers was an inland family. She puzzled it out for herself—CCCP— her charming low brow frowning under her still raven widow's peak. She gave it up. 'The world,' she said, 'is melting into initials. Alphabet crackers in its soup.'

'Their C is our S,' said Paul, always eager to explain, 'and their P is our R. It stands for *Soyuz Sovietskikh Sotsialistichyeskikh Respublik*. Which means literally USSR.'

'There was a big oak back home,' she said, 'that was scarred with initials. "JBW loves LJ." Funny it should come into my mind just then like that. "BH loves S." Ah hell, what's the use?' She pouted viciously, for some reason, at the bright Baltic outside. 'That bitch,' she said, and Paul still couldn't understand the viciousness. Besides, he wanted to explain the Russian alphabet to her.

'Their pi is our pee,' he said. 'The letter, I mean.'

'I didn't ask for a letter,' complained Belinda. 'A card would have done.' And then, 'Ah hell, I'm going out. Who do they think they are, anyway, making us stick in like this? I'm going to see that man Stroganov

38

or whatever his name is. Some mail may have come aboard.' She strode energetically to the door. As soon as she opened it a female voice shouted:

'*Nye mozhna, nye mozhna!*'

'Hell, what's that she's saying?'

'She says you can't,' said Paul. 'We've got to wait in here.'

'But it's so goddamn childish.' Nevertheless she came back into the cabin, as though the corridor bristled with knouts. Frowning and restless, she lit one of her king-size cigarettes and blew smoke at Paul. 'I suppose,' she said, 'I ought some time to tell you——' Paul looked up, smiling kindly, from neatly printing the C in PASTERNAK. 'Ah hell, what's the use?' she said. And then the knock came and Paul's heart jumped. The door opened and a Soviet official walked in.

'*Dobriy dyen.*'

Paul had already suspected, from his brief experience of the sea-Russians, that here was a people he was going to have to love. Now, with the ambling in of his first land-Russian, the suspicion was confirmed. For how was it possible to hate or fear this harassed clerk in a customs uniform as ill-cut and skimpy as coolie-dress? (Of course, this was high summer; the effect of the winter uniform might be different.) He was middle-aged, lined, he had his worries; you could see him going home from them at the end of the long Soviet day, fat kisses from his wife, the samovar bubbling, the kitchen reeking of beetroot, children running to lisp their sire's return. A family man, he assessed the ages of Paul and Belinda, then decided to be their uncle. He kept his pungent *papiros* in his mouth, he smiled, he enfolded their right hands in turn in two warm paws. And then he wanted the cases opened.

'We wear all these,' said Paul, his voice tight and high. 'At least, my wife does.' The customs-man peered

39

in at the chemical dresses, nodding, spilling *papiros*-ash on to them. 'A matter of perspiration,' said Paul. '*Pot*,' he translated. Dissatisfied with that, which sounded vulgar, he tried '*Potyeniye*'.

The customs-man understood. 'Shvet,' he said.

'It's this book I'm really worried about,' said Paul, presenting *Dr Zhivago*. 'Can I bring this into the Soviet Union?'

The customs-man examined it with little interest, flicked through the pages as if looking for old tram-tickets, then handed it back. '*Mozhna*,' he said. 'Can.' Then he went back patiently, making crooning noises, to the dresses, counting them gently like some old Chinese laundry-hand.

'Oh God,' said Belinda.

And then, to his huge relief, Paul saw that the customs-man was not really interested in the dresses; he accepted Belinda's alleged hyperidrosis with rather insulting readiness. He was looking for something else. Paul frowned, puzzled, as the blunt warm Soviet fingers dug into a sponge-bag. They pincered out a full and a near-empty tube of Dentisiment.

'Ah,' in triumph. '*Narkotik*.'

'No no no,' smiled Paul, 'that's a substance for making loose false teeth stick to the . . . What I mean is, I have these four bottom false teeth here in the middle, look, and what with the shrinking of the gums, you see . . .' The Dentisiment advertisement had been rather more coherent; the customs-man looked not at all convinced. 'Denture,' said Paul, showing. '*Ryahd zubof*. That stuff is a sort of *klyey*, if that's the word, for loose *ryahd zubof*.' Belinda began to laugh, showing teeth all her own. 'It was for you I lost them,' cried Paul hotly. That was true. Borrowing that bicycle that time on their French holiday to go and get the doctor because she said she had appendicitis and then wheeling smack (wrong

•side of road) into a Renault. It was he who'd needed the doctor; her appendicitis turned out to be only wind.

'*Narkotik,*' persisted the customs-man.

'*Nye . . .*' Paul said, and went through the motions of lathering. '*Nye . . .*' he said, clenching his teeth and shaking his fist at mouth-level.

The man shrugged: what else could it be except some narcotic? Anyway, to be on the safe side, he was going (and no hard feelings, he evidently hoped) to confiscate. He put the tubes in an inside pocket.

'But what am I going to do?' cried Paul. 'The damned things will fall out.' And he tried to wrest the Dentisiment back from the customs-man; the customs-man, a reproving uncle, slapped him sharply, though without rancour, on the wrist. Belinda laughed.

'Ah, damn it all.' Paul was angry. 'I won't be able to get any more, not in Russia. The blasted thing won't stay in.' He blushed, hearing himself say that. Perhaps, then, yesterday, after the Russian cognac there had been no roast beef of Old England for an effete Yankee. He hadn't asked her and she'd said nothing. Perhaps the holiday hadn't really started yet after all. And now teeth were going to drop out.

The customs-man asked Paul how much foreign currency he was bringing in and recorded his answer on a form. He chalk-crossed the suitcases, humming and smiling, and, before leaving, again wrapped both his warm paws round each right hand. But he would not return the Dentisiment.

'Come on,' said Belinda, following the reek of his fresh *papiros,* 'let's go and get some nice cool Soviet air. And see that man Stroganov.'

Paul groused to himself. In the corridor he saw teeth, Soviet teeth and teeth of Soviet satellites, flashing in the flash-bulb's instant from the wall-newspaper near their cabin-door. There had been wall-newspapers all

41

over that RAF camp, he remembered, tacked up by a grim commissar of a flying officer, also portraits of a wet-lipped sulking bulldog, their war-leader. It had really been a kind of Russia, really, the Services. This ship's wall-newspaper had the usual punning heading —'*MIR MIRU*'. The Russians seemed proud that *mir* meant both 'peace' and 'world', as though that were a specifically Soviet achievement. There were glossy press photographs of Khrushchev embracing emergent revolutionary leaders all over the peace or world—bearded, in fez or songkok, all well-teethed. Paul's quaternion of false ones was, he knew, soon going to be loose.

There was nobody around the administrative area. The saloon was full of Immigration, Intourist, expostulatory arms. Paul had had their joint passport stamped already, so that was all right. As for their hotel, well, that was Mizinchikov's responsibility. Poor dead Robert had kept in touch with occasional pen-pal letters in Russian, describing the Changing of the Guard and the British Weather; Mizinchikov had replied in primary-school English, saying that everybody was very happy in the Soviet Union. That was just to keep the engine ticking. And then the cable, only this time Paul had sent it: 'DOUBLE ROOM PLEASE ASTORIA JULY 4 REGARDS.' Robert's signature, of course; everything could be explained later. Mizinchikov knew what the cable meant, as well as what it said; Paul knew what Mizinchikov looked like: he had a snapshot given to him by Sandra—Mizinchikov embracing Robert in Leningrad Port, a background of gantries, sunlight, hammer-and-sickled ship's funnels, gulls. Poor dead Robert, slim till death and no grey in hair which, had he been a woman, would have been called honey-coloured. Fat laughing Mizinchikov, a Mongol-straight lock over a Coleridge-type brow, roaring his happiness. Russia seemed a great place for happiness. It was a colour-photograph, taken by some third unknown. First seeing it, Paul had realized with a shock that the Soviet Union must be coloured like anywhere else; it was not just grey, as in spy-films. One was learning all the time.

Meanwhile the ship rode steadily in, the great city's skyline becoming more and more clearly defined. *Chaika, chaika* went the gulls, announcing that they were Russian gulls or *chaiki*. They screamed and wheeled, beaked hungry maws planing on the wind, their greed as whining under one régime as another. Buoys, tramp-steamers, launches, brown faces laughing up, teeth white and gold. And the gold breast of St Isaac's flashed like an old dull filling. Paul and Belinda leaned on the taffrail, squinting at that distant relic of Holy Russia. Students leaned too, sullen and still hangoverish, but Paul recognized no one from the Atheists' Ball. And then Belinda was tapped cheerily on the shoulder. They both turned to see the ship's officer she called Stroganov, the purser, a young man whose sad Asiatic eyes belied his brave smile. He had a fistful of mail. 'For you,' he said, 'a postcard. From Sandra. You do not mind if I read, it is good for my English.' So even Sandra was being folded into the great Russian family. Belinda snatched it, saying:

'Oh, you . . .' She devoured it like a potato crisp. Paul saw a Lake District view. 'The bitch,' went Belinda. 'She's gone to Keswick with that bloody ——. I knew all the time she would.'

'Who, darling?' said Paul. 'Let me see.' But she angrily tore the postcard quarto, octavo, then scattered the scraps over the side. The gulls came mewing, dipping.

'That is astonishing,' smiled the purser. 'I can say "astonishing", yes? That will be with sudden rage at this Sandra.' And he pointed to Belinda's neck. The rash, with chameleon-speed, had flared up to a kind of burning purple, the texture of porridge.

43

Five

'I MEAN, what concern of yours is it really, dear, Sandra's morals, I mean? Morals surely don't come into it, do they? What if she has gone off on a little holiday somewhere with somebody? She must be very lonely. Especially with us away.' Something about 'or ere those shoes were old'. 'I just don't understand this new-found posthumous concern about Robert,' said Paul, thinking he *did* understand it. Or perhaps did. 'Sandra's got to start a new life, hasn't she?' No reply from the bunk.

The ship's doctor, looking in drilon not merely beautiful but desirable, had repainted the rash and administered a mild sedative. Paul's stomach rumbled. He'd neglected the flat unresonant gong-call to an early disembarkation dinner to sit here by Belinda. He fidgeted. The luggage was piled outside cabin-doors like rubbish. Starboard now had a monopoly of sea; to port was the strangeness of diminished light, landfall's obtrusion. To arrive anywhere was unpleasant, imposing small responsibilities which were harder to bear than the great moral and civic ones: the winches' squeal and the shore-voices sounded derisive. Soon they would have the pain of having to start to know a new city. He wished Belinda would be fit and lively and cheerful and awake. His little wedge of false teeth was as loose as toffee in his mouth. He knew he could understand all this Sandra-and-guilt business if only he had the time and lack of distraction to mine deeply enough. He could almost press down that first charge now, feeling that if she and Robert, Robert teaching things in

44

bed, that is to say, Robert would at least be alive again if they were . . . What he meant to himself was, no need for Belinda's guilt really, certainly no transference of self-reproach to Sandra . . . Oh, now was no time for thinking about that sort of thing, was it? He wished to God she'd wake up and blink and smile, rub her neck in wonder to find the rash gone, then say, 'I feel wonderful. Let's go.' But all she did was start to snore gently, as though settling down to a night's sleep. This would not do at all.

And this nervous hunger. He had repeatedly pressed the button which should summon the stewardess, but the whole ship, as a working organism, seemed to have gone dead now, except for the trundling away of the baggage. And where was Yegor Ilyich, his adoptive nephew? Ashore undoubtedly, telling laughing stories, his lower lip a ruby, of how he'd drunk quarts of a silly Englishman's cognac. Belinda went on snoring in relaxed slow rhythm. Paul fancied he could hear excited noise in the distance, the noise of disembarking passengers. There was no need to panic, he kept telling himself; the ship, having butted to the end of a blind alley, was not going to sail on anywhere; the day after tomorrow it would turn around and be outward bound for Tilbury; there was plenty of time. But he wanted them both to be normal, to join the disembarking queue like everybody else. A nervous hunger for conformity was what it was.

Paul couldn't keep still. He went out into the corridor and found his luggage had gone. It would be awaiting his collection, he assumed, in the Sea Terminal. Supposing, he thought confusedly, the little customs-man had started to talk about somebody who had what would seem to any ordinary person an excess of drilon dresses (it was none of his business, of course; the lady apparently sweated too much; still, it was something

45

new and perhaps amusing, a topic for gossip) and somebody brighter and higher up had decided to have the
bags opened up again because there'd been a lot of this
smuggling in of capitalist consumer goods lately and
attempts to wreck the Soviet economy, and this, a large
number of dresses, seemed to be it at last, a genuine
catch and perhaps—who knew?—leader of the smuggling
ring and a little torture under strong lamps, bald
bullet-heads looking on, the reek of *papirosi* which was
really the smell of prison, would perhaps elicit the names
of everybody involved on this side, and so——

Help! Paul almost ran to the comfort of decent
laughing disembarkers who thronged the port side of
the ship. Everybody was looking down, laughing. Paul
pushed in at the rail and saw that the androgynous
doctor was being carried ashore, well-rugged and
wrapped, despite the sunny warmth of an evening that
promised to be endless. The wheelchair was being
bumped down the steps of the gangway, Madox blowing at the rear, a surly blue-denimed porter at the front
taking the weight, bowing to it as to imperial whips,
the wattles and cheeks of Madox and the doctor
chattering at each jolt. The doctor cried to the jeering
students:

'Louts! Board-school scum! You will learn, all of you,
never fear!' The skinny silver hand held a dog-headed
Malacca stick at its ferrule, shaking it in impotent
threatening.

It was, Paul now saw very clearly, too much of an
act, something for a masque; there was something fishy
going on. To his relief he saw also a sort of bogie riding
up a ramp, its load passengers' baggage; he thought he
recognized theirs. There would be time, time, if he could
drag her ashore now. 'Leningrad,' he breathed. He
devoured the port in a single blink: the people waiting
to greet with flowers, their clothes ill-cut as by prentice

46

dressmakers and tailors. Crates, cranes, a film-team of all girls in deplorable flowery frocks—clapper, camera, director. That Iron Curtain was a mere fright for children, then. Smoke, haze. They were here, and it was the same as anywhere else. The bogie reached the ramp's summit and entered the port building. Bogey was the word; Russia was a Hallowmass bogey. It was just people waiting, smoking, with flowers, their shoes or sandals abominably made. Dr Tiresias now entered it, the first, pushed by Madox, up that ramp. The students cheered. Paul ran back to the cabin. Everything changed at once; time changed, place changed: a cabin was a room where you were suspended between departure and arrival. Leningrad disappeared, and there was only Belinda, still snoring.

'Dearest.' He shook her roughly. 'Come on, we've got to go ashore.' She did not respond. Shaken on to her back, she presented an open mouth to him. It said only a snort. She seemed well out, that sedative was not so mild after all. He shook her quite violently and heard strange words, words from the underworld: 'Gart . . . fairgow . . . lublu . . .'

How strange! She knew no Russian, and yet here was an approximation to the Russian word for 'love' bubbling up from the depths, as though James Joyce had really been the inventor of everybody's unconscious. Earwicker was Everybody. Robert had been, for a time, keen on that. Robert had taught him quite a bit, he supposed. He shook and shook and shook Belinda, but soon saw it was going to be hopeless. He sat down in the airless cabin and lit an English cigarette, then, between puffs, tongue-juggled with the denture, now completely loose (wedge it with a pledget of cotton wool perhaps?). Mizinchikov would probably be waiting at the hotel, aware of time of disembarkation. It would be a relief to get all this dirty business over quickly. Of course, she would be awake in an hour or so, but still . . .

Even if Mizinchikov were not waiting, even if he did not come to the hotel tonight, it would be safer· to get those bags out of the shed out there and lock them in a hotel room. He could leave Belinda here, taxi to the Astoria, taxi back to the ship (the ship could *not* move off; it was all laid down in the agency's time-table: two days here, then Helsinki, Rostock, Tilbury, Le Havre. The ship would still be here, Belinda asleep in it, when he got back.) He tore out a page of his diary and ball-pointed a message: 'Darling, have just gone to hotel to make all arrangements, don't worry, will be back at once, hope you feel better. NOT TO FEEL GUILTY.' After three seconds of deliberation he deleted that last injunction. He shook her two or three times more; she did not stir. Satisfied that he was doing the right thing, he went out, carrying his raincoat. At the purser's office he saw a small rounded officer he had never seen before and suddenly lost all confidence in his Russian, he could not tell why. He performed a brief mime against a background of disembarking students (haversack-carrying, grown long-haired and scruffy for the occasion; he saw that delectable fallen angel of last night, now jerseyed and sluttish, her accent coarser). The little officer watched with patience, his brown eyes compassionate, while Paul mimed that his wife was ill and under official Soviet sedation and she had better stay on board asleep while he . . .

'*Da da da da*,' went the officer like a baby, laying comforting hands on Paul. Paul joined the disembarkation.

He was jostled down the gangway and then tripped, for he suddenly found himself in the middle of a confusion of hearty Russians, smelling of Georgian wine, *borshch*, harsh tobacco, most of whom he seemed to

48

know. It was the Soviet musicians being welcomed home—Korovkin, Yefimovich, Vidoplyasov, Kholmsky, others, all looking like decent artisans on a day out, carrying brown-paper parcels and cardboard suitcases, greeted by women with thin bunches of sweet william and smacking kisses. He, Paul, Pavel Ivanovich Gussey, was somehow all mixed up in this loving group, so that a little girl leapt on him like a dog and washed him with a fury of affection, and a toothless *babushka*, lined and tanned like a gipsy, cackled and held out brown arms that were all intertwined cables. Clap went the clapper-girl, another girl brought a hand-mike, Paul could see sound-recording going on in a lorry, film began to whir on the sprockets. Paul was in it, a sizable chunk of Soviet newsfilm, and couldn't get out. '*Uluibka, uluibka!*' the film-girls were calling, meaning they wanted a smile. Paul obliged, showing a fair upper row and a bottom row whose middle four, unsecured by Dentisiment, were ready to drop on the quay at any moment. Behind him he heard a voice, female, Manchester, saying loudly, 'That's a bit of a mockery, him being a friend of Opiskin's.' Comrade Korovkin seemed to recognize him as somebody who, though a foreigner, had something to do with Soviet music, and grabbed him with a beefy friendly hand. The camera recorded all this, the sound-apparatus Paul's shouting 'Oh hell', running away up the ramp and escaping into Russia.

Six

IN THE great Sea Terminal old and new Russia met amicably. Posters offering *chasse* and *Jagd* in civilized forests jostled loot from the walls of the Hermitage—a fleshy Raphael, a still-life of unplucked game, a monstrous Rembrandt convocation of burghers. The waterjugs and glass goblets on the bright brochure tables were obviously filched sacramental vessels. Jaunty girls from Intourist called cowed blue-clad serf porters *tovarishch*; ill-dressed and handsome, ear-rings jingling, they strode among the crowds of disembarked. With relief Paul saw that his and Belinda's luggage stood disregarded by the money-changing desk. He joined the queue for roubles and kopeks. A fat man in braces for the heat, his bare gums like polished coral, said to his wife: 'Stands to reason you'll be able to get a nice steak and chips in a big place like Leningrad. Stands to reason, it does.' For his ten-pound traveller's cheque Paul was given, by a really sweet girl, a few notes that he took at first to be meal-tickets. But they were roubles all right. He had heard that one could do better with black-market touts in hotel lavatories. Tomorrow.

Paul took his meagre fistful of money across to a sort of small snack-bar that stood open about half a mile off over the luggage-packed floor of the Customs Hall. The little eating-room was full and he had to join another queue. His stomach rumbled as he watched with kindly interest the cheerful serving-girl swishing the beads of her counting-frame. She was plump and ginger and shouted as though on a farm. He took in the vases of sweet william, the open sandwiches of ham and smoked salmon and red caviar, the Russian champagne and cognac. A self-sufficient country. His spirits rose with the excitement of one who knows he is at last again on foreign soil. It was important to note the most trivial of details: the single blond hair that lay coiled on that dark man's back; that other man tugging at his nose as though trying to milk it; the match-sticks on the floor; the rich tobacco that smelt like Christmas. He surveyed the ranks of Soviet cigarettes, some of them celebrating Soviet scientific achievements—Sputnik; Laika (that intrepid space-bitch laughed happily, like Mr Khrushchev himself, on the packet); Vostok; Vega (their ambition was limitless). But an older Russia was represented in Troika, Bogatuiri (bearded Cossack heroes on shaggy steeds), Droog, meaning 'friend' (a fiercer-looking dog's head than Laika's). And then there was . . .

The serving-girl whoaed cheerfully at Paul. He jumped, and his tongue jumped with him, and his quaternion of teeth leaped out of his mouth. He fielded the little pink wedge skilfully, but various Soviet citizens, including the serving-girl, saw and were startled. 'National Health,' Paul tried to smile, feeding it back in. For some reason, now he was on Russian soil, his Russian had deserted him.

'Never cry stinking fish, mate,' said a known voice. Paul turned to see Madox, secretary-companion to Dr Tiresias, standing in the crush, a bottle of Budvar in his hand.

'I should have thought . . .' Paul began to say. And now, the fall-out of teeth having made some customers step to one side (foreign secret weapon; foreign dangerous jape), he could see the Doctor itself, in wheelchair still, right in the corner by the bar, talking animatedly to a surly strabismal man in a dingy suit. 'I had the idea . . .' Paul wanted to say that he had expected Dr

Tiresias and Madox to be whisked off immediately on disembarkation in an official car, but he was finding that any attempt at speech threatened to propel once more the tiny pink machine into the crowd. Besides, the serving-girl was urging him with louder whoas to say what he wanted. He pointed to a couple of open sandwiches and a bottle of beer and put a single rouble on the counter. When he turned round Madox was not to be seen. A flesh curtain had been drawn again to hide the Doctor and the surly man: a Mongol woman in summer frock and great bare shaking arms; a tragic Caucasian giant, brawny chest exposed for the heat. Paul shrugged the matter off (he had his own concerns to occupy him fully) and, like Laika herself, took his food into a corner to wolf it. He had to take the teeth out first. Something must be done about that, and quickly.

Sucking his real teeth and belching on the hurried draught of Budvar, he turned right outside the buffet and strode to the lavatory. It was a rough substantial kind of lavatory, not too clean, typically Russian perhaps, and it was empty. Paul took out his matches and began to make hasty experiments, cleaving match-sticks lengthwise, trying to contrive little wooden wedges. Mad, it was mad; here he was in the Union of Soviet Socialist Republics at last and all he could find to do was to split matchwood with his thumbnail in the port lavatory. At length he managed something that would serve: a pine-tasting splinter that he drove between denture and left canine. He tested with his finger gingerly. That ivory portcullis held fast enough between the yellowing towers. Good; it would do.

Now there was the question of a taxi. He went down the steps on the land side of the Terminal and saw many shabby motor-coaches with students and elderly conducted tourists getting into them. There was an official car or two. But there was no taxi. He asked a busy pyknic-looking man with wrestler's shoulders, a man in whom many seemed to have great confidence. 'Outside the gates,' said this man, 'you may find a taxi. Or there is a number 22 autobus. But here is nothing.'

'It's a question of my luggage, you see,' said Paul.

'It is not a big walk,' said the man. 'A mile perhaps only. This is not London.' He pronounced the o's round and deep, making that city sound like a great capitalist dungeon, crammed with wasted cabs; then he turned his back on Paul. Paul saw Miss Travers counting the students aboard one of their coaches. She gave him a look of grim triumph.

'I wonder if it would be possible . . .' began Paul. 'You see, there's a certain transport difficulty for those of us who are not under the aegis of any particular . . .'

'Twenty-seven, twenty-eight. It would not be,' said Miss Travers. She was atrociously dressed as if for eventual camouflage. She spoke with a mock-patrician accent.

'Or even just some of my luggage,' said Paul. 'I could pick it up from wherever you're being taken to. And my wife's ill, you see. Please.'

'Thirty-two, -three, -four. That seems to be the lot.' The students aboard jeered down, up-your-piping and I'm-all-right-jacking like truck-riding troops at route-marching troops.

'I didn't mean what I said, whatever it was, about Opiskin,' pleaded Paul. 'It was my friend who admired him, you see, not me.' Meanwhile, the coachload of conducted tourists was already bumping off to its specially packaged Russia, waving. Miss Travers said:

'You'll have to make your own arrangements, chum. It's nothing to do with us.' And she began to follow her charges up the coach-steps.

'You and your bloody brotherhood-of-man hypocrisy,' called Paul. The holiday was really starting well.

'Sod you and yours for a start. Opiskin for ever,' he shouted, as the gears ground and filthy smoke poured from the exhaust. The students fat-baconed, old-Roman-signed from their safe if dirty windows and shot jerkily away to their mission. Paul wondered about Dr Tiresias and Madox and how they proposed to get to town, then he determined to ask no more favours. What he would do was to carry the two dangerous suitcases as far as the bus-stop or taxi-stand and leave the harmless ones in the Terminal for later collection. He saw activity in the office marked 'INTOURIST', a man searching manically for a lost document, a goddess in a faded rose dress yelling '*Allo, allo*' into the telephone. Nobody heeded him as he carried the two safe bags into an inner chamber, dark and smelling of crumbs. With confidence he said, coming out of it, '*Bagazh.*' Distractedly they thanked him. That was all right, then.

It was a wearisome walk to the dock gates. This high northern summer evening was hotter than he would have thought possible, brought up as he was on the Western image of Leningraders always dressed in furs. After the tramlines, bales, vistas of ships, there came enclosed sad little lawns, a modest fingerboard stating that it was pointing to (but where else was there now the sea was at his back?) the city. Then the peeling archway, the monstrously blown-up portraits of the Leningrad Soviet, like a committee of welcome with no welcome in any stern governing face; the squat small official who, his concern more aesthetic than bureaucratic, admired and admired the blown-down portrait of photogenic Belinda on the joint passport Paul showed; then out to a vision of appalling shabbiness, a lack of paint on the Manchester-docks-style buildings under a magnificent gold-blue quattrocento sky; a sooty stunted garden, decayed ornamental urns filled

54

with butt-ends, shabby folk resting, exhortatory posters; Soviet workers waiting for buses or taxis. For the first time Paul became aware that there was capitalism in the very cut of his clothes. Neither the new cavalry-twill trousers nor the quite old Harris tweed sports-jacket could be absorbed easily into this scene. Here was the capped tieless proletariat with a vengeance; he had never really, he realized, seen the proletariat before. He wanted a taxi quickly, to escape to the decent normal luxurious world built, however ephemerally, by capitalist tourists (safe drinking round a table, laughing in conscious superiority to the natives outside). Ashamed as, he remembered, his father John Hussey had been ashamed when in work at a time of mass unemployment, he joined the taxi queue at a post marked with a large T. The queuers ate his shirt, tie, shoes, even the greasy raincoat over his arm. But, damn it, they had Yuri Gagarin and the Bolshoi and Kirov Ballets. They had Comrade Khrushchev's sky-pie promises, they had the monopoly of truth, beauty and goodness. What more did they want?

They wanted his clothes and pigskin suitcases, that's what they wanted.

Waiting, Paul tried to smell Soviet Russia, knowing that only to the rawest newcomer does a country reveal its smell; after a day it becomes deodorized. He smelt his schooldays in Bradcaster—a whiff of brewery, tannery, burning potatoes, dust, a bourdon of tobacco which suggested Christmas, the pantomime, for, with the British, only festive smokes were aromatic. He saw himself in a queue of his own poor relatives—Uncle Bill and Auntie Vera, little Nell and Cousin Fred, unwilling to talk to him now because of his appearance of opulence—but all in the past, in the thirties, for now one did not have poor relatives any more. Odd forgotten images grew, sharply remembered: sixth-form

holiday swotting in the sooty People's Park of Bradcaster; the filthy shop-window of the RAF Recruiting
Centre and one day no more swotting in the People's
Park; himself in uniform; then the evening on the
Russian course when, the gramophone playing Opiskin's bell-music, Robert had started shivering with
fright, remembering the beam attack and the starboard
engine on fire; then Paul's wrapping Robert in his arms
and going 'There there there there there . . .'

Startled, Paul found himself at the head of the
queue. He had to fight a feeling of guilt at an achievement that, after all, only time and patience had
brought. And, anyway, there was no need to feel guilt
at entering the broken-down home-grown jalopy that
eventually came, its dirty buff flanks enlivened only by
the statutory T-in-a-circle-and-a-row-of-dots, its driver
shirt-sleeved, sweaty and smoking. 'Astoria,' Paul said.

He was shocked to his soul as the grimy past enfolded
him deeper and deeper. He had expected, he could not
think why, a fresh clean city of glass and modern flat-
blocks. He found wide streets enough, empty of traffic
as for an English provincial Sunday, but carious,
cracked, in cynical disrepair, as though Soviet eyes were
focused only on outer space. And the buildings were
wounded, all tattered bandages of peeling stucco,
windows starred, the diseased walls crying for paint.
Childhood Bradcaster, yes, but an even older Bradcaster, heard of in childhood, uncovered. Despite the
canals that suggested a factory-worker's Venice, the
bald Cyrillic signs saying 'MEAT, FISH, MILK, VEGETABLES',
as though the town were a vast house and these shops
the larder, Leningrad was not a foreign city.

But then the taxi sailed bumpily into Byzantium—
over the Neva of Byronic Pushkin to St Isaac's Square,
a prancing equestrian statue, the vast barbaric cathedral itself with its dull gold dome like, in the sun, an

army of Mussorgskian brass, the sparse traffic, the pigeon-moaning piazza, the feel of the centre of an imperial city.

Getting out at the Astoria, his eyes still on that fiery dome, Paul paid the driver a rouble. He pulled out his luggage himself and then his heart dove to find he had brought the wrong bags. Later he would be able to call it an understandable mistake, hiding what was forbidden in a dark cache for Intourist to guard. But now he cursed emphatically, dislodging his denture again.

Seven

THE entrance-hall of the Astoria had a dusty ecclesiastical smell, and Paul was not really surprised to find, at the still centre of the bustle, a peasant man and woman sitting on the edges of their chairs, eyes closed, hands joined. Perhaps they were on their first visit to the great city and thought this was St Isaac's. Or one of the railway termini, and peasants were notorious for liking to pray while waiting for trains. Paul dumped his bags quietly near them and then blinked round at the huge Edwardian ornateness. There were high unwashed chandeliers of the most painful workmanship, gigantic vases into which it seemed permissible to chuck cigarette-ends. The décor was fussy, stuffy yet spacious, all gilt and plush with stone and metal tormented into unnatural curlicues; the carpeting was deep and well worn. Well, this was what it had wanted, that pack of yapping middle-class revolutionaries, the tied-on tincan proletariat clanking obediently behind. It had wanted Dad's monogrammed silver hair-brushes and leatherbound travelling flask. In 1917 it had got the lot. And now it had to go on having them. Paul was quite sure that at the bottoms of those monster floor-vases there would still be fag-ends of the Tsarist régime.

Nowhere, among the ill-dressed natives and the smart tourists, was there anybody to be seen who might be Mizinchikov. Anyway, let's have one thing at a time. Paul took a long walk down a corridor, found the gents, then, in the cool dark of a *cabinet*, made another matchstick wedge for his denture. Then, kicking his heels back in the entrance-hall, waiting for the queues at the desks

58

to grow smaller, he had leisure to kick himself about that blasted mistake of the bags. Mizinchikov? There was certainly no Mizinchikov around. To be quite sure, he took out that sunlit photograph with poor dead Robert embracing Mizinchikov and prowled around the great vestibule, covertly comparing the image with various incurious Slav and Mongol faces. No good. Then a very bald man called to him from behind a desk:

'Eh!'

Ah, something was moving at last. 'Yes?' said Paul, his heart quickening, going over. The bald man pursed shapely Russian lips at him and said:

'What is right to say—*in* a corner, *at* a corner, *on* a corner?'

'How,' asked Paul, 'did you know I was English?'

'You are English,' said the man, 'so you know what is right to say.' He said this grudgingly, as though Paul had an unfair advantage.

'Well,' said Paul, 'it all depends, doesn't it, on the context? For instance . . .' He was not a trained teacher, and the lesson took rather a long time. The bald man called other hotel employees over—a waiter in white coat and tennis-shoes, a woman who had the look of a governess, the pretty dark girl from the magazine kiosk. 'Stand the naughty boy *in* the corner,' said Paul.

'Please, what is *notty*?'

'That will be for another lesson,' said the bald man impatiently. 'One subject, one lesson. Continue,' he told Paul.

' . . . is situated *on* the corner of the street. Look,' said Paul, 'I have to see about the booking of a room. A double room. My wife and myself.'

'You cannot do that here,' said the bald man. 'At the Intourist counter you must do it.' He dismissed this need of Paul's, frowning, as a frivolous interruption, and said, 'So I cannot say, "I am *in* the corner of the

59

street"? *Da da da, ponimaiu,* I understand. So. Now we have another difficulty, whether to say "*in* the bed" or "*on* the bed". You will explain, please. Shhhh,' he beetled to the now large class. A sort of fish-chef was breathing heavily over Paul's shoulder; a pencil had been shoved into Paul's hand. Paul said:

'Look, the queue's going down. I'd better get over there quick.'

'I do not think you can say "quick" like that,' said a woman in black with a large key-ring. The bald man said reproachfully:

'In the Soviet Union we all want to learn. We want to know *everything*,' he said with passion. 'Very well.' He dismissed the class grumpily. There were some murmurs against Paul. Wait, was that fat back the back of Mizinchikov? It was not. Mizinchikov, then, would have to be contacted at the only address Paul possessed, that of the Dom Knigi or House of Books. There Mizinchikov, it seemed, had some undefined job. To-morrow morning. Paul saw an empty space at the Intourist counter and rushed to claim it. The praying peasants were now asleep, the man snoring slightly. A freckled snub-nosed girl was ready for Paul, her wide-set speckled eyes turned mildly up at him, on her desk a down-turned Penguin Margery Allingham. She had a snivelling summer cold and kept dabbing her nose with a soaked ball of a handkerchief. Paul was now aware of a well of compassion for the Russian people rising slowly in him; he wetted his lips from it and smiled.

'A double room,' he said. 'A friend of mine was instructed to book a double room here for me and my wife.' He corrected that before it could be corrected for him. 'My wife and myself. The man's name was Mizinchikov.'

The girl sniffed, wiped and looked confused. She had a great number of pieces of paper on her desk, like betting slips, and she did a quick addition sum on one of them. 'Mizinchikov?' she frowned. Then she looked up again. 'Yes yes yes, I think somebody here knows about that.'

'How well you speak English,' smiled Paul. 'And you read it also I see.'

'Yes? Oh yes.' Raising a swan-neck arm high to signal to a colleague across the wide area of desks and telephones, she used the other hand to wipe her sore nose sadly. With a sudden eagerness she said, 'Gemingway. The death of Ernest Gemingway. It was a great disgrace.' Paul was surprised to see her eyes fill with tears. She gave him a form to write his name on. 'All the girls here were lovers of Ernest Gemingway.' When Paul had written his name she examined it closely. 'Gussey,' she said. 'Mr Paul Gussey.' An aitchless race. Her colleague came over, a plain pigtailed girl with utility spectacles, one whom Paul could imagine taking earnest piano lessons. 'You have changed your name, she says,' sniffed the snub-nosed girl. 'It is not what she has on her list.'

'Exactly,' smiled Paul eagerly. 'This is what happened——'

'The porter will take you upstairs. It is the third floor.' She did not want to hear. She seemed suddenly bored. Perhaps it was common for patrons to change their names between booking rooms and claiming them.

Paul followed the little man in shabby uniform to the lift. In it, going up, the two harmless suitcases at their feet, they looked at each other. Paul had seen this porter's type before, in many countries: the small unskilled artisan who wears glasses and has a cheeky talkative face, moronic butt or sea-lawyer. He was not, reflected Paul, unlike his dead Uncle Jim, the plumber. Getting out on the third floor, they were met by the floor-concierge, a fat frowning waddling woman, fearsome, all bulges.

The porter nudged Paul privily, as to say: 'Yon's a reet boogger, yon is.' Paul was given a massive key, as to the whole of Imperial Russia, and the woman said sternly:

'Go to your room.'

It was not a bad room. The evening streamed in golden through great dusty windows, a tap dripped, an antique telephone stood on a desk scattered with hotel notepaper, the beds were roughly made. A past time seemed arrested here, as in the cabin of a ship that has made its port, having sailed into the future. Such a room might be an exhibit in some revolutionary museum (here Leyontov was arrested; here the joint manifesto was signed). Paul gave forty kopeks to the porter, who had the look of a man whom a tip would not insult, and was then left alone. He sighed, flopped on to one of the beds, washed quickly in cold water, and then prepared to go downstairs for a taxi and a drive back to the ship and poor Belinda. He opened the door and was surprised to see the concierge standing there, grim and akimbo, great peasant feet astride on the corridor carpet. 'Go back to your room,' she ordered.

Of course, she couldn't really mean that peremptoriness, could she? A question of not knowing much of the language. Nuances and so on. Paul smiled, pawing his tie, collar, chin, ears. If she was perhaps, in a motherly way, dissatisfied with his toilet . . . He tried to get past her. She would not let him, coming closer to him, ready to be another door. 'Please,' smiled Paul, 'I have rather a lot to do . . .'

'To your room, go.'

'This,' snapped Paul, 'is not funny.' He tried to push her aside, using both palms. He met heavy flesh, a complication of cheap corsets. Her peasant feet didn't budge a centimetre. And now she pushed him, using one hand, saying:

'Your room. Go back.'

Paul blazed. Anger did not give him a chance to be puzzled. A solvent of proletarian uppishness was needed. He raised his right hand and smacked her left cheek. It did not even redden. She took no notice.

'Back. To your room. Go.'

'And I bloody well will,' cried Paul. 'And I'll get on that bloody telephone.' He stumbled back in to the desk. She said:

'Good.'

Paul swore. He picked up the ancient instrument, trembling. Static crackled at him, whirring like wings, the firing of a distant six-shooter. On the dial was a segment of the Russian alphabet; he fingered a letter at random. At once he was let into the world of the dead—parrot-voices of ghosts, the Military Revolutionary Committee, perhaps, stuttering orders from Smolny. 'Hallo,' said Paul. '*Allo allo.*' The ghosts stammered on and on.

'*Khorosho, khorosho,*' a kind voice was saying from the door. Two men with suits bequeathed from the time of Lenin, each with a zip-portfolio, one stocky and boxer-ish, the other drawn and intellectual-looking, both smiling kindly. The huge woman complained at length and loudly about Paul's striking her on the cheek. She used the term *zhestokosty* several times. 'Brutality, she means,' smiled the drawn man. 'She accuses you of brutal behaviour.'

'I'll give her brutal bloody behaviour,' shouted Paul. 'What I want to know is, what the bloody hell's going on here?'

The woman waddled off down the corridor, still complaining. The two men came into the room. 'Zverkov,' said the drawn man. 'And this is Karamzin. Now we shall all sit down and be comfortable.' He spoke English with a composite accent hard to anatomize:

there were shadows of Sydney in it, flashes of New-castle-on-Tyne, a peppermill-grind of the Bronx. It was as though he had made a pilgrimage in search of an English accent. Paul rather liked his face: the many lines, the fleshy mouth, pale eyes, an Audenesque forelock. Karamzin brought chairs to the desk, humming. He was very pyknic-looking: neckless and bull-bodied, he showed in eyes and mouth a more dangerous volatility than his mate. The light from the window seemed in love with his head: it polished its nudeness and was an auricome for the stubble above the folded nape. Paul was frightened. He knew himself, after all, to be no innocent tourist. He had already committed a crime. But he took one of Karamzin's White Sea Canal *papirosi* and said jauntily:

'*Spasiba, tovarishch.*'

'Ah, so you speak some Russian,' said Zverkov. 'But that, of course, we knew. From your letters.' He un-zipped his poor cheap brown portfolio.

'Letters?' said Paul. 'I've written no letters in Russian.'

'Oh yes,' said Zverkov. 'Oh yes indeed.' He waved a sheaf of them humorously at Paul's nose. Paul could see clearly Robert's painfully printed Cyrillic (*Dorogoi tovarishch*—dear comrade) and, at the right, above, Robert's address in Roman script. 'To your friend Mizinchikov,' said Zverkov. 'Him you will not see, if at all, for many many many many years.'

'It's all perfectly simple,' smiled Paul. The air be-tween them was full of smoke from three *papirosi*, the scent of a cheap pathetic Christmas. 'Those letters weren't written by me. Look at the signature. See, here's my passport. A different person altogether.' He put his left hand into his inner pocket (Karamzin went tense, ready to draw) and produced it. (Karamzin relaxed.) Paul now realized that something unusual had

been nagging him ever since leaving the Intourist coun
ter: that girl's failure to ask, following the normal Con-
tinental procedure of hotels, for his passport. The pass-
port-ploy had been deliberately reserved for something
more than a formality. They'd been waiting for him.
Mizinchikov? 'What's happened to Mizinchikov?' he
asked. The two Russians were poring over his passport.
Karamzin raised his head and said, in a sobbing kind
of German-style English:

'In the lavatories. It was very wrong. He sold roubles
to tourists on the black market. A black market, you
understand, in the vaysay or *tualet*. But he was caught.'

'How many to the pound?' asked Paul.

'Five to the pound. Two to the American dollar.
Illegal,' said Karamzin. 'Very illegal. So as to ruin the
financial, the financial—*nye znaiu slovo*,' he said impatiently to Zverkov.

'Structure,' said Zverkov. 'Or fabric. Or framework.'

'Framework,' said Karamzin, smile-nodding his
thanks swiftly to his colleague. 'Of the Soviet Union.'

'I see.' Paul was having difficulty in getting all this,
along with its various implications, to settle in his mind
and breed disquiet. 'So Mizinchikov is in prison.'

'He awaits trial,' said Karamzin. And then, 'Gussey,'
he said, looking, with Zverkov, into the passport. 'That
is not the name we have.'

'The name you have,' said Paul, 'is the name at the
foot of those letters. My friend. My friend is dead.'

They looked up with interest. 'So,' said Zverkov.
'Death seems to be a hard punishment. But the number
of capital crimes in England is very large.' He asserted
that; he didn't just suggest it. 'To die, to sleep, no more.
For offences of smuggling or black-marketing or similar
crimes. Mizinchikov will get some years in prison or be
sent to a correction centre or a labour camp, but his
crime certainly does not deserve the death penalty.'

'My friend,' protested Paul, 'was no criminal.'

'No criminal?' said Zverkov. 'Mizinchikov was very glad to confess everything. He saw that he had done wrong and he was sorry for it right away. Immediately. And this friend of yours had done wrong with him. One of many, perhaps all friends of yours, for what do we know about you? Smuggling capitalist goods into Soviet Russia in order to ruin the economic structure or fabric. Watches, toys, cigarette-lighters, clothes. And you say he was no criminal.'

'Under British law,' Paul said, 'he was no criminal.'

'He wished,' said Karamzin, 'to ruin the economic framework of the Soviet Union.'

'Oh,' said Paul, 'he merely wanted to give people what they wanted. They were only too ready to take what he had to give. Your citizens are shockingly dressed.'

Karamzin did not like that. He boiled up at once, dinging his mottled fist on the desk, making the telephone leap in its cradle and the hotel notepaper languidly fly. 'Rudeness,' he bellowed. 'You come here pretending to be tourists. We are too easy with you. *Nyegodyay*,' he snarled. Paul did not know that word. '*Podlyets*,' added Karamzin, his throat full of blood.

Zverkov calmed him with a long brown hand. 'A criminal is a criminal,' he said. 'Your friend was obviously a born criminal type. Rudeness and bad manners we can ignore. Criminality fights at the very roots of society. But your friend will never be criminal again. And he has paid *shockingly*,' he mocked, 'for his criminality.'

'My friend,' said Paul loudly, 'died of a weak heart. He was shot down by the Germans. He was exposed to bitter cold in a dinghy on the open freezing sea. The Germans,' he said more loudly. 'Your enemies as well

66

as ours. You were long enough coming into the bloody war, weren't you?

'We will be calm,' said Zverkov. 'One thing at a time.' He nodded at Karamzin, as though Karamzin was in charge of the official tranquillizers. And indeed Karamzin, though shrugging and pouting, handed round again the coarse cigarettes with their attached cardboard holders. The two Russians crushed and bent their holders before smoking. The three of them puffed silently a space and blew up blue fumes at the little chandelier. A spider was giving an exhibition of Soviet arachnidial engineering up there: catwalks between the pendent glass rods, a fine suspension bridge. They admired silently. Then Zverkov said gently, looking down at the passport again:

'You have brought your wife with you?'

'Yes,' said Paul. 'She's still on board the *Isaak Brodsky*. Ill. Under sedation.' He looked at his watch. 'I must get back to her.'

'Is it, do you think, fair to your wife to carry on this kind of work?' asked Zverkov.

'What kind of work?' said Paul. 'My wife and I are here on a visit.'

'Yes yes yes yes yes,' said Zverkov with humorous weariness. 'We are big men, all of us, not little children. Why did you try to contact Mizinchikov? You are trying to carry on where your friend left off. Let us have no foolishness and pretending. Life is very short. What do you have in those bags there?'

'There's a divinity that shapes our whatsits, we're looked after, we really are, God works in a mysterious way,' Paul sang within. 'Open them up if you like,' he said. 'The customs have already examined my baggage. I don't know what you think you'll find, but open them up by all means.'

'I see,' said Zverkov. 'You are too ready.' He and

Karamzin seemed to embark on a brief exchange of humorous proverbs. Then Karamzin said:

'The rest of your luggage will be on board the ship.'

'No,' said Paul readily. 'Not at all. On board the ship is only my wife.' He frowned at that; that did not seem idiomatic.

'It will be a pleasure,' said Zverkov, 'to run you back to the ship. We have,' he said proudly, 'a car outside. It is a Zis. 1959.'

'Thank you,' said Paul. 'I'll get a taxi.' They both smiled at that, as at engaging youthful innocence. Zverkov said to Karamzin:

'As a formality we ought to examine his baggage. Remember, he is a guest in our city. Do not make the contents too untidy.' Karamzin sighed, stubbed out his *papiros*, then got up and clicked open one of the cases. Paul said hotly:

'Look, who or what are you, anyway? You barge into my hotel bedroom without knocking, you interrogate me, you insult the memory of my dead friend, now you start examining my luggage. I have a right to know what you're supposed to be.'

'We can take you,' said Karamzin, puffing as he rummaged among shirts, 'to our headquarters. There you can be told what we are. And after that we can take you to the port to see your wife.'

'You have,' said Zverkov, 'a customs declaration form showing how many pieces of baggage. Please let us see that.'

'My wife has it,' lied Paul. 'I asked her to keep it in her handbag. My pockets are already stuffed with forms and traveller's cheques and things. I tend to lose them if I carry too many of them.'

'Well, then,' said Zverkov, 'we had better all go to the ship together.'

'What exactly am I suspected of?' asked Paul in

reasonable calm. 'What exactly am I supposed to be doing or proposing to do?'

'Carrying on your friend's bad work,' said Zverkov. 'Bringing in capitalist goods in order to sell them and thus upset the Soviet economy.'

'But,' said Paul, 'I could sell anything. I could sell that pair of shoes there or those ties or that dirty shirt your friend so seems to like the colour of. It's the selling that's the crime, isn't it?'

Karamzin said, 'This is all ordinary baggage.' He began to shut the cases petulantly.

'Of course it's all ordinary baggage,' said Paul. 'My wife and I have come to Leningrad on an ordinary visit. As I've been trying to tell you.'

'And Mizinchikov?' asked Zverkov.

'A contact,' said Paul. 'A man my friend knew. My friend had asked him to book a room for himself and his wife. Then he died. So I took up the booking instead. How was I to know that Mizinchikov was a great criminal? I had understood that crime no longer existed in the Soviet Union.'

'Yes yes yes,' said Zverkov. 'It is the selling that is the crime. I agree. You have spoken with logic.' He began to nod and nod and nod. Karamzin, back in his chair, caught the nodding, like yawning. 'Don't sell anything,' said Zverkov. 'Your time is better taken up with seeing our city than with trying to sell things. There is much to see. The Hermitage, the Field of Mars, the Admiralty, the railway stations, the Decembrists' Square, the Karpinsky Geological Museum, the Dokuchayev Soil Science Museum. . . . Oh,' he cried, seemingly suddenly depressed, 'there is a terrible amount to see.'

Eight

THERE was a taxi-stop on Ulitsa Gertsena, just over the way from the Astoria. Paul joined the queue there. It was a delicious summer evening; for some reason, though not a Catholic and knowing himself in a God-less land, Paul saw the huge sky as of our Lady's colour, maculate but elegant above the shabby patient group. Perhaps it was something to do with the great family archetypes which brooded over this strange yet familiar country. Paul felt his face soften with pity at the old woman who carried dried fish and warty potatoes in a string-bag, the family-man who was taking home, smiling with excitement, a big carton marked *Televideniye*. A Red Army officer first frowned at Paul, then saluted grudgingly; something to do, presum-ably, with the smart capitalist-or-commissar clothes. Weighing down a jacket-pocket was the key of his room.

Well, they had parted very amicably, he and his two official visitors. He had even seen them off in their 1959 Zis. It was not altogether improbable that they would be waiting for him at the port, even in the cabin, but Paul did not think it very likely. A certain tired depression, very Slav, had come over both of them at the end. But there were new problems which Paul now had plenty of time to think about: how to dispose of the drilon dresses now Mizinchikov was gone; how not to be caught and made (for this was the price exacted of those apprehended selling illegal imports) to enter a Soviet spy-ring. And of course, even before he started trying to sell, there was the possibility of the confisca-tion of the goods on suspicion. That would be awkward.

He would have let himself down in the dead eyes of Robert and the all-too-live eyes of his widow; he did not, anyway, have all that much money in traveller's cheques, hardly enough to see Belinda and himself through the five days before their booked return to Tilbury on the *Alexander Radishchev*. They would just have to turn around with the *Isaak Brodsky*, if that ship had any spare berths. Not much of a holiday, whichever way you looked at it.

When, after about an hour, Paul thankfully climbed into a taxi, he found that the driver was not, as he'd expected, grudging and morose but lively and hospitable, as though nearing the euphoric crest of the Slav manic-depressive cycle. He was hairy, tall, and dirty-shirted, the spitten image of an out-of-work called Fred whom Paul sometimes met in a Sussex pub. On the seat beside him were scattered very many torn-open packets of Soviet cigarettes, as though he had only recently started smoking and was still trying to find out which brand he disliked least. He saw at once that Paul was a foreigner and insisted on treating him to a tour of the city. Paul didn't want that, he wanted to get back to the ship and so kept saying, '*Parakhod, parakhod,*' but the driver refused to understand Paul's Russian. Paul, the driver decided, should have the foreigner's privilege of being unintelligible. So Paul was shown the Lenin Monument in front of the Finland Station, the Peter and Paul Fortress, the Cottage of Peter I (with special protective covering), the cruiser *Aurora*, the Summer Garden, the ornamental grille round the Summer Garden, the Hermitage, the Palace Square and Triumphal Column, the Arch of Triumph at the General Headquarters, the armoured car from which Lenin once delivered a speech, the Strelka, the Pushkin Academic Drama Theatre, the Metro and other monuments. Paul kept saying that everything was beautiful—'*Krasiv, krasiva, krasivo*'—varying the ending occasionally and arbitrarily, as he was never sure of the gender of anything he was being made to admire.

Eventually they reached the shabby dock-gates. The light was going now, not fast, but going. There were the delicate hints—pink, magenta, gamboge (poised between resin and powder)—of the possibility of the eventual oncoming of full night, but no more than that, as though in this high latitude of summer full night were an obscene suggestion. Paul showed his passport and the poor shabby taxi shook and jolted through, a thin dust of tobacco rising from the driver's displayed packets of cigarettes. In this dock-world of bales, gantries, tramlines, Paul could not see where the *Isaak Brodsky* was hiding. The driver shouted cheerily for directions—'*Gdye* Isaak Brodsky, *tovarishch?*'—and odd white sentry-figures pointed. And there at last it was, at rest, most still, bare working lamps already glinting on it, Paul's home for five days but grown unfamiliar and menacing. The driver shook his taxi towards the gangway.

'*Odna minuta,*' said Paul. 'One minute only. I must fetch my wife. *Moya zhenah.*' The words sounded strange, even the English ones. It seemed revealed to him that he had not got a wife.

And so it was really no surprise to find, passing the callow sailor at the gangway-head who alone appeared to be on watch, feeling a sudden warmth for the familiar posters of Khrushchev and Our Little Yuri, padding breathless down the port corridor, opening the cabin-door, no surprise at all to find that Belinda was no longer there. Both bunks had been stripped of linen, blankets lay folded at the foot. No Belinda, no sign that Belinda had ever been there or he himself for that matter. He checked the number of the cabin again—122. No, no mistake. He sniffed the enclosed air, small and dry. No ghost of perfume. And on the table no hair-clip, no black-silk filament, no hint of powder. She had been abducted. The word slotted at once into his brain, straight from a spy-story. He left the cabin and ran down the corridor shouting:

'Hey! Hey hey hey!'

The young sailor on watch appeared, only faintly interested. All the time Paul was trying to explain what his agitation was about he kept feeling that he'd seen that sailor before somewhere, some time far in the past (but that was impossible), and while still stammering out his stiff Russian he discovered where he'd seen him before, and that was in the film *Battleship Potemkin*, one of the young mutineers, all for a spoonful of *borshch* full of maggots, and he and Robert had seen the film together, one evening of that Russian course. The sailor went over to a ship's telephone, dialled, then spoke into it softly but at length. ''*Chass*,' said the sailor to Paul. 'Wait.'

Paul waited. He paced, shouted twice, 'What the hell's going on?' lit a cigarette, threw it almost at once into a sand-bin. The poster of Khrushchev and Major Gagarin laughed at him, the ship hummed deeply. At last a girl came, chewing and dabbing her mouth with a napkin. She was in a summer frock, her face was long, her hair frizzed; Paul had never seen her before. She said:

'Ah, and how do you like our city?' It was good, cool, smiling English.

'My wife,' said Paul. 'What have you done with my wife ?'

'Oh,' said the girl. 'So it is you who are the gentleman. The doctor will be very angry with you. She was very ill and she should not have been left alone.' Her eyes grew large with remembered drama. 'A terrible rash and then her leg swelled up. It was terrible. She was terribly ill.'

'Where is she?' gibbered Paul. 'Please, where is she? Tell me, please, where she is. Please.'

'An ambulance was called,' said the girl. 'The ambulance took her away. She was very ill. She was fighting with the ambulance-men and the nurse and the doctor. She did not wish to go. She was in the-word-is-I-think-delirium. Yes? Delirium? She was crying out all the time for a ball. "Ball ball ball," she was crying out.'

'Oh Christ,' he said. 'That was me she was crying out for. Paul, that was. My name's Paul. Paul is me.'

'Aaaaah.' The girl smiled brilliantly. 'Paul, not ball. Now it is explained. A mystery is solved. That is a relief.'

'Where is she?' asked Paul, his hands claws, his voice almost no voice. 'Where did they take her? What have you done with my wife?'

The girl pondered in a conventional pose—hand cupping elbow, hand cupping chin, eyes turned upwards. 'It is one of the clinics,' she said. 'Polyclinics we call them. No, wait. I think I heard the doctor say the Pavlovskaya Bolnitsa. That is one of Leningrad's finest hospitals.'

'Pavlov . . . ?' Paul was stabbed by a swift vision of Belinda being used for behaviouristic experiments, salivating as a bell tinkled. 'Where would that be?' he asked.

'Where would that be? That is very funny English. It would be where it is, I think. That is to say, somewhere near Ploshchad Mira, which is off Sadovaya Ulitsa. You must go there at once to your wife and tell her you still love her.' This was said not archly but seriously, almost clinically, love being everybody's need and hunger in this land where none was enough beloved.

'I'll do that,' promised Paul. The girl smiled and nodded goodbye as he stumbled out on deck and then clattered down the gangway. A broken neon-sign on the dock buildings announced to the sea that this was Leningrad. Paul's denture was loosening again. The taxi-man was shambling up and down below, hunched and smoking furiously, his meter clocking up kopeks for that sub-department of the State which was concerned with taxis. He was now, Paul could see, dipping down into his depressive phase. But he expressed willingness to try and find the Pavlovskaya Bolnitsa. Over the tramlines and rough cobbles in the thickening air. Paul and the passport-man at the gate were becoming old friends. Meanwhile, behind them in the Intourist office, a large number of drilon dresses lay snug and dangerous.

As they drove south Paul's heart ached, but not for Belinda. In his soul was a great plangent song for Russia, Russia, Russia, a compassion hardly to be borne. But why? It was not up to him to feel anything for Russia, these grimy warehouses, these canals, the Venetian Salford on which an irrelevant and perhaps disregarded metaphysic had been plastered. But with an inexplicable sob in his throat he gathered to himself the city, all the cities, all the lonely shabby towns he had never seen, the railway trains chuffing between them with wood sparks crackling from their funnels, the wolves desolate on the steppes, the savage bell-clang of Kiev's great gate, dead Anna Karenina under the wheels, the manic crashing barbaric march of the Pathetic Symphony, hopeless homosexual dead Tchaikovsky, the exiled and the assassinated, the boots, knouts, salt-eaten skin, the graves dug in the ice, poor poor dead Robert.

Lights were coming on on Nevsky Prospekt, string (as someone had called it) to the Neva's bow. Lights in the trams showed, like mediaeval guild pageants, tableaux of life since the Fall: embracing lovers, tired families, a wild-haired single drunk. Shabby workers off duty were obedient to the blue-glow crossing signs (*Idyetye:* they went; *Stoyatye:* they stopped). Paul's driver was sinking deeper in depression, head hunched as he turned right into Sadovaya Ulitsa. Grinding up to the hospital, which, as that girl had promised, was quite near the Square of Peace, he looked, haggard and drooping, himself a fair candidate for a bed there. The Slav temperament was really an illness. He refused to wait any more, shaking his head sadly. Paul gripped his shoulder; the driver gripped the gripping hand and squeezed it. Physical contact comforted them in their sickness. But, paying the many roubles and kopeks which the clock said, Paul added a decent tip. Tea-money they called it, but this man needed more than tea. He drove off back to the great thoroughfare, every corpse its own hearseman.

The Pavlovskaya Bolnitsa was authentic municipal institutional. How firmly Soviet Russia was planted in, say, the England of the Webbs! Leningrad was a planet of another galaxy reproducing a long-dead, say, Borough of St Pancras. Dirty brick, eroded stone steps, worn corridor. Entering, Paul was at once met by a little man all in white, white cap on his head like a soda-jerk. Corridors buff and nigger-brown, institutional smell, a stringy-haired old woman wheeled by in a chair. 'Ah,' said this little man. He, Paul was sure, was no doctor—the face too earthy, an artisan's hands. Paul said:

'*Moya zhena. Anglichanka.*' That seemed enough. Before the man could reply, point, lead him, there came a loud cry of protest from down the corridor:

'I won't! I won't, I won't, I won't, I tell you! Lemme go! Take the goddamn thing off!' It was not, properly, the voice of an *Anglichanka*; it could be assigned to Amherst, Mass., more easily than to any of the ancestral territories. Except for that 'goddamn', the little American girl had come out fully, naughty, resentful, unhappy at home. (But what sort of childhood could it

76

have been—only child, no mother, professorial father?)

Paul said, '*Spasiba*,' and the little man said, '*Pozhal'-sta*.' They both followed the direction of the noise—louder American cries of anger, then a crash, a splintering of some glass vessel, Russian bellowings and bear-growls. Paul opened the obvious door.

Light, light, light. Clinical light and white. Faces, all with soda-jerk caps above them, turned at his entrance. The little man told them rapidly what Paul was. 'Aaaaah,' some of the faces went. Not Belinda's. Belinda, hair a mess, make-up smudged, mouth square for crying or yelling, near naked, being roughly handled by two powerful nurses who were trying to put her into a strait-jacket, no, a hospital night-dress, Belinda went, 'Oh, Paul, Paul, Paul, Paul, oh, where the hell, what the hell . . .'

'Darling,' said Paul, and was with her. She sobbed mascara on to his shirt. A dark angry man began sweeping up broken glass, shouting. 'Ah, shut up,' snarled Paul. Belinda was on a wheeled trolley. Embracing Paul desperately, she tried to kick off the trolley as if it were a shoe with a roller-skate attached. It was impelled into the back of the sweeping man. He shouted louder. 'Her clothes,' called Paul. 'What have you done with her clothes?'

'*Bett, Bett*,' cried a sister. Paul tried to adjust himself to the bad German. '*Hier muss sie bleiben.*'

'We think it is better she stays here,' said a woman with a strong face, youngish. 'It is something that requires investigation.'

'Thank God,' said Paul. 'You speak English well. I've ceased to have any confidence in my Russian. What do you think is the matter with her, then?'

'Dr Lazurkina,' said the woman. 'That is my name. I do *not* speak English very well. Not yet. Soon I will speak it as well as an English person.' She was clean,

77

smooth, a little too firmly handsome for a woman. She smelled subtly of antiseptics.

'I'm sure,' agreed Paul patiently, 'quite sure. And what do you think is the matter with my wife?'

'Where were you?' sobbed Belinda, still clinging to him. 'Why did you go away and leave me? Owwwwww.' She looked ugly, howling like that. A frowning woman like a very old and cantankerous nanny tut-tutted at the row. Seated on a little stool, Paul now noticed, was a hunchbacked man, all in white like the rest, humming contentedly some dreary song of the steppes, a kind of miniature clinical model of calm.

'It wasn't my fault, darling,' soothed Paul, smoothing her cold shoulder. 'I got held up by a couple of officials. And then I had to keep waiting for taxis. And then . . . Oh, do be quiet, darling; there's nothing to worry about now.'

'You don't love me,' snivelled Belinda, 'you never have.' At least she had stopped howling. 'I've never been loved.'

'Love,' said Dr Lazurkina. 'We have all, even here in the Soviet Union, a great deal to learn about love. That is to say, the therapeutic values of love. The sense of being not wanted, deprivation, the effect of unfulfilled emotions on the body. A great great deal to learn.'

'You speak English admirably,' said Paul.

'Psychosomatic,' threw in Dr Lazurkina, as an added earnest of the total command of the language she would (how many years her plan?) eventually achieve. And then, 'You have a small piece of wood embedded in your gum. Has that perhaps some magical or superstitious meaning? Or is it there fortuitously? It can be taken out with ease if you wish.'

'Thank you,' said Paul. 'It's to do with our National Health Scheme. I'll explain more fully another time.'

'All right,' said Dr Lazurkina. 'I am interested. But

78

your wife is of first importance.' She took over the stroking of Belinda's shoulder.

Belinda wriggled away, then relaxed, then said, 'I want my clothes. I want to go home.'

Dr Lazurkina said, 'She ought to stay. We cannot be quite sure of what is wrong until she is under observation. It will be interesting to us to have a capitalist patient.'

'I'm not staying,' cried Belinda, breaking away from the stroking hand (cleanly scrubbed, firm as a man's). 'Somebody give me my clothes.' She tried to get down to the floor. 'Ouch,' she went. Then, 'It's better, a lot better, really it is. Ouch. See, I can walk.' She could, too, just about.

'It only seems to be this rash,' said Paul. It was still there, a patch of flame like scorched turkey-skin. 'They said something about swellings. I can't see any swellings.'

'I'm all right,' winced Belinda, limping around in her underwear. 'I feel fine. I never felt better in my life. I want to go.'

'We gave her the usual injections,' said Dr Lazurkina. 'We are making great advances in antibiotics in the Soviet Union.'

'I should have thought penicillin——'

'Exactly. She has had penicillin. Already it is taking effect. But there is something deeper. There was the danger at one time that our new antibiotics would liquidate the art of diagnosis. Can you understand that? Good. They cured and knew not what they cured.' Paul felt he would treasure that utterance. 'And now,' said Dr Lazurkina, looking with professional hunger at Belinda, 'we have here a case that invites very very deep probing. She is not well, your wife.'

Belinda, whose clothes had been grudgingly handed back to her by the cantankerous champing nanny, was now dressed and ready for make-up. 'I'll show you

79

whether I'm well or not,' she said, clinking and rustling in her handbag.

'Well,' said Dr Lazurkina, 'I think you will be back. And I shall be waiting here. If,' she said to Paul, 'it is the cost that is on your mind, if so, I must tell you that medical attention in the Soviet Union is free.'

'In the United Kingdom also,' said Paul.

'Oh yes?' said Dr Lazurkina. 'But in the Soviet Union medical treatment is *free*.'

'And with us,' said Paul, 'dental treatment also is very nearly free. Which it is not here. There are many members of your Kirov Ballet who are doing *entre-chats* in British false teeth. They collect them when they come over to dance at Covent Garden. We do not begrudge them these teeth, far from it. Let us give to each other and take from each other.' He gave a little stiff bow at the end of this little stiff speech.

'In your case,' said Dr Lazurkina, 'I do not like those four teeth you have there at the bottom. They seem as if they will fall out at any given moment.'

Paul prepared to explain about these teeth, the Dentisiment and the customs, but he suddenly felt rather weary and in need of a drink. 'There is a reason for everything,' he said. 'We are not such fools as we seem.' Dr Lazurkina inclined her head. Belinda was glowing with lipstick now, her cheeks feather-finished and her hair tamed and sleek. 'Ah,' said Paul. 'Would it be possible,' he asked Dr Lazurkina, 'for someone to get hold of a taxi for us? Then I could take my wife to the hotel and put her to bed.'

'I'm tired of bed,' proclaimed Belinda. 'I feel fine now. Food is what I want. Food and drink.'

Dr Lazurkina gave orders for a taxi. Then she looked sadly at Belinda's perkiness. 'Euphoria,' she said. 'Temporary only, I would say. Well, I am on duty all night.'

Nine

BOTH, then, had official intrusion to complain to each other about, bumping along Sadovaya Ulitsa in Paul's third taxi of the evening. '*Restoran*,' Paul had ordered, and the driver had at once suggested the Metropol, which, he indicated, making a crucifix of himself, lay on that arm of Sadovaya Ulitsa which was north of Nevsky Prospekt. He was a kind of Cockney Leningrader with an Old Bill moustache, the East End bazaar-whine in his voice. He was quick with his limbs, ready to mime everything, so that he illustrated 'Metropol' with a swift montage of piano-playing, drumming, trumpeting, dancing, love-making, eating, drinking, getting drunk, and all this without seeming to take his hands off the controls.

'I don't like that at all,' said Belinda, when Paul had finished his story. 'The best thing you can do is to disown those bags. Sandra doesn't deserve our help, anyway, the bitch.' This new-found bitchiness of Sandra was a line still to be pursued. 'Just leave them where you've left them. Pretend they belong to somebody else.'

'With our name on the labels? Do me a favour.'

'Go and get them early in the morning, then. Throw them into the harbour. Anything. I knew,' she mourned, looking fearfully out at the big dirty street, 'I knew all the time we shouldn't have come. I had this presentiment.'

'Chuck away all those potential roubles and nickers?' said Paul. 'Do me a favour.' He was shocked at his speaking in that pert slangy way. The Cockney spadger of a driver, that was what it was; he had always been

81

suggestible. 'No,' said Paul. 'What I shall have to do is to turn myself into a retailer. Sell the dresses in lavatories and so on. They'll go like hot cakes, man. Woman, I mean. Darling,' he said, taking her hand, 'how are you really? Are you really all right?'

'You shouldn't have left me like that. In a strange country. You should have known better. Going down that goddamned gangway on a stretcher. I was *ashamed*. And they had this very old female nurse in the ambulance—it was a terribly small ambulance, no bigger than a minicab—and she had my head in her lap and was crooning old Russian lullabies or something. And, oh yes, the two other nurses were male nurses, and one of these kept cuddling me, but not in a sexual way at all. Anyway, the whole thing wasn't right. It was as though they were just taking me into the family as some of these big slum families were so big already they used to take in just any poor kid from the street. That street,' she said of Nevsky Prospekt which they were just crossing, 'seems a pretty big street. That, I would say, is really imposing. But shabby. And kind of anonymous.'

'What do you mean by that?'

'Well, no names. No sky-signs and advertisements and things. It's not a bit like London. Or New York, for that matter. No,' she said, 'it's very far from being like the States.'

He saw better than she probably did what she meant by anonymous. It was all nameless the way everybody in a family was nameless; names were for strangers. All the shops and stores and warehouses here were in the family. 'One thing it's not meant to be like,' he said, 'is the States. Do you mind about that?'

'And yet,' she said, 'I kept getting kind of a whiff of when I was a little girl. I wonder why that was. Do you know what I mean?'

82

'Perhaps,' said Paul, 'Russia is really everybody's past. Not everybody's future but everybody's past.'

'Oh, that's crazy,' said Belinda. The driver found himself entangled in people who were trying to board a tram; he mimed that he was so entangled, his back very vigorous. Then he neatly drew up outside a dark place with dirty glass doors, the name 'Metropol' (in the current script that was so unlike print) sprawled across them. If light and gaiety were here they were well wrapped in darkness; it was as if the war were still on. An old man like the postman of Douanier Rousseau was on guard. When Paul had paid off the taxi-driver this old man opened up a dim passage-way. It reminded Paul of a municipal library after closing-time, the local literary society gathering upstairs. And then, seeing on his left a sort of inset rough eating-shop that was shutting and being angrily swept, he remembered that disastrous war-child of Winston Churchill—the British Restaurant, with its sour-faced servers, floors filthy or else wet from the mopping, the diarrhoeal niff of liquid cheese from the kitchen. But, as they mounted the bare curving stairway, they could smell the heat of gaiety above, like some guffawing popular magazine in its drab public-library folder. Belinda seemed much better; she ascended jauntily towards the noise of jazz which wasn't quite jazz—*dzhez*, rather: it was fiercely Russian under the corny sax-and-trumpet configurations of 'Lady, Be Good', some desperate martial melancholia brewing up.

Here it was again—the old solid Russia preserved in Tsarist décor: piano nobile, vista of white napery, complex chandeliers like ice-palaces shaking to the thud of the dancers. The dance-floor steamed with fox-trotting engineers, electricians, transport workers, all with bulky unsmiling wives; there were small uniformed men, whom Paul took to be cosmonauts, twirling with girls who glowed as from the farm, their firm bodies apparent through skimpy summer dresses; here and there were the very young, thin-legged in jeans or tights, jiving. A rich though grubby drawing-room, fussy with plush and mirrors, separated the dancers from the diners. At the moment it was loud with Italianate waiters in white jackets and tennis-shoes, all combining to throw out two Dostoevskian drunks. By the door of this room was a cigarette-machine glowing the letters 'ABTOMAT'; it had gone mad and was whirring out free cigarettes to a gleeful group who were cramming them into their pockets. 'Follow me,' said Paul. He thrust through, Belinda clutching his sleeve, to the dining-room.

White, white, light—just like that hospital revelation. There was even the smashing of glass, but this was in drunkenness, not rage. Paul could see at once that formidable drinking was going on. *'Pozhal'sta, pozhal'sta,'* he kept excusing himself, pushing, squeezing.

'My God, the heat,' went Belinda.

As with the heat, the eating and drinking groups at the tables had expanded into the aisles, sturdy legs wanting leg-room, elbows needing space for the swilling act. The heat bounced back from mirrors and chandeliers; heat danced in the vodka-glasses. 'Here,' cried Paul. It was the table from which, to judge by the swilling mess on the cloth, unsmoked cigarettes opening like flowers in a pool of beer, the drunkards had been evicted. But it was a table for four, and opposite sat a young artisan, his arm round his wife or girl, forking up fried egg from a kind of cakestand with the hand that was free, while she—not a pretty woman, her hair gollywoggy and a top incisor missing (thank God, Paul's bottom quaternion still held, but how sore the gum was)—poured beer and giggled. 'Well,' said Paul, as he helped to push Belinda in, 'now at least we can have a drink.'

The corks of Russian champagne-bottles exploded: bubbly for the workers. Their table companions had bottles of Budvar, a flask of vodka, a pinkish viscid liqueur which the young artisan—putting down his egg-fork—sipped with fat red lips. Over in a far corner a wild-haired giant stood up to toast something amid his table's roars. There was a group of young men who seemed to be students, but not Russian students, singing something that sounded nevertheless Slavonic, their spilling beer-glasses swaying in rough rhythm. A serious man and his family celebrated something, all seriously drinking. 'Oh God,' said Belinda, 'I'm so dry.' Waiters, having disposed of the drunks, went leisurely to and fro with trays of beer, Georgian muscatel, warm-looking champagne, vodka, cognac. Paul made ingratiating gestures, lolling out his tongue, heaving his shoulders in the metre of desperate panting, pointing to his wife's thirst, swooning up his eyes in death's throes. Two respectable-looking citizens meanwhile seemed to have a vodka-drinking competition of two minutes' duration; another champagne-cork popped and sweet warm champagne spurted; a man emerged from his beer-glass with frothed lips.

Paul panted more shallowly, his hand on his heart, crying to the nearest waiter, '*Pozhal'sta, tovarishch.*' All waiters continued to ignore his pleas.

'I shall die,' threatened Belinda, 'if I don't get a drink soon.'

Waiters cheerfully or solemnly gurgled wine into glasses and levered off crown-corks. They smirked at Paul and Belinda indulgently as if they were a television play about dipsomania which they hadn't time to watch. Then Paul noticed the source of the tray-loads—a zinc-topped counter at the end of the room, a white-overalled masseuse of a woman presiding, on her hair a tiara-shaped white head-dress. He pushed his way ('*Pozhal'sta, pozhal'sta*') towards her. The woman got behind her cash-register, frowned, then tried to shoo him away. 'Beer,' begged Paul. '*Piva, piva, piva,*' he translated, crescendoing like some desperate bird. The woman beetled more nastily and sneered, '*Nyet.*' Paul was becoming tired of all this bossing by stocky females. He saw where the beer was, crated duodenes of it stacked between counter and wall, and went to help himself. The woman came, raised two formidably muscled arms, and began to hit him. Paul, who had had enough for one evening, wanted to cry. All he asked was a bit of peace over a couple of cold beers. He felt tears of self-pity pricking his eyes as he backed away, weak, done, arms at his sides.

'What you must do,' said a male voice, 'is go back to your table and wait till the waiter comes. You both wait, dig?'

The speaker was a young man, tall, in a sports shirt unbuttoned at the neck, its rolled sleeves pushing up into the very armpits. His denim trousers were skin-tight. Paul, wiping his eyes, saw hard-as-hurdle arms with a broth of goldish flue breathed round, scooped flank, lank rope-over thigh. The blue eyes were wide-set, the nose had generous wings which were now, in time to the *dzhez* from the next room, twitching independently and alternately. The hair was hyacinthine, curling over the shining brown forehead. The mouth was good, wide, meaty, gently smiling. This young man, without changing his relaxed stance, shot out an arm like a chameleon's tongue for speed and caught a passing waiter. He spoke rapid Russian which Paul partly understood.

'Thank you,' said Paul. 'I do appreciate that. We're both dying of thirst.'

86

'He'll bring it to your table, dad,' said the young man. 'No trouble at all. Though maybe you could spare . . .' He made rapid V-signs to and from his lips.

'Cigarettes?' Paul searched himself and found, next to the massive room-key which was weighing him down like a lateral pregnancy, a crushed ten-packet of Player's.

'Cigarettes,' said the young man, accenting the word, in the Jewish-American manner, on the first syllable. 'Thanks, dad.' He examined the bearded sailor, the lifebelt, the sea and said, 'British.' Paul frowned, trying to assign the young man to a national group. American? But he was no tourist (too relaxed, settled, ill-dressed). He had spoken Russian like a first language. And now it was spoken to him, angrily, by a cross dark girl with a Chinese fringe and kohled eyes, wooden beads chattering round her neck, dressed in a puce sack-like garment and black stockings, the left knee with a hole in it.

'As for *your* nationality . . .'

'It's a long long story,' said the young man. 'Remind me to tell you, but not now.' Hearing a waltz strike up, he twitched his nostrils in triple time. The girl spat more angry words. 'Relax, relax,' said the young man easily. He winked at Paul and then pulled his girl towards the dancing, parting some fresh quarrelling drunks like a curtain on the way. Paul breast-stroked back to Belinda. High was the term, high; everybody was getting a bit high.

'Look,' complained Belinda, 'what they brought was these. I didn't order them. They brought nothing to drink, either. I'm *parched*.' On the table were some salty-looking fish, shining in oil. The young artisan opposite had finished his fried eggs and was pungently, his right arm still engaged, boring into an orange.

And then—'Thank God,' Paul prayed, *Slava Bogu*'—
a waiter brought Budvar beer, glasses, a hundred-
gramme flask of cognac. 'The same again,' ordered
Paul before even pouring. And now the young artisan,
apparently pricked by that '*Slava Bogu*', took notice of
the Husseys. In mime (indeed, it was hard now to make
oneself heard above the singing, shouting, toasting) he
seemed to indicate that there was, in spite of the official
line, a *Bog* somewhere up there in His heaven, but that
this Bog was not a very good one, as He allowed
poverty, pain, H-bombs. His girl or wife, whom he still
held embraced, looked shocked. He used the near-ruined
orange as a prop, dripping juice from it from a height
to symbolize rain or fall-out or mercy, solemnly making
it gyrate in orbit to show that the world or the moon or
the man-made satellites danced roundly on in Bog's
spite. Paul found he could now talk very fluent Russian,
but he had to shout to be heard and that made him
cough and drink more. The waiter, the point now
being established that the Husseys were to be served
like everybody else, was prompt in refilling the cognac
flask and fetching more beer. The evening was now
really beginning.

The young artisan could not pay his bill. He was two
roubles thirty kopeks short. His girl-wife hit him and he
sulked. Paul told the waiter that he himself was willing
to make up the difference, but the waiter frowned that
that would not do, there being the question of face.
The wife (now vividly, dull gold ring and all, revealed
as such) shouted very clearly that she would bring the
money tomorrow. The young artisan's eyes filled with
tears. The waiter, now turned brutal, shoved him away
unresisting, from the pathetic scraps of his feast—little
cakes, sweets wrapped in paper, orange-peel. And his
wife joined in the pushing, reviling him as he shamefully
tottered off, pitiable in his drab workman's clothes.

A phase of brutality seemed, in fact, to have broken out all over the restaurant. The tough woman from the counter was going round with a pledget of cotton wool soaked in ammonia (its smell rang astringently like some denouncing Puritan) and this she rammed up the noses of those who snored in drunken sleep. They woke crying and swearing. She rubbed the sour rag in the eyes of the harder cases and they woke dancing in great pain, blinded. A small group of waiters seemed to be kicking a customer, but their tennis-shoes could do little harm. The students were brawling. A young bearded man had climbed on to the empty bandstand, crashing music-stands over, and was punching the piano in vicious boogie-woogie. Two men started dancing together in the narrow aisle, and their clumsy animal fox-trot thumped into tables and sent bottles flying. Parents began taking children home.

'I,' Belinda suddenly announced, 'want to dance too.'

Paul looked at her curiously. She seemed dangerously well; her eyes were like gems. 'We can't,' he said. 'Not here. And that place next door looked terribly crowded.'

'You had your fun,' said Belinda, 'and now I want to have mine. You danced last night and I'll dance tonight.'

'Alone, you mean?' Bog knew what drugs these mad Russians had been squirting into her. 'Look, dear, are you sure you're feeling all right?'

'Fine, just fine. Come on, let's dance.' She said this last word in film-American.

And then there they were, fox-trotting away in the aisle (but the aisle was fast losing its definition) with Paul murmuring '*Pozhal'sta*' to tables they bumped into.

The students ceased their brawling and cheered; one blond god shouted, 'Oh yes, I dance you.' The boogie-woogie expanded to symphonic length, reached a manic climax of repeated discords, then abruptly changed tempo and became a blues.

'I hate to see,' sang Belinda, 'that evenin' sun go down.' She was too well to be true. There seemed no sign of the rash, her legs moved in easy rhythm.

'Enough,' said Paul. 'That's enough.' The pianist thought so, too. Like a child he grew tired of his music, the instrument, and slammed his hands anyhow—crash thud crump—on the keyboard.

'Temper temper,' said Belinda.

'St Petersburg Blues,' said Paul. 'Come on.' He led her back to the table and there, having taken the chairs of the young artisan and his wife, were the dark kohl-eyed girl with the chattering beads and her boy-friend, that young man who had been so helpful at the zinc counter. 'Well,' said Paul.

'If you don't mind,' said the young man. He V-signed, as before, from and to his lips.

'You've got through those already?' said Paul. He searched his pockets. 'It looks as though I haven't . . .' That big room-key bruised his fingers.

'You sound American,' said Belinda, frowning, puzzling. She took a packet of king-size cigarettes from her bag and offered them.

The girl shook her head impatiently; the young man said, 'Thanks.'

'My wife,' said Paul, 'is from Massachusetts.'

'What is an American?' asked the young man, jetting out smoke from his nostrils after a long draw. 'What are un-American activities?' He looked with sudden be-wilderment at his girl, as wondering whether she might be one of them and, if so, what his attitude should be. 'This,' he said, 'is Anna. My own name is Alexei Prutkov. Is that an American name?'

'So,' said Belinda, 'you *are* from the States.'

'I was born,' said Alexei Prutkov, 'in Brooklyn. My

dad came from Smolensk. *His* dad came from Nisso-gorsk. He took him, that is, his dad took my dad, to America when he was only five. My dad. Five years of age.' He looked from Paul to Belinda and back again, twiddling his left forefinger at them in a gestuie of doubt as to whether he was making himself clear.

'Well, that makes you one hundred per cent American,' said Belinda, smiling. 'And this is the Old Country and this is you paying it a visit. Glad to know you, Alexei.'

'Alex will do,' said Alexei Prutkov. 'And I'm not paying it a visit. Dig?' He looked from Belinda to Paul and back again, shyly. 'Is that right?' he asked. 'I pick up what I can, here and there, from tourists and newspapers. Dig. Way out. Crazy, man. Cool. Things like that. I'm a bit cut off.'

'There are certain things,' said Paul amiably, 'that I don't at all dig. If you're not paying the Old Country a visit what are you doing here at all? Studying? In business?' The little world of aisles and separate tables was fast disintegrating. The more violent drunks had gone. Other young men, though none with girls, were drawing up chairs to the Husseys' table. The students who had been brawling were now marching about like convicts, hand on the shoulder of the man in front, singing.

'My dad had cancer,' said Alexei Prutkov sadly. 'He said he wanted to die on his native soil. And there was only me left, dig, as my mother had eaten something in what they called a hash-joint and died. My mother, my mom that is, was what they called a Bohunk. So there was me and my dad and my dad never got further than here. He never saw Smolensk. He died in the Pavlovskaya Bolnitsa.'

'Ah,' said Paul, glancing swiftly at Belinda. The name evidently meant nothing to her.

91

'He'd had some very special ideas,' said Alexei Prutkov, 'as he got more and more ill. He said he didn't like the way things were going in America. They kept using this word "Commie", which was like Jew or nigger, because his name was Prutkov. Then there was this man Senator McCarthy. My dad said there was no taste in the food. He talked a lot about Smolensk as he got more ill. It was as though he knew a lot about it, but he left when he was five, just like I told you.'

A saturnine youth in glasses breathed heavily on Paul and said, 'Ernest Gemingway. Murder or suicide?'

'Oh, murder, I think,' said Paul. The kohled girl gave a loud yawn, a huge red capital O. 'Something to do with Cuban politics, probably. Political assassination, perhaps.' This was seized on thankfully and hissed— *'Politicheskoe ubiystvo'*—round the company.

'Oh, Paul, you idiot,' said Belinda.

'There was my Uncle Vadim in Leningrad,' said Alexei Prutkov. 'He looked after me. I speak Russian and I speak English. I have this job of interpreter with Intourist.' He looked defiantly at Belinda and Paul, as daring them to congratulate him. 'But,' he said, 'where am I? Where are all these? Where are we all going? I don't know where I am or what I am.'

'You mean,' said Paul, 'you're unsure of your allegiances?'

'I don't know what I mean,' said Alexei Prutkov. 'I hear these stories about people waiting for the bomb to drop. Little groups of people in America and Western Europe living together and listening to jazz and waiting for the bomb to drop. And who is it who's going to drop this bomb? That's what I want to know.'

'That's what we all want to know,' said Belinda.

'It's the State that's to blame,' said Alexei Prutkov. 'It's the State that wants to kill off everybody inside it just to show it's more powerful than they are.'

'Oh, nonsense,' said Paul. 'Besides, you shouldn't talk like that. Not here in Russia you shouldn't.'

'Russia or America,' said Alexei Prutkov, 'what's the difference? It's all the State. There's only one State. What we have to do is to get together in these little groups and start to *live*.'

'Can you do that here?' asked Belinda.

'We've got to try,' said Alexei Prutkov. 'Life is the important thing, isn't it?' he said gloomily. 'Wine, women, song and having a good time. While there's still time to have a good time, dig?' He twitched his nostrils in rumba rhythm, like an earnest of having a good time.

Ten

IT ALL became very friendly. The faces of the young Leningraders grew names—Vladimir, Sergei, Boris, Feodor, a Pavel like himself; it was the cast-list of a Russian novel coming alive. Smoke rose; *borshch* and herrings were eaten. The restaurant was still full, but the drunken, frog-dancing phase was spent; it had given place to the discussion and poetry that were more fitting for these small hours. So now Sergei, a student of engineering, spoke a poem of Pushkin's to Belinda, a luscious growling poem of infinite lyric sadness:

> '*Ya vas liubil; liubov yeshcho, buit-mozhet,*
> *V dushe moyey ugasla nye sovsyem . . .*'

' "I loved you," ' translated Alexei Prutkov. ' "Perhaps this love has not completely died in my heart, dig? But let it no longer be any trouble to you. I don't want you to be sad about anything. I loved you silently and without hope, sometimes nearly dead with joy and sometimes with jealousy. I loved you so sincerely, dig, with such tenderness, as God may allow that you be loved sometime by somebody else." '

> '. . . *Kak day vam Bog liubemoy buit drugim.*'

Paul's eyes were wet; Feodor was openly weeping; the waiter stood by with bottles still to be opened, his face drooping with sadness. Only Belinda seemed unaffected. 'Love,' she sneered. 'What some call love is all take and no give.'

'Not with me, dearest,' said Paul, and he tried to slide an arm round her, but she shrugged the arm off. She had reached an irritable, awkward, truculent mood. She said:

'And there aren't any more decent cigarettes. There are only these horrible cardboard Russian things,' pouting. 'I gave all my decent American ones to you,' she accused, pointing at Alexei Prutkov. And then, to Paul, elbowing him viciously, 'Go and get some decent cigarettes somewhere.' Paul saw that the sooner he got her out of here and to bed the better. He said:

'In the hotel, darling. Perhaps we'd better be going.'

'I'm not going. I'm staying. This is my holiday as much as yours.' Sergei began to recite more Pushkin, a long speech from *Boris Godunov*. Belinda said, 'If that's more about love, as they call it, I just don't want to know.' Sergei's voice crunched and honeyed on. 'Ask *him* about love, I don't think,' she said, jerking her shoulder towards Paul. 'You try and see how much he knows about loving a woman.'

'That's quite enough now,' warned Paul.

'Enough is right,' said Belinda. 'I came here for a good time and not a lot of poetry. Clear all that muck off the table and I'll do a strip-tease.'

'Come on,' said Paul very sternly. 'We're off.'

'I'll do it on the table. Somebody go up there and play the piano. A strip-tease to music. I bet,' said Belinda, glowering at Anna, 'I've got as good a figure as hers. Better. More voluptuous. Not,' she said, 'that *he'd* ever do anything about it.' She turned nasty blue eyes on Paul again. The rumbling flood of Pushkin stopped. Vladimir said:

'*Bien entendu, nous autres Russes ne voyons presque rien des mœurs occidentales——*'

And then Belinda went 'Ouch', clapping her hand

on her neck as though a horse-fly had stabbed at it. 'The goddamn thing's paining again,' she said.

'Look,' said Paul urgently, 'you're not well. Whatever they gave you's wearing off. I'm going to get a taxi.'

'A taxi?' Alexei Prutkov shook his head slowly. 'You won't get a taxi. Not now. Not at this time.' He talked Russian with Boris, Sergei, Feodor. 'No,' he confirmed. 'No taxis now, dad.' But Pavel laid his finger to his nose, straight out of Gogol, and said something. 'Pavel,' said Alexei Prutkov, 'is in the Secret Police. He said he'll take over somebody's private car for you. In the name of the Secret Police. Not,' he added in gloom, 'that there'll be any private cars around at this time. Nor any time for that matter. Crazy, man.'

'Oh,' said Belinda, in time to a new stab. 'Oh oh ouch.'

'We'll find something,' said Paul. 'Come on.' But when she stood up she found herself lame. The drama of her sudden physical distress appealed to the young Russians. There was a loud skirring of chairs as they rose. Anna, however, remained seated. 'I'd better pay my bill,' said Paul.

'The only way to pay your bill, dad,' said Alexei Prutkov, 'is to get up and go. If you just sit and wait it will take a long long time.'

And indeed, in the big shabby drawing-room, as Belinda—well-supported by strong young Leningraders —limped through, groaning, a waiter was only too ready to present a bill. It was unitemized and huge but Paul didn't argue. On the ABTOMAT cigarette-machine he saw a notice hanging—nothing improvised, something printed and evidently taken from an ever-ready stock: '*Nye Rabotayet*'—It Works Not. He was to see it often in Leningrad. And now he was able to say '*Nye rabotayet*' to the waiters who expressed concern about

Belinda's groans and limping. The grim masseuse-like woman with the ammoniac cotton wool frowned from the stairhead; a dwarfish attendant from the ladies' *tualet* was with her, nodding and saying '*Pyahnaya*'. Paul was annoyed and growled, 'She's not drunk, blast you.' And so they got Belinda painfully downstairs and placed her on a chair in the shadows by the manager's office. A hellish noise of bawling and banging and smashed glass came from the street; there was frenzied hammering on the front door. Paul was momentarily frightened. A Biblical phrase came into his head: 'Bring us the strangers, that we may know them.' Drunken Russians were after foreign blood. But Alexei Prutkov reassured him:

'Those are only *stilyagi*. They want to be let in.'

'*Stilyagi?*' That had something to do with style, dress. 'Oh yes,' Paul remembered, 'teddy-boys.' And then, to Pavel, 'What about some transport?' But Pavel was ready to take his time about it. He laid his finger to the side of his nose again, went 'Pssssss' gently, then pointed towards a dim light and a stench of urine. All the men prepared to go there, nodding, as though this question of transport had to be debated by an *ad hoc* committee to meet *in camera*. Anna, who had followed sulkily at the tail of the procession, stood in shadow with her arms folded, affecting to ignore Belinda's distress. 'Shan't be a minute, dear,' said Paul, going with the others. He had a need, he realized, a definite need.

In the urinal two very small men were fighting. A large cloakroom official remonstrated with them but took no physical action. A student from upstairs was pounding his full stream at the stones; he recognized Paul, smiled with beautiful teeth, and said, 'Peeeeeace.' Phonemic confusion; it was nothing to do with *mir*. The place was filthy. Alexei Prutkov turned urgently to Paul and said:

97

'What have you got to sell, dad?' Vladimir, Sergei, Boris and Feodor seemed to associate themselves with this question; they looked keenly at Paul.

'Sell?' His heart jerked up in hope, but he remained cautious. Pavel of the Secret Police was talking earnestly to a man with Tarzan-length hair. But it still might be a trap.

'Yes, yes, sell,' said Alexei Prutkov impatiently. 'Watches, cameras, Parker pens. All tourists have something to sell.'

'As for that,' said Paul carefully, 'that has to be thought about. There's the question of the law. The immediate need is to get my wife to the Astoria. She's far from well, as you've seen.'

'Your wife also,' said Alexei Prutkov, 'might have things to sell. Brassières, for instance. Russia is in great need of brassières.' He looked gloomy.

'Might I ask,' said Paul with continued care, 'what or whom you represent? I mean, is it some Government department?'

'Oh, dad, dad,' said Alexei Prutkov, his nostrils writhing, 'you're just not with it. You're not hip. (Hip —is that the right word?) People need things, not ideas. Ideas mean bombs. People want a few things to play with before the big bomb goes off. Now then, what have you got to sell?'

'That would depend,' said Paul. 'My wife, for instance, might have a dress or two. If she sold, who would buy? The exchange rate isn't very helpful to tourists. She might need a little extra money and would be willing to sacrifice one or two of her dresses. But she'd need cash, not promises.'

'Oh,' said Alexei Prutkov, 'there'd be cash, dad. There's plenty of cash around. I don't have much myself, but there's plenty around.'

'It's something to think about,' said Paul. He was

now at the stones, steaming away, Alexei Prutkov un-
buttoning next to him. The two men who had fought
now sang, arms entwined. 'In the meantime there's the
question of——'

'Yes yes, transport, I know. We'll get you there, dad,
never fear. I work,' said Alexei Prutkov, 'in the
Hermitage. Do you know where that is?'

'I've seen it,' said Paul. 'Very imposing.'

'They have these old professors who are with it, dig—
art and sculpture and history, but they don't know any
English. That's where I come in. I translate what they
say for the tourists. Sometimes I get it all wrong, but
nobody seems to notice. Sometimes I just ball it up on
purpose, dig, but nobody seems to care. What I want,'
said Alexei Prutkov, 'is to *live*. The Hermitage is dead.
I'm there every morning around now,' he added,
buttoning up. 'From ten o'clock on.'

'So now,' said Paul, 'I know where to find you.'

'That's it, dad. You know where to find me. And
some time,' said Alexei Prutkov, 'you might like to
come round to my pad.' He looked both shy and
daring. 'Pad. Is that the word?'

'That will do,' said Paul. 'Pad will do very well.' He
was taking a liking to this strange mixed young man.

'There's just Anna and me living there,' said Alexei
Prutkov. 'Anna's married to a man in Georgia.
Russian Georgia, not the one where they hang all the
niggers.'

The group reassembled at leisure around Belinda—
Vladimir with the glasses, consumptive-looking Sergei,
fattish Boris, Feodor with the collar and tie, enigmatic
Pavel. Belinda railed at Paul; the pain was as bad as it
had been on board; the rash—Alexei Prutkov struck a
match to peer at it—was angrier if anything. 'Do something,' cried Belinda. 'For God's sake do something,
damn and blast you.'

The *stilyagi* were still raging to be let in. Two sweating bulky commissionaires swore as they lent their weight to support the straining portals. 'We want to get out,' said Paul. 'Please open up.' To his surprise they did, promptly. To his greater surprise the *stilyagi* took no advantage. Young toughs in shirt-sleeves (this being no season for *stylo*), armed with coshes and bottles, they politely made way for the leaving party, waited for the doors to be bolted again, then resumed their batterings and yells. Something to do with the chess-mind. 'Where are the police?' asked Paul. There seemed altogether too much freedom in the Soviet Union—no licensing laws, teddy-boys rampant and unreproved, and now a raincoated prostitute under a dim lamp.

'Police?' said Alexei Prutkov. 'We don't dig police here much, dad.'

Nor taxis. 'Is nobody doing *anything*?' moaned Belinda. She let herself collapse gracelessly on the edge of the pavement, her lame leg stretched into the gutter. Huge northern summer night above, belled fire and the moth-soft Milky Way. Sergei began murmuring more Pushkin. The road was empty as though drained; there was no London hum of distant traffic. Pavel went off, muttering he would be back with something. Alexei Prutkov and Anna were snarling at each other.

'Somebody will fix up something, dad,' Alexei Prutkov said. 'She says we've got to be going. See you around.'

'See you at the bridge,' said Paul.

Alexei Prutkov liked that. 'At the bridge,' he repeated. 'Crazy, man. Cool.' Paul wearily joined Belinda at the pavement's edge; he felt they were both now being deserted. All right, they would just wait and wait and go on waiting. 'You can teach me a lot, dad. You know where to find me.' And he was pulled off by Anna. The *stilyagi* were quietening now, tiring. The prostitute clicked up and down her lonely beat. Belinda said:

'I'm in such pain. I shall just lie down here and *die*.'

'*Attendez*.' Vladimir clicked his fingers. '*Zéro trois*.' And he ran off. A telephone number?

'What's all that about?' asked Belinda. But she seemed past caring; she even drooped on to Paul's shoulder.

'If only,' said Paul, 'there were some *police*.'

He snivelled inwardly at the image of a nice cosy English nick, a fat old desk-sergeant bringing tea in mugs, somebody on the telephone taking care of things. He looked up. Sergei and Boris saw him looking up and made delicate good-night gestures with their fingers. '*Da svidanya*,' said Feodor. The three went off towards Nevsky Prospekt. All the *stilyagi* seemed to have gone. Late revellers came from the Metropol; the prostitute picked up one of them, a neckless laughing man. Soon Paul and Belinda had the Leningrad street to themselves. Belinda slept on his shoulder, making dream-noises of pain. Twice the pain woke her. Paul's teeth had lost once more their tiny splint, but he didn't care. He was wretched, wretched, wretched.

And then Vladimir returned, saying, '*Ça vient maintenant*.' He was excited.

'A taxi?' said Paul. 'You've actually managed to get a taxi?' Vladimir was right to be excited; to conjure a vehicle out of these desolate streets, at this desolate hour, was an act of thaumaturgy potent enough to excite anybody. And there was the noise, something to be savoured, just round the corner and coming nearer. Vladimir bowed and danced off. 'Oh,' cried Paul, '*spasiba, spasiba*.' He foresaw a bed in that hotel room, unbroken sleep till tomorrow's noon, Belinda better. The taxi drew up about fifty yards down the street. '*Slava Bogu*,' prayed Paul, thanking the God of the

Russians. And then out of the taxi emerged three white-coated figures, two of them carrying a stretcher. 'Oh no,' groaned Paul.

'What? Where?' mumbled Belinda, waking. Then, 'Ouch. Oh my God.' She was ill all right.

'So,' said a familiar voice, 'it is just as I predicted.' It was Dr Lazurkina, ghostly in the dark. 'When the telephone call came through I was quite sure. And how,' she said, bending to Belinda, 'is our little English flower?' The two men were picking up Belinda by her four corners and she was too spent to protest.

'Ouch,' she went.

'I'm coming too,' said Paul. 'I must come.'

'The ambulance is very small,' said Dr Lazurkina. 'Besides, you can do no good. Go to your hotel and sleep. Sleep, sleep, sleep,' she intoned, breezily, hypnotically.

'Paul, Paul,' went Belinda, being slid into the little vehicle on her stretcher and looking as if she were being crammed into a boot. 'Paul.' But her voice was faint.

'Tomorrow you shall come,' said Dr Lazurkina. 'But now you shall go.' She shook hands with Paul.

'Paul,' came Belinda's voice from under the noise of the ambulance starting up.

Dr Lazurkina leapt athletically into the front passenger-seat. Off they went to Bog knew what voluptuous probings.

Paul, desperately weary, faced the prospect of walking to the Astoria. To inch along on his bottom would take far too long. He felt he would pay any number of roubles to whatever kopekless *mujik* would drag him thither by the heels. Or he could sleep here on the pavement, safe in the knowledge that no police would come to stop him. Finally he decided to pluck up courage and slide forward on his feet.

Eleven

PAUL woke to a brilliant Russian noon marching in through the window with swinging elbows. No secret police had come for him in the small remainder of the night; he felt free and refreshed and guiltless as waking Adam; then, as he sighted his denture on the table—a morsel of ham-pink and ivory in the sun—the day of burdens and responsibilities fitted in its own full set and gnashed at him. But, first, breakfast: one difficulty at a time.

In shirt, pants, shoes and raincoat, the denture riding free on his gum, he went out into the corridor, which was quite empty. After some searching he came to a sort of still-room in which two old women sat happily with ample elevenses. It was squalid and cosy, very much mum's kitchen at home; only the copy of *Pravda* on the table proclaimed foreignness. The main head-line said: '*MANCHESTER RUKOPLESHCHET Y. GAGARINU*'—Manchester acclaims Y. Gagarin—so the foreignness was a little mitigated. Paul wished the two women good morning and said, '*Chai.*' They took no notice of him, so he began to seek out tea-things for himself. The bigger of the two women shouted and pre-pared to hit him. He shouted back, being rested now and ready for any Russian nonsense. '*Zavtrak,*' he demanded (such a hard word for breakfast) and the big woman shrugged and filled him a tray with open blood-sausage sandwiches, glazed pale caviar, and a glass of tea that was milkless but spilled into a saucer of grey wartime sugar. He grunted, took the strange breakfast back to his room and ate and drank while he dressed.

The first thing, obviously, was to go and see poor Belinda; the second, to do something about those blasted drilon dresses.

The horrible scowling concierge insisted on taking his key, grumbling with deep curses like some Eisenstein historical character but offering no real violence. He showed her his lower teeth, the middle four of which were reasonably secured with cotton wool from an aspirin bottle. The lift said '*Nye Rabotayet*', which was just as well, for he didn't propose to trust it anyway. Going down the lovely imperial staircase he thought, 'A present. I must take poor Belinda a present.' In the busy hall he saw a sort of boutique staffed by pretty, ill-clad girls and displaying bits of sorry jewellery and toys. It seemed to him that a *matrioshka* might amuse her as well as anything. A *matrioshka* was a wooden peasant-woman doll inside which was a smaller peasant-woman doll inside which was a smaller peasant-woman doll again, and so on until the innermost peasant-woman doll, which was the size of a walnut. This was probably deeply significant of something in the Russian psyche. He tried to pay with roubles and kopeks but was told, very prettily, '*Nyet nyet nyet*.' The girl said, in French, that, all these things being for foreign tourists, only foreign currency could be allowed. Paul took out his English money, and the girl searched madly through a cyclostyled international price-list as thick as a thesis. Eventually she announced:

'Twenty-two shilling, seventeen penny.'

Paul sighed and said, 'We can't have that, can we?' He began to give the girl an £ s d lesson, and all the other girls crowded round, glowing with interest.

An American matron or, from her shape, *matrioshka*, grew angry and banged on the counter with a wooden bear-riding-a-bicycle she was trying to buy. 'Inefficiency,' she kept nasalizing. 'You get no more dollars outa me.' But the girls didn't seem to want even these dollars.

'So,' said Paul finally, 'the cost of this article should be expressed as one pound, three shillings and five-pence.' The girls were charmed. Paul's heart ached for all that wasted work of the price-list. He handed over two pound notes. His salesgirl was desolated but regretted that there was, as yet, no change available in foreign currency of any sort. The purpose, she seemed to say, of this whole enterprise was to get foreign currency, not give it. 'Well, then,' said Paul, 'let me have my change in Russian money.' But that, said the girl, was not allowed. What, she said, Paul must now do was to buy further articles which would bring the total cost of his purchases up to two pounds. Paul sighed again (time was getting on) and chose an enamelled brooch from Czechoslovakia. That was listed at 6s. 14d. He recapitulated the s. d. part of his lesson, administering, to charming giggles, some gentle schoolmasterly knuckle-rapping with a ball-point. And still he had not spent enough. He spotted a kind of neck-chain from which hung a space-rocket blasting off in cheap cast-iron. That was seven shillings. 'So,' said Paul, 'you can buy yourself *du chocolat* with the little bit of change.' The girl was horrified; everything, she insisted, must be spent. So Paul bought a shilling Yuri Gagarin badge and was given a handful of boxes of Russian matches. The girl was overjoyed at the satisfactory completion of the transaction and kissed Paul warmly on the cheek. They were really, God help them, most charming people.

Even, really, the two who now approached him and whom he would have missed had it not been for this long currency business at the boutique—Comrades Zverkov and Karamzin, his inquisitors of that evening before, which already seemed more than a month old.

There was nothing like eventful foreign travel for lengthening one's life. 'Ah,' said Zverkov, 'it is Mr Gussey.' He smiled. 'Perhaps,' he suggested, 'we could all go into the restaurant there and drink some vodka together.'

'I should like nothing better,' said Paul, 'but I have to go and visit my wife. My wife is at present in one of your hospitals.' He smiled rather smugly, as though the fact of his wife's being now (he presumed) in a Russian hospital night-gown vicariously elevated his own status to something more than a mere visitor's. He had a gently thrilling sense of being accepted; why, even these two (discount their probable motive for a moment) were calling him by his name in its Russian version and inviting him to drink vodka.

'So,' said Karamzin, 'and what has she done to get herself put into hospital?' His mind seemed to have few tracks.

'Your friend Mizinchikov,' said Zverkov, 'has talked more. Ah yes, he has talked really well. All last night he talked.'

'Yes,' said Karamzin, 'he talked.' And he nodded vigorously as he saw a broken man in bandages and on crutches swing into the vestibule, as though this were an actor entering dead on cue in an impersonation of Mizinchikov having talked.

'He talked,' said Zverkov, 'of consignments of garments coming from England, all to be sold in Leningrad in order to disrupt the Soviet economy. He talked of his English friend coming to Leningrad solely for that purpose. He talked with great passion and emotion.'

'I'll bet he did,' said Paul. 'But what's all this to do with me? I don't even know the man.'

'We would so very much like to see these dresses you have brought,' said Zverkov, almost wistfully. 'They are not on the ship, for we have confirmed that in person. They are not in your room here in the hotel. We have but newly checked that. So in what place which seems to you safe have you put them? There are so many places,' he said in an aggrieved tone. 'There are the baggage places in the railway stations, for example. There is the Metro. There are cloakrooms in restaurants and hotels. It is very difficult for us, you can see for yourself, Mr Gussey.'

'What is meant,' said Karamzin, 'is that we will make a bargain. If you give us these things, then you will hear no more about it. It is Mizinchikov we are concerned with. When he comes to trial in the People's Court it is a good thing to have evidence that can be seen and touched. You are a visitor, you are our guest. You we would not want to harm.'

'Our guest,' agreed Zverkov. 'I beg and implore you to come now and drink vodka. A lot of vodka.'

'A lot of vodka means a lot of talk,' said Paul, going through the motions of downing slug after slug after slug of it. 'Some other time,' he said. 'I really must go now and see my wife. I'm seriously worried about her.'

'But you would very much like to know that Mizinchikov is severely punished,' said Zverkov in a pleading tone. 'After the things he has said about you. He has said horrible things. He has blamed everything on to you so that he could say he was really an innocent party.'

'But I tell you,' Paul told him, 'that I don't know the man from Adam.' Karamzin frowned suspiciously at that name.

'Well, your friend, then,' said Zverkov easily. 'He said some terrible things about your friend and about his bad habits. He said he was gomosexual.'

'He did, did he?' said Paul. He thought. He said slowly, 'This Mizinchikov was a friend of my friend. I

107

wouldn't like to do anything that would harm a friend of my friend.'

'Do nothing, then,' said Karamzin, reddening for a swift journey to anger. 'Do nothing. You will not drink vodka with us, so do nothing.'

'I have to see my poor sick wife,' said Paul. Karamzin snorted, as though to indicate that he'd heard that tale before.

'What my colleague means,' said Zverkov quite gently, 'is that what you do you must do of your own will. We will not force you to do anything. You are free to come and go. You will not be followed. I promise that. And Karamzin promises, too.' He put his arm round grumpy Karamzin's shoulders. They were very wide shoulders.

'Ha ha ha,' laughed Paul to himself. 'Not followed, eh?' He wondered whether he ought to do what Belinda had suggested, namely throw the damned things into the harbour. That was one thing, anyway: nobody had thought of searching that little dark room at the back of the port Intourist office; that was the last thing in the world anyone would think of. And then he thought, damn it, why should he throw them into the harbour? The name Alexei Prutkov came into his mind suddenly; at the back of the name a little computer seemed to be ticking away. He said:

'Let's have that drink another time. I should love to have vodka with you, really.' He would, too; that way he'd learn a lot about Russia. Modern Russia. The police methods of modern Russia.

'Believe us,' said Zverkov, his arm still round Karamzin's shoulders, 'you will not be followed, Mr Gussey. You are a free man, free to come and free to go.' It sounded like an exoneration. 'And we shall certainly drink vodka together another time. Won't we, Karamzin?' he said, shaking his colleague with lively affection.

'*Da svidanya*,' said Paul, saluting with his parcel of gifts. So. What gomosexuality, as they called it, had Robert, omnifutuant Robert, been up to here? But it was a lie, of course, an item in the standard litany of vilification. Paul decided, for several reasons, to walk to the hospital (taxis difficult at this hour, with lunch-time hurry beating all round him; the need for post-drinking exercise; the inadvisability of hanging around waiting and letting Zverkov and Karamzin renew their importunities). He walked out into the great radiant square with its blazing dome and quiet throaty whirring of doves, the sun blessing the prancing black statue. He turned into Ulitsa Gertsena, then into Ulitsa Dzershinskovo. Lunch-time Leningrad was everywhere, in dour suits with open necks, skimpy wartime frocks, no city gents or smart idle ladies to be seen. He felt a moment of fear, the stranger from the West alone and unprotected among the proletariat, fear that he might be recognized for the Enemy, leapt on and torn asunder, and no police to stop this happening. Leningrad had, moreover, at least the *look* of Orwell's fantasy world; in it one could see how a schizoid parallelism was possible—reality in the collective mind of the Party, Hegel upside down, but still Hegel, so that the buildings could become ruins with tarpaulin flapping for roofs and the vision the more shining for the decay of the matter it transcended. And, deliberately forgetting he could read Russian, he let the hieroglyphs which were imposed on the old capitalist buildings become the strangeness of the future or of other planets, the symbols of a monstrous unacceptable mystique which affected hardly any of the lunch-time walkers in the sun. Despite the sun he shuddered, turning right into Sadovaya Ulitsa and seeing Ploshchad Mira ahead. There was the hospital, less fearsome in the light. Still, his heart beat hard as he walked in and said that his wife was there, the Englishwoman or American, as they pleased, admitted last night and could he, would it be possible . . . ?

' '*Chass*,' said the girl in the glass office.

Paul sat down on a horsehair sofa that had once belonged to his Aunt Lucy in Bradcaster. He smoked a cigarette and lighted another, and then Dr Lazurkina came to him, smiling, in crisp white, her hair parted in Madonna-style and drawn back to a bun, her ear-rings jingling like tiny chandeliers.

'Come,' she said, 'you and I must go and talk.'

'How is she?' asked Paul. 'May I see her? Look, I've brought a few little presents.'

Dr Lazurkina took the presents from him gently and unwrapped them, examining them with care. 'Yes,' she said gravely, 'these will do no harm. I will give them to her.' It was as though they were things to be eaten.

'And how is she?' pressed Paul. 'Please, I must know how she is.'

'We will go and talk.' And Dr Lazurkina, in deplorable jumble-sale high heels, led him to what seemed to be her own office—small and workmanlike as a builder's on the site—and bade him sit facing her at a plain deal table. 'Now,' she said, 'we will have your name.'

'*My* name? Oh, very well. Paul Dinneford Hussey. But how is she, please, how is she?'

'Dinneford?' She was writing it down in fair Roman characters.

'My mother's maiden name. *Please*——'

'She is no worse,' said Dr Lazurkina. 'She needs a lot of rest. At present she is sleeping, under very heavy sedation. So today you cannot see her.'

'And what precisely is the matter with her?' He was relieved, anyway, that she was no worse.

'That will take time,' said Dr Lazurkina. 'But do not worry. She is in very good hands.'

'Oh, I don't doubt that,' said Paul, 'but there's the

question of how long we can afford to stay. There's the question of visas and documents . . .'

'That is no worry at all. It can be arranged for you to stay here as long as is necessary. How long will be necessary I cannot say now. Perhaps two weeks, perhaps three, perhaps a month, perhaps many months.'

'But one needs money to stay here,' said Paul desperately. 'And there is my business to run. We have to get back.'

'What is your business? Tell me about your business. You are a capitalist, yes? Who looks after your business now?'

'I sell antiques. Books and ornaments and bits of furniture. If by "capitalist" you mean, do I own the business? the answer's yes. If you imply "rich" I just laugh,' said Paul, 'ha ha ha ha ha.'

She looked at him with faint interest. 'I see, I see,' she said. 'Not to be rich makes you all very bitter. Well, it is your chosen way of life.'

'At present,' continued Paul, 'my young assistant is looking after the business. But he can't be trusted for very long on his own.'

'I see, I see, I see. Well, we must have first things first, yes? Your wife must be restored to health and then there will be time for all your other problems.'

'Look,' said Paul reasonably, 'can't you just arrange things so that she's fit enough for the voyage home? Back home I can put her in the hands of her own doctor.'

'It would be a great pity. Not,' said Dr Lazurkina, 'that I believe English doctors to be bad. Some of them are very good. I had a six months' tour of English hospitals, so I know what I am saying. Well, we must see how things go. I cannot give you an answer yet. And today I am not here to give answers but to ask questions.'

'All right,' said Paul. 'Ask questions.'

'First, about yourself and your childhood and your upbringing. You have in England still social classes. From which class do you come?'

'Working class, I suppose. My father was in the building trade. My mother came of a family of very small shopkeepers. We lived in a slummy part of Bradcaster. Is that the sort of thing you want to know?'

'And you would say that the kind of English you are now speaking is the kind of English spoken by your English working class?'

'Well, no,' admitted Paul. 'I try to speak what could be called upper-class English.'

'Why do you do that?'

'I wanted to rise above the working class. I wanted to be acceptable in that kind of society which is concerned with books and music and *objets d'art*. Can you understand that?'

'No,' said Dr Lazurkina frankly. 'I cannot see why one should exclude the other. Here we are all working class. And,' she said shrewdly or naively, it was hard to tell which, 'was your desire to rise above your class the reason why you married an American woman?'

'Last night,' said Paul, 'you called her English. And in any case I don't see what any of this has to do with——'

'She has talked,' said Dr Lazurkina. 'She has told me one or two things while under a little dose of pentathol. I suppose I should have listened more carefully to her dialect. But in Russia we do not have dialects. I find the dialects of English very puzzling.'

'Pentathol?' said Paul. 'Are you trying to psychoanalyse her or something? Why are you doing that? I should have thought that what's wrong with her is purely physical. I don't think I like what's going on at all.'

'I wanted her to relax and talk freely. She seems a

112

very unhappy woman. No,' said Dr Lazurkina, 'we do not believe in your man Freud. A Jew from Vienna. He believed all mental troubles came from an unhappy childhood. He said more. He said that everybody had an unhappy childhood and that some recovered from it and some did not. That would be nonsense with us. In Russia there are no unhappy childhoods.'

Paul nodded slowly and sincerely. He could genuinely believe that. 'But you're trying to dig into her mind or something,' he said. 'All she needs is a course of penicillin.' Then he added, 'I'm sorry. That was silly. I don't know what she needs.'

'Nor do I, nor do I. But I shall find out. Now I must ask this very important question. Why did you marry your wife?'

'Why? Because I loved her. I still love her,' he added somewhat defiantly. 'Very very much.'

'Yes? But she told me she hated men. All men.'

'Oh, under a drug . . . It's nonsense, of course. She did once have a thing about men, but that was a long time ago. Uncles and cousins and so on. She hated them all. And also one of these freckled-faced kids they have next door in American towns. It was all her father's fault, of course.'

'She said nothing about her father. I do not see what her father would have to do with it.'

'Figure to yourself,' said Paul, frowning and wondering why he was using a French idiom, 'what your attitude to men might be if your father got into bed with you. At the age of seven, that is.'

'I was often in bed with my father,' said Dr Lazurkina. 'We were all in bed with him often. He was very warm.'

'But this was different. She woke up to find that her father was calling her by her mother's name.'

'The names were different?' said Dr Lazurkina.

'I see I don't make myself clear. Her mother had died. Her father was demented with grief. He was a professor of English literature and never very stable. As a widower he had no real resources.'

'I see. Yes yes yes, that is quite interesting. Incest.' She wrote the word down in Russian. It seemed a long and complex word.

'She got over it,' insisted Paul. 'She was old enough to feel compassion for her father. Of course,' he added, 'in Amherst, Massachusetts, the Emily Dickinson country, one is perhaps not brought up to take incest in one's stride. It was different in the Bradcaster slum where I was brought up. Dragged up,' he amended. 'The father and the daughter and the edge of the kitchen table after throwing-out time on Saturday night. . . . I don't,' he said primly, 'really think it's very profitable to pursue this subject.'

'No,' she said, smiling very faintly. 'You have risen above all that. Well, now, while we are on this question of sex, what is it, do you think, that makes her say she hates all men? Under this drug, as you will know, people tell the truth. What sort of sexual life have you been giving her?'

'That's a very personal question.'

'Oh yes, it is. Very personal. So please answer it.' And she waited, tap-tap-tapping her teeth with the tip of her pencil.

'I'm not,' mumbled Paul, 'what you'd call a very highly sexed man. There was a time, of course . . . But we really haven't bothered much lately with that sort of thing. Companionship, intellectual intercourse— these are the important things in a marriage. To be honest,' he said with sudden boldness, 'there's never been any real *rapport*. Not, of course, that that makes any difference to my feelings for her.'

'No?' said Dr Lazurkina. 'No. You are aware that

she has been going with women? Or rather with one woman. One woman at a time.' She admired Paul's open mouth while she dug into a side-pocket, drew out a scrap of paper and read from it. She held it up briefly to Paul, like a flash-card. CAH— 'This woman Sandra. Do you know of such a woman?'

'Well,' gaped Paul. 'I had no . . .' But of course he'd had an idea, he realized. Lugging it up to the light brought shock, but the shock was, for some reason, not all that unpleasant. He tried to feel humiliation but couldn't. Still, he gazed aghast at everything leaping in order to its station.

'There is no reason why she should not go with women,' said Dr Lazurkina. 'There is nothing criminal in it. Women are very good at giving sexual pleasure to each other without danger of unwanted conception. Women,' she pronounced reasonably, 'cannot be conceiving all the time.'

'Poor girl,' said Paul, but didn't really mean it. 'Her father, that's what it is.'

'In some societies,' said Dr Lazurkina, 'including the Chinese, the act between man and woman is used solely for conception. For sexual pleasure it is man with man or woman with woman.'

Or perhaps it all came from Sandra's side. But not because of Robert, oh no. And now this question of Robert's final heart-attack. It was like entering a library full of books that would have to be read some time. When there was time. 'I suppose,' he said, 'it's all easily enough explained.'

'Oh yes,' said Dr Lazurkina. 'In your Western society you cannot plan your lives very reasonably. You are rational but not reasonable. Not like the Chinese or the Indians. From those people you once enslaved you have learnt nothing.'

'Oh, come——'

'So I explain what your wife has been doing by saying that it is all because you are homosexual and are not honest enough to admit it.' Paul gaped to the limit, but still noticed that she did not pervert the h of that bomb of a word to a g. 'You have made yourself unaware of it,' she smiled in cold scientific triumph.

'No,' said Paul, 'I've never . . . That is to say . . .' But he wasn't, he was quite sure he wasn't.

'It is nothing to be ashamed of,' said Dr Lazurkina. 'So long as one is honest. Some friendships between men can be very beautiful.'

'You mean Robert,' said Paul. It seemed best to assume that she knew everything. 'But our friendship wasn't just that. And it was during the war. He was in a terrible state. A flier, you know. It seemed natural. But not since. I swear.'

'You are not being accused of anything,' smiled Dr Lazurkina. 'We are what we are. Your own fault has been in pretending to be something you are not. The only real crime,' she said sententiously, 'is to be unwilling to face reality.'

'But it was only with Robert,' protested Paul. 'And only in those special circumstances. He was under very great strain and suffering terribly.' He was going to say that she would know nothing about that, but that wouldn't be fair. Leningrad had had its siege, guns, a grey mouthful of bread, frozen fingers, corpses preserved by winter. 'It happened a lot during the war. All life is a matter of adjustment and readjustment. And then men went back to their wives quite happily and were quite normal ever after. I don't think you're being fair to me.'

'Fair? It is nothing to do with fair and unfair. All you people in the Western countries are full of guilt, and it is always guilt about the wrong thing.'

'And afterwards,' went on Paul, 'when he and Sandra

came to live near us. Well, there was nothing. He was a man of very large sexuality. Unlike myself. We were close friends, but now we had our wives and our sexual duties to them.'

'Yes,' said Dr Lazurkina, with an exactly English sarcastic intonation. 'Sexual duties. You English are very different from us Russians. But,' she said, 'this time of homosexuality with your friend meant more than any relationship you have had since.' Paul said nothing. 'Large sexuality,' she quoted. 'That is a very good phrase. And you could perhaps feel both proud and guilty that you had taught your friend so much.'

'I don't understand you,' said Paul.

'Ah well, as we say—*nichevo*.' She gathered Belinda's presents and her own notes together. 'But all this is very interesting. It is most interesting to be in contact again with the Western mind. Incest,' she said without irony. 'Men with men and women with women. Of course, you all really wish to die. We are quite different here. Well, you must come again.'

'And when do I see Belinda?'

'Oh, you can wait a little. One day, two, three. You will find plenty to do in Leningrad.'

But the plenty to do was ignored for the rest of that day. Paul spent the remainder of the afternoon getting drunk. He joined the queues of men at the little side-street beer-kiosks. He found a couple of charmingly dirty champagne-and-cognac bars below street-level. He was cushioning his shocks very well. He thought he was not fundamentally a homosexual at all. He tested his reactions muzzily to the attractive young of both sexes whom he passed in the street. He was quite sure he felt more for the female than the male.

Still fairly drunk, he went later to the Barrikada Cinema on Nevsky Prospekt. The place stank pleasantly of proletariat. The main film was, as far as he could tell, brilliant technically and most dull in content, being concerned with happily married meteorologists in Siberia who rushed eagerly home on snowshoes to hear Party pronouncements on Moscow radio. A little boy in the film, the son of somebody, sang a song about the Red Star shining over everybody. Paul blinked at the brilliant and wearisome snowscapes. It was hard to tell what the rest of the audience thought. Nearly asleep, he came to with a jolt to find the screen filled with somebody who looked strangely familiar. It was himself, a huge sulky face opening up to show a full set of teeth parting to shout 'Oh hell' before running up the ramp of the sea terminal. He recognized other faces, smiling, those of the Soviet musicians. He could not understand what the newsreel commentator was saying about him, but it made some of the audience laugh. 'Shut up,' he said to the man next to him. 'I am no laughing matter. I am Paul Dinneford Hussey, English tourist. My wife is in hospital. *Shut up.*' He was smiled on good-humouredly. In this country drunkenness was no offence.

Twelve

HE dreamt that a telephone was ringing and woke up wondering pleasantly that a dream should so promptly be fulfilled in the world of consciousness. J. W. Dunne or somebody. J. B. Priestley or something. Then he grinned ruefully at the split second of sleepy imbecility and, in the rest of the second, was able to note that he had no feeling of crapula and that this had something to do with the bite of ammonia in his nasopharynx and the fishy oily eggy taste in his mouth. He tried to dig up from somewhere the memory of eating ray caught in its menses. Also in his mouth was his denture, very loose; by some miracle he had not snored it in and choked in his sleep. For the rest, his mind carried nothing except the sense of a valet standing always just out of line of vision presenting purpose like a clean starched shirt. Then it caught at the skirt of Belinda, tore off the skirt and bundled her groaning into a hospital bed, then in panic he stumbled to the telephone. He was interested to see that he was stark naked.

'Mr Gussey?' It was a girl's voice, and he instinctively sought to cover himself with a towel. 'Will you have them both sent up to your room or are you perhaps not staying with us here any more?'

'Let's,' panted Paul, 'have that again.' What folly had he committed last night, what couple rashly invited? Why did it seem to be implied that the management wished him to leave? 'I didn't,' he said, 'quite——'

'Intourist at the port,' said the girl's voice. 'They tried this hotel first and they were first time lucky. They said you were right to have your name on them but wrong to be so careless and forgetful. Do you want them to be sent up?'

'What?' cried Paul. 'Oh God. Wait, wait, I'll be down.' He was as wide awake now as ever in all his life he would expect to be. 'Don't touch anything,' he warned, like some TV police inspector. 'I'll be right down.' As he dressed, snoring through his mouth, Zverkov and Karamzin kept appearing on the wall in a static smiling pose, hugging each other. He rushed out and the concierge bawled '*Kliuch*' at him near the stairhead. Paul threw the ridiculous ceremonial key at her desk, missed, and was railed at. The lift was still not working. He ran with clumsy toes down stairs meant for Tolstoy beauties, swan-necked, gliding like swans. In the hall he saw them, both cases, neatly stacked near other cases in the luggage-space between two pillars. Zverkov and Karamzin were nowhere to be seen. The time? Nearly ten, his watch said. Early enough, early enough to get lots done. From the reception desk, uncluttered as yet by complaining tourists, the girl with the cold, admirer of Hemingway, cried cheerfully:

'Ah, it is Mr Gussey. The gentleman of the bags.'

'I must take them now,' he panted. 'I've left my others upstairs. I'll be back later to pay my bill.' For he'd decided that the only way to rid himself of Zverkov and Karamzin was to get out of here and go to . . .

'Eh!' It was the bald man with the shapely lips who was so eager for free lessons. He called very clearly, 'What is right—"in the belly" or "on the belly"?' God knew what context of action he had in mind; or perhaps he too admired Hemingway.

'Both are painful,' said Paul. 'No time now. Must go.' Zverkov kicking him in, Karamzin on. He picked up the bags and hurried towards the swing-doors. The bald man's voice pursued him in anger, like that of a kennelled dog cheated of a walk. In the street Paul noticed that the weather was changing: rain to come, a stiff breeze from the Baltic. He crossed to the taxi-stand and saw with relief that only three people were waiting. Zverkov and Karamzin were still craftily out of sight. When, after ten dithering minutes, Paul's taxi came, he said to the driver, '*Ermitage.*' He felt better: the name seemed to carry connotations of sanctuary. He tore the name-tags off his bags.

The Neva was all dull metal today. As he looked up at the northern façade of Rastrelli's baroque monster his heart sank at the prospect of having to search for Alexei Prutkov in a place so vast. The hundreds entering with him eyed his cases curiously. He smiled re-assuringly at them all: he was bringing no bombs, he didn't want to steal the Sword of Marengo. Once in the entrance-hall that was full of Soviet eyes and mouths awed at the wedding-cake ceiling, the blind salt-coloured caryatids, Paul was glad to surrender his luggage at the cloak-room. And now, with indecent prodigality, the Hermitage tried to make drunk again one who had woken sober. And empty, he noted, as well as sober: nothing in or on the belly. The miles of rooms made him giddy. His feet and eyes ached and his belly grumbled at the gilt and malachite and agate, the walls of silver velvet, the rosewood, ebony, palm and amaranth parquet, the frozen Arctic seas of marble veined and arteried like some living organism. The size of things, and no place too big for the swarms of Soviet workers on an instructive morning-off. The for-midable parade of portraits of whiskered victors of 1812, the mad painted ceilings, the mosaic map of the USSR in precious stones like a giant squashed pearly king, the statues, cameos, intaglios, the mediaeval weapons. Chandeliers impended like glass-forest helicopters. Verst after verst after verst of Rembrandts, French Impression-ists, Titians, a whole Prado of Spaniards—loot for the shabby dazed workers and their women. Paul's head and feet raged. And then, in the fiftieth room (but the surface of the hideous mounds of treasure hardly scratched), *Slava Bogu*, the voice of one he was seeking.

'This clock is the size and shape of a goose-egg, dig, and it's got more than four hundred separate parts. It was made between 1765 and 1769 by the watch-maker I. Kulibin, dig, and I. Kulibin never had a lesson in his life.'

Paul limped to the periphery of a large group of American conducted tourists, nearly all of them middle-aged. There was Alexei Prutkov all right, translating with little vivacity the rolling rich commentary of a big bear of a professorial man in a very old suit.

One of the Americans said, 'Well, whadya know?'

A young woman asked, 'A lesson in what?'

Alexei Prutkov replied, 'How would I know a lesson in what? You better ask him, chick,' nudging towards the professorial man, who was now talking about a yashma vase that weighed nearly nineteen tons.

Alexei Prutkov translated dutifully and dully.

'He's a living doll,' said a painted woman in early middle age, ogling.

Alexei Prutkov looked hopefully at her, and Paul could see in his face the desire to ask her about the habits and vernacular of beatniks. 'A dreamboat.' But it was no good; he was cut off, the hungry eyes cheated of a sign, a word, a feeler; he was part of a Russian raree-show to be recollected later in the boisterous tranquillity of Wisconsin. The group prepared to move on to fresh rococo monsters and Paul went up and caught at Alexei Prutkov's sleeve. It was the sleeve of a thick sports jacket, overpadded at the shoulders, a sick green peppered with domino-pips of purple ink, obvi-ously very expensive. A red tie, a yellowish sports shirt with bunchy unironed collar, worn-out sandals, the denim trousers of the night before last with thigh-pocket's white stitching making clear blue-print lines—these completed his conformist costume. To Paul he looked very wholesome, very delectable. After a two-second frown Alexei Prutkov said, 'Oh, it's you, dad.'

'I've got to talk,' said Paul.

'I'm busy right now, dad. Can't it wait?'

'I'm moving in with you,' said Paul. 'Just for a time. I'll help with the rent. I want to move in today.' They looked each other straight in the eyes. Alexei Prutkov's nostrils began to twitch in a complicated metre.

'Well,' said Alexei Prutkov, 'as far as that goes, dad . . .' And then, quickly, 'My pad's very small. What's gone wrong, then? Did the hotel give you the bum's rush?' The professorial voice called him loudly from a painted dynasty of Tsars and Tsarinas, blank cruel eyes trapped on a long wall. ' *'Chass*,' he called back. 'Well,' he said to Paul, 'you can go there. To talk about it anyway. I shan't be finished till four, dad. Or you can wait till then. *All* the rent, did you say?'

'Something like that. Look, I've still got two suitcases at the hotel. I'll have to go and get those. I've left two more in the cloak-room here. Here,' said Paul, handing over a flimsy buff slip. 'Could you take care of those?' And he winked with a great bunching of his face's left side.

Alexei Prutkov played a tiny concertina tune on the cloakroom slip. Then, as though satisfied it was not made of rubber, he nodded, though frowning a little. 'I'll do that,' he said. He was called again, louder, more imperiously. 'Ah, drop dead,' he said, taking care not to shout. And to Paul, 'We can talk about it anyway, dad.' He drew out a black leatherette wallet which looked as if it had been long left in the rain and carefully stowed the cloak-room ticket. Then, as carefully, he fingered out a sort of visiting-card. 'Here's where it is,' he said. 'You'll have to take the Metro. Can you read Russian, dad?

'Enough,' said Paul. 'I'll find it, don't worry.' The Cyrillic letters on the card, which seemed to have been cut out with scissors, were in duplicated purple typescript, not stationer's print. 'Thanks. I'll go there as soon as I've had some lunch.'

'Not before two-thirty, dad. Anna's got the key. Anna won't be home till two-thirty.' He was hailed a third time; a facetious American voice joined in with 'Alexeeeee, oh, Alexeeeeee.'

'Right,' said Paul. '*Khorosho*. You won't regret it.' And they looked each other once more straight in the eye. Alexei Prutkov ran off to resume his duties. Some of the Americans cheered.

Well, that was it, then. Paul had a long walk, finding his way out of the Hermitage, half-shutting his sore eyes against a reprise of its bludgeoning splendours. His heart beat easier. He had some difficulty in finding his way back to the Astoria. Taxis were full of men with parcels and dwarf trees in newspaper, unresponsive to his cheerful hail. Eventually he boarded a tram which, he was assured, would take him to Nevsky Prospekt. Wedging a bit of tram-ticket between right canine and false quaternion, he thought of what he would say to Zverkov and Karamzin. They would be there waiting, undoubtedly they would be there. He would invite them to lunch and tell them he was leaving Leningrad. They would be quite welcome to watch him paying his bill. Yes, in one sense leaving. In another, just arriving.

Part Two

One

'You look,' said Belinda, 'just *terrible*. I'd say you haven't shaved for days and days and days. And you're dirty with it. Not a bit like God's Englishman abroad.' She was sitting up in bed in a Soviet hospital night-gown, a woolly bed-jacket on, her black clean hair bound in a coarse blue fillet.

'I'm growing a bit of a beard,' explained Paul, fingering the bristles. 'It saves trouble, you see. We're not too well off for water where we are.'

'And where exactly are you?'

'Oh, it's all right really. A bit rough, but it's all right. Cheaper than a hotel, that's the main thing.'

'But *where?*'

'Not far off the Kirov works. You have to get the Metro. The suburbs you could call it.'

'Poor Paul. This has all been a bit unexpected, hasn't it?'

'I'm all right. It seems funny to be called Paul again. I've got quite used to being called Pavel. This last week seems like ages and ages.' He took her forearm, egg-smooth, egg-warm, and squeezed it. 'Poor darling,' he said. 'I've missed you.' He thought about that and added, 'When I've had time to, that is. I've been busy one way and another. It's been more difficult than I expected, you know, selling these damned things.

You've got to be very careful.' He swivelled his head instinctively to look, with narrowed eyes, at the other patients of the ward. They were all somnolent or surveying, straight in front of them, vast Russian wastes. 'And what,' he asked, 'are they doing to you exactly? And when are they going to let you out?'

'Oh.' Belinda let the vowel drop and shrugged her shoulders vaguely. 'Drugs and things. Tests and so on. And Sonya talks to me a lot.'

'Sonya?'

'Dr Lazurkina. She's been wonderful.'

'I see,' said Paul warily. 'Wonderful, is she? A great one for talking, I'll say that. And what precisely does she talk to you about?' He frowned jealously. Belinda smiled. She said:

'Happiness. The meaning of happiness. The need to belong somewhere. My childhood. Her childhood.'

'But,' said Paul, 'what in the name of God is supposed to be wrong with you? Talking about happiness doesn't seem to be much of a sort of treatment. That rash seems to have gone.' He spoke with increasing heat, *crescendo poco a poco*. 'I should imagine you're able to walk now, too. When are they letting you out? I had to go and see about an extension of our stay here. It took a long time. What the hell's going on?'

'That was nothing much, apparently,' said Belinda. 'It was just something to do with mixing barbiturates with wood alcohol or something. Have you ever heard of that before? I hadn't, either. It seems we've been drinking a lot of wood alcohol. No, all that's all right. I'm ill in a deeper way, she says.'

'It sounds to me,' cut in Paul brusquely, 'like a bit of brain-washing. They're trying to get at you because you're an American.'

'Is that what it is?' said Belinda languidly. 'It sounds rather nice.'

126

'Oh, come off it,' scowled Paul. 'Indoctrination. Are they trying to get you to say that Western democracy's no good and that it's made you unhappy and there's a fundamental contradiction in it and all that jazz?' Belinda said:

'Where did you pick up that expression?' Then, ' "Wash the stone, wash the bone, wash the brain, wash the soul." That comes in *Murder in the Cathedral*, doesn't it? I always liked the idea of getting absolutely clean. Mr Eliot, too. My father met Mr Eliot at least twice.'

'I don't seem to be getting through to you,' sighed Paul. 'It must be the drugs.'

'From your boy-friend, I suppose. That's where you've got that expression from. Are you happy with your boy-friend?'

Paul blushed. 'Alex,' he said, 'is *not* my boy-friend. Not in the sense you mean.'

'How do you know what sense I mean?'

'I'm going to see Dr Lazurkina,' said Paul. 'She's been putting ideas into your head, hasn't she?' He made as if to get up right away from his visitor's chair, but the gesture was half-hearted and he knew it. And Belinda said:

'She's not here today. And I won't have you running to her raging and complaining. She's helping a great deal. Sonya's a wonderful doctor.'

'For the fifth time,' exaggerated Paul, 'when are they going to let you out of here? There's a shop to be run, remember, back in good old capitalist decadent England. And the money won't last for ever.'

'If,' Belinda said, 'it's dear Sandra and her goddamn widow's dower you're worried about——'

'I know all about that. I know all about you and Sandra. But it's Robert I'm concerned about. I've got to do my duty to poor Robert. I've got to take back a good thousand quid in memory of poor dead Robert. I won't be able to do it if we stay here much longer.'

'Oh,' said Belinda, 'if you take it nice and quiet and easy . . . You don't *have* to spend much money, do you? Living out in the slums of Leningrad or wherever you are. And I'm not costing you anything. They look after me here very well.'

'But,' Paul said with force, 'don't you want to get out of here and back home again? Do you *like* being stuck here in a Soviet hospital?'

'It's nice to be able to lie back and dream a bit,' said Belinda dreamily, pushing herself languidly back down into the bed. 'I lie here and dream about the past, you know, and then Sonya comes and talks to me and asks me questions. It's a bit of a rest. Soon, she says, I'll be able to get up and go for little walks. She'll go with me and show me things.'

'There's one little walk you can take,' said Paul viciously, 'and you can take it with me. That's a walk back to the ship.' Silly: that ship had long gone; nobody could call that a little walk. 'What I mean is,' he said, 'I'm going to have a word with your precious Dr Lazurkina about getting you out of here. To-morrow,' he said. Then he saw he had to be realistic. 'Or the next day. I'll get these dresses off my hands somehow and I'll book on the next available boat.'

'All right,' said Belinda levelly. 'That's fine. Nobody's complaining, then. No hurry at all, is there? Just leave me here till you've finished doing what you came here to do. I'm having a nice little rest. Do you know, I'm reading all sorts of books I never read before. *Uncle Tom's Cabin. Three Men in a Boat.* They have them all here. In English.'

'But it's not right,' said Paul. 'Can't you see that? It's just not right at all.' A farmer's wife of a sister came to the bed, red, jolly, affectionate, with a glass of tea in which seemed to float segments of apple. She smiled on Belinda and hugged her, saying:

'*Krasiva Anglichanka.*'

Belinda smiled up her thanks. 'Did you understand that?' said Paul. 'Did you get what she said?'

'She said I was a beautiful Englishwoman,' said Belinda. 'That, I should think, is about half right. I'm learning a few words,' she said complacently. The sister, though still jolly, made briskish chicken-shooing gestures at Paul. 'It would seem,' Belinda said, 'that visiting-time is over. It was nice of you to come and see me, dear. You must come again.'

'Tomorrow. I'll be along tomorrow.'

'Kiss Momma, then.' She kiss-pouted. Paul, scowling, kissed. Then, taking up his brown-paper parcel from the locker-top—one drilon dress, his day's wares—he said:

'Do you want anything?' A few days before, still forbidden to see her, he had left a Spenserian bag of needments at the hospital office. 'I'm afraid I've run out of English cigarettes.'

'You mean American,' said Belinda. 'There's no such thing as English. I don't,' she said, 'seem to have the urge to smoke these days. I've lost the old craving. And, you know, I feel better for it.'

'I don't like that,' Paul said. 'I don't like it one little bit.' He juggled his parcel clumsily from hand to hand. 'It's not quite so easy as I'd expected,' he said, 'selling these things retail. I'm lucky if I manage one a day. I've let two go on tick and I can't quite remember who the people are.'

'Poor Paulovich,' said Belinda rather indifferently. She drank off her glass under the sister's smiling eye.

'People are always willing to buy, you see, but they never have any ready cash. They seem to spend it all on drink.'

A thinner sister came rattling along with syringes, cheerful though and humming something simple.

'Alex,' said Paul, frowning at this, 'keeps promising to put me in touch with people. But I'm still waiting,' he complained. 'This is a terrible place for putting things off.'

'All life is putting things off,' said Belinda sententiously. Paul thought he heard a faint distant chopping of a cherry tree, but it was the sister breaking open an ampoule. She plunged a syringe in, then frowned at Paul. 'Ah,' said Belinda, 'this is my dreamland stuff. You *must* go now, you know.'

'I don't like it,' said Paul.

'But I do,' said Belinda. Her upper arm was gently bared and then swabbed. 'I like it fine,' she said, with mock nasality.

Paul was rather glad to get out. On his way to the main entrance he had a look at himself in a fine old blue mirror, Tsarist loot, on the wall. Dirty open-necked shirt, no jacket because of the return of the heat, sloppy unpressed sports trousers, brown shoes unpolished, hair ill-combed and in need of a trim, the beard slow in coming. Putting on dark glasses, he grinned at himself and said, '*Tovarishch*.' The teeth were all right, the false four plugged in today with a very tasteless kind of chewing-gum given to Alexei by an American tourist. Pavel Ivanovich Gussey, dealer in illicitly imported drilon dresses. He slouched out into the sunlight, appraising with a vendor's eye the few comrades who walked in Ploshchad Mira. But the streets were no good; the best place seemed to be a little champagne-and-cognac dive called the Kukolka, a pretty name. There he had sold two dresses, though he had not yet received the money for them. Today he would be firm: no cash, no goods. Twenty roubles seemed a reasonable price to ask but, in his present financial state, he would be willing to go down to Mizinchikov's fifteen. Walking towards Ulitsa Plekhanova, he counted his pocket's meagre contents: two roubles, forty-five kopeks. His traveller's cheques had all been cashed: hotel bill, lavish drunken lunch for Zverkov and Karamzin (they had been there, waiting; oh, thoroughly predictable), loan to needy Alexei Prutkov, back rent of Alexei Prutkov's flat, food, drink, cigarettes: money didn't go very far, especially not in this gay city. He smiled in the sun, remembering that lunch with Zverkov and Karamzin, their affection growing with the vodka, the loud toasts to Anglo-Soviet friendship, the final sentimental tears of farewell and vigorous hand-pumping. 'Only connect,' someone had once said; connection was the thing, whether through bed, bottle, grand inquisitorial session. And supposing now he were to meet Zverkov and Karamzin again? They would not, he thought, recognize him, a tramp, bearded. Besides, Leningrad was a very big city. Besides, even if they did meet, what wrong was he doing, having—through sad circumstances all open to the checking of the suspicious—been obliged to delay his departure? What they must not find out, of course, was where he was now staying. It was up to bloody Alex to help him get rid of those dresses. Any day now, he kept saying. There was somebody, he said, very definitely interested.

Paul came to the Kukolka and entered, his heart thumping away with fear and excitement; the holiday, he was sure, must be doing him good. The Kukolka was neither attractive nor clean, despite the delightful name which meant 'Dolly', but it breathed a sort of vigour of drinking. There were, apparently, no pure drink-shops in Leningrad; the fiction that drinking was ancillary to eating was maintained everywhere, but in the Kukolka it was a comic fiction: food was minimal

—the bread brown stone, the fish scaly rags in old oil. It was a place of specialist drinking: sweet champagne to chase the rawest of native cognacs: those only. Paul entered as a pedlar, whining, '*Platye, platye—ochin dyeshyovuiy.*' That was meant to mean: 'A dress, a dress— very cheap.' It was not a place—with such open and hearty drinking going on—in which to make a furtive approach. As he exhibited the dress, or rather a cognacgold tongue of it lolling out of the parcel, he looked around for his debtors. A man with a known face and two statutory bottles nodded cheerily. Paul approached with '*Dobriy dyen, tovarishch,*' working out a polite and grammatical request in his mind. ('Are you, comrade, now perhaps in a position to . . .') Russian grammar was terrible.

'There's no point in you speaking Russky to me, mate,' said the man, 'though it's a fine language and a worker's language.' Paul frowned, taking in now the clothes too smart (though not in themselves very smart) for Soviet tailoring, the thinnish East London tones. 'Unless, of course, you're playing some very deep game in which you're supposed to be pretending to be a Russian.' And Madox, companion to the strange bisexual doctor of the voyage, winked. 'Sit down,' he said. 'Strangers in a strange land, mate, but both workers, as I take it, and hence entitled to sit here drinking champagne in a worker's country. So perhaps not so strange.' He whistled to the sullen whitish- aproned glass-washing curate, shaping with his fore- fingers the image of another glass. 'Pretty,' he said, 'the way they've got the walls done up.' He showed Paul a prominent larynx as he looked up at the crudely painted, flatly gambolling dolls in an open-square fresco near the ceiling. 'There's some nice little places in St Petersburg.'

'You use the old name,' smiled Paul, 'like your . . .'

Perhaps this fundamental matter had better be settled first. 'Is it,' he asked boldly, 'master or mistress? Both? I feel it's one of the things one has a right to know.'

Madox shrugged, as though the question of a person's sex were of little importance. 'It depends,' he said. 'Depends what the job is.'

'Job?'

'I see I've said too much already.' A glass was brought and Madox poured sugary froth. 'Though I can see you're up to something yourself that's not quite above board, as the saying goes. Not that the Doc is doing anything wrong, far from it. Far far far from it, mate. Nothing but good the old Doc is doing, and you can take that from me as gospel.' He frowned at Paul's scruffiness and the parcel gaping brandy-gold cloth on the chair between them. The frown said that Paul seemed up to no good at all.

'What does it say,' asked Paul, 'on your—on the Doc's passport? About sex, I mean? And, while we're at it, what is the Doc a doc of?'

'You do want to know a lot of things and no mistake.' Madox smiled and rocked the smile from left to right as though it were a cradle for Paul's curiosity to be cosseted indulgently in. 'Well, you could always ask the Doc personally, couldn't you, mate? You do that thing—you ask the Doc personally. We're here in Petersburg for a week more yet.' He surveyed comfortably the comfortless little dive as though he proposed to pitch his tent there. 'Only got back from Moscow last night. There's a dump of a place for you, Moscow. Wait,' said Madox, and he began to search his pockets. 'I don't see why you shouldn't—I've got the damn things here somewhere if I can only . . . I think these are the bug . . . Ah.' His jacket seemed to have more than the usual allowance of pockets; it was from one somewhere near the back that he pulled out a deck of gilt-embossed cards all engrossed in old-time copper-plate print. 'After all,' said Madox, 'you are, in a way, one of our race.' Paul didn't understand that qualification. 'More so than any of these Polish fur-buyers and engineers and the like. And the Doc took a fancy to you, I could see that. You had guts, sort of. You shouted out about old what's-his-name that time on the boat. Old Buggerlugs—you know who I mean.' He handed Paul a card; the card said, in the guest-space, 'Colonel D. Y. Efimov'; the pleasure of his company, so curlicued the formal print, was requested at dinner at the Evropa Hotel at 8.30 p.m. on the . . .

'But this isn't me,' said Paul. 'I'm not Colonel Efimov. Opiskin is the name you mean,' he added. 'On the boat, that is. Look, I don't see how I can really . . .'

'Opissoff or Efiskin,' said Madox, 'makes no diff-erence. The Doc won't know and won't care who comes. All these names are much the same,' he con-fided. The card, Paul noticed, gave no clue to the sex, name or precise academic qualifications of the Doc; the invitation was extended by something called baldly 'ANGLERUSS'.

'So,' said Paul, 'you're something to do with Angleruss, whatever that is. Something to do, I should guess, with improving Anglo-Russian relations.'

'Never look a gift horse in the mouth,' said Madox obscurely. 'It could be that, and it could be other things. But, whatever it is, it's not the sort of thing *you're* doing, mate.' His nose rabbited at the rough parcel as he poured out more champagne and then more cognac. 'And when you come,' he said, 'do try and come a bit less untidy. There'll be women there,' he added. 'The Russian women are very old-fashioned in some ways. They don't like being at posh parties with geezers who haven't shaved. This place,' he said, 'seems to have got you down a bit, if I may make so bold.'

'I'm growing a beard,' explained Paul, scraping his chin with the flat of his hand: skurr skurr skurr.

'A disguise, eh?' said Madox. 'Dark glasses and all. But I would have spotted you anywhere. It's the walk, you know. A man can't disguise his walk.'

'Is that,' said Paul, in a sudden bold inspiration, 'why the Doc goes about in a wheelchair?'

'That,' said Madox, unperturbed, 'might in some circles be regarded as clever. But it's not clever enough, not by half, my old mate. No, you leave the Doc out of it as far as those speculations are concerned. It was your walk we were talking about, wasn't it? I'd spot your walk a mile off.'

'What about my walk?' asked Paul with heat. 'What precisely do you mean by that remark?'

'Take it easy,' said Madox easily, pouring. 'And if you can't take the drink it's best to leave well alone. Sex,' he said, 'is nothing to do with me.' He seemed to toast that observation, taking a frothy swig. 'You live your own life. Nobody else can do it for you.'

'You seem,' said Paul angrily, 'to be implying something that nobody has any right to imply about another man. I resent it, that's what I do, resent it.'

'This talk,' said Madox, still calm, 'is taking what you might call a sexual turn. Now why can't we leave sex out of it, eh? Let's be like the Doc, how about that, eh? Sex,' he said, shrugging with his clerkly face puffed out smugly, 'sex—I've had it all ways and I never talked about it. And now it's all over for me. But if it's not all over for you, mate, then what I say is: jolly good luck to the girl who loves a sailor. And now let's finish this lot, because I've got to address some envelopes.'

'Look,' said Paul, red, aware that his neck was growing thicker, 'I didn't like what you said then about sailors. The song was about soldiers and you know it.

And I was in the RAF.' 'Poor dear Robert,' he thought; he wanted to cry very quietly somewhere now. Sweet champagne and cognac. Grapes that were like sugar-plums; wood alcohol with burnt sugar. Or to be sick somewhere. 'I've got to sell this,' he said, bunching the brown-paper parcel up in his hand. 'You don't know what it's like, having to go round selling this. With my wife in hospital and no money left. Trying to sell dresses to bloody Russians with no money.'

'In hospital, eh?' said Madox. 'And you being forced to sell her dresses. Poor old devil. This,' he said, putting out very white fingers, 'seems a nice bit of material. How much do you want for it?'

'Thirty roubles,' said Paul, 'and that's very cheap.'

'You do drive a hard bargain, don't you?' said Madox. 'Still, anything to help a fellow-subject of Her Majesty.' He took out a wallet of Russian leather, fat with notes, and counted out four fives and a ten. 'There you are,' he said. 'I know a barmaid back home I can give it to. A present from Russia, I can say.' Pocketing the money, Paul nearly cried with gratitude.

Two

PAUL walked none too steadily (he wondered if he had
been eating enough lately) to the Baltic Station. In the
entrance-hall he nodded briefly at the bas-reliefs of
Ushakov, Lazarev, Kornilov, Nakhimov and Makarov
—Russian admirals all, and they looked it. He was
getting to know them well. The ocean-coloured marble
from the Urals in the underground hall, the ceiling
that billowed like a sail, 'The Shot from the *Aurora*'
represented in Florentine mosaic—these made his
nausea seem marine and healthy. But on the brief
journey (there was only Narvskaya Station in between)
to the Kirov Works stop, he had a sensation of quarrying
going on in the Urals of his brain, or rather a bas-relief
of the true Paul Hussey being laboriously hammered,
also urgently (day and night shifts) because the un-
veiling to slow hand-claps and ironical Prokofiev music
was not far off. It was not right that a time for down-
right no or yes should have dawned when he had never
been more aware of everything necessarily containing
its opposite. What was he, then, and what was he in
the world for? He had a partial answer to that: there
had to be people presiding with rubbed hands and
smiles (part-false) over dust accumulating, veil over
veil over veil, on Elizabethan pennies in plush, sailing-
ships in bottles, some volumes of Jacobean and Caroline
sermons, a page—framed—of a Civil War *Courier*, a
Roundhead pennant: 'I AM A JEALOUS GOD', a beautiful
oak sideboard of 1689, some genuine Queen Anne silver
candlesticks, a set of *The Rambler*, a first edition of
Cowper, a Regency brocade waistcoat and a battered

Regency striped sofa, some regimental table-pieces showing tarnished silver savages subdued by gun or Bible, whatnots, meticulous taxidermy, a sadistic and a sentimental Landseer, starry Pre-Raphaelites with very strong female noses . . .

Kirov Works Station. Up to light-grey Caucasian marble, the fluorescent square ceiling lamps like natural daylight; the workers like so many *papiros*-smoking Bottoms amid the airy delicacy. Then out into sunlight and, soon, the familiar landmark of the eleven-storey tower of the Kirov District Soviet; there was a cinema there, and that was where Anna, the dark mistress of Alexei Prutkov, had once worked as a projectionist. Alexei had told some story about her snarling up several thousand feet of some epic of the steppes during a gala performance or something; now she helped clean up the tiny workshops of the Children's Technical Station at the Kirov Works Club. Ah, Russia.

Paul walked near the thirty-acre Ninth of January Park, where the workers of the Narvskaya Zastaya had assembled to take a petition to the Tsar and had been shot down instead. (The slim shiny topboots, the careful aim, the Eisenstein black holes of bloody mouths and the cracked steel-rimmed spectacles.) It was all a fair, modern, smiling district, but the flat-block Paul now approached dated from the nineteen-thirties and had become as sorry, stained, peeling, as anything built in England during that flimsy period. Crowning the edifice was the bas-relief image of some hero in overalls, his face nibbled away and his body striated with weather-stains. There were little verandahs with washing on them; several radios were bleating the same contralto recital. Paul sighed and began to climb the stairs.

He was panting and palpitating when he reached the door of the flat; he opened it (it was never locked). Anna was there alone, lying on the one bed. Paul frowned at that, not being quite sure what he felt about Anna or she about him, panting. She had very black eyebrows which she would beetle at him, as she did now, flipping through a sports magazine (Amazon weight-lifter on cover) on the bed, fully dressed in black stockings, thick pepper-and-salt skirt, baby-blue ribbed sweater. Paul had offered her a drilon dress, but she had rejected the gift. She resented his being there. Paul panted. He had never before, now he came to think of it, been alone with Anna in the flat. The prospect of being with her now, until Alex came home, didn't greatly please him. What he really wanted was to lie down on that bed, quietly and alone, and snore. It was curious that the image of a desirable nap should come to him in the form of a snore. There was only one bed in the flat; he had, so far, slept in the cane chair (fleas in it, he was sure) that stood by the summer-empty stove, his feet up on an old box that—according to the stencilling—had formerly held cucumbers. At night, that was, or what was normally left of it after drink, argument, poetry, jazz. During the day, when not visiting Belinda or trying to sell drilon dresses, he would take a grateful flop on the old charpoy, alone and quiet save for the flies buzzing and odd noises outside— children not at school, water drumming into a bucket from a tap on the landing, trucks changing gear on the corner, Radio Leningrad. Now, just after three in the afternoon, he would have to attempt a doze with the fleas, but there could be no uninhibited snoring. Anna was critical of everything that came out of his mouth, everything she understood, anyway. She would sneer faintly at his Russian accent, wait with mock patience and lifted eyes while he struggled with spoken syntax; she would open her mouth at his laughs, hums, sighs, as if these too were not being properly declined or conjugated; and once, when his little denture, tongued out in sleep on the chair, had fallen to his lap, he had awakened to see her picking it up with coke-tongs, sneering.

He looked down at her now, still panting, and attempted a smile, then said in careful Russian:

'You are having a rest after your labours?'

She examined that offering with a look of distaste, as though it were a broken transistor radio or something; anyway, she did not seem pleased with it from the point of view of its phonetics, its grammar, or its propriety. Paul, panting more slowly now, sat down in the cane chair and took out his packet of Bulgarian cigarettes. He made a noise at her and an offering gesture, but she shook her head. 'Sod her then,' he said to himself, lighting up. She turned over a page. He picked up the day's *Pravda* from the top of the stove and yawned out smoke. Oh, glory be to God, what was he doing here? How the hell had he managed to get himself in this position, dirty and near-bearded, smoking a painfully aromatic Bulgarian cigarette in a flea-haunted cane chair in a miserably small Leningrad flat that smelt of cabbage, aniseed, kvass, and now the vague muskiness of a dark woman from Georgia lying, breathing up at her sports magazine, on a bed with a dirty flowered coverlet? She had her black legs flexed, apart, as for the heat. Her shoes had been kicked off and there was a hole in one foot-sole. She scratched an armpit and the magazine flapped shut. She shook it open impatiently. 'Anna,' said Paul. 'Anna, Anna.'

'*Chto?*' She responded to that, giving him a dark suspicious questioning look. Paul realized that he'd had no reason at all for speaking (it wasn't really calling) her name. '*Nichevo,*' he said. But, of course, it was because of Belinda, nymph of *The Rape of the Lock*, and Hampton Court, where thou, great Anna, whom three realms obey—'*Chai*,' he suggested; he could do with a cup, or rather a glass, of—'*Chai mozhna?*' She shook her head very forcibly; the little bitch resented his having anything in that flat, despite his payment of the rent. 'Right,' said Paul, 'I'll make some bloody *chai* myself.' And he got up, puffing Bulgarian smoke, to go to the little cupboard by the stove to get the *chainik* and the tea, and then to see if there was any water in the filthy electric kettle that, because it leaked, was all clumsily bound up in sticking-plaster. He shook it and heard only the dry rattle of broken-off bits of calcium deposit; but there was water from the landing tap in the old-fashioned rosy wash-jug. Ready to pour, he was astonished to find himself set upon from the rear, not only with irritable words but with one hand in the hair at his nape, the other—stubby, he saw clearly, and with bitten nails—trying to wrest the electric kettle from him. The latter went down on the bare floor, clattering. He turned on her, saying, 'Damn and blast it, who pays the bloody rent here? And if this is your idea of bloody Russian hospitality . . .' He couldn't understand a word of what she was saying, but he got a fine close-up of her opening and shutting mouth with the red meat of her tongue darting up all the time to her palate for the y-y-y-sounds which were called iotization, the straight and (now he came to think of it) Burne-Jones-type nose with the promise of an eventual woman's moustache beneath it, the speckled nasty eyes, the moving black wedded brows above. 'Oh, shut up,' he said and gave her a light back-hander. She recoiled back towards the bed, though with no show of outrage: perhaps she was used to being hit—though not, Paul thought, by Alexei Prutkov; probably the man in Georgia whom she'd left.

Which from the neighbouring Hampton—Hampton, hampton: how had the word come to describe, in the vernacular of vulgar men, the cory or Master John Thursday? Paul felt there was a well-damped-down fire of excitement somewhere round his perineum. He said, in softer tones, to the girl on the bed who was rubbing her cheek and spitting odd words at him, 'All right, I know I shouldn't have done that. I won't have any tea, then. Let's say no more about it.' He must get Belinda on the next available bloody boat, whatever the doctor said. 'Here, have a Jezebel,' proffering his packet. That was his little joke; the cigarettes were really called Djebel. But she struck the packet out of his hand. Jezebel? He generated no current in her, that was evident. He'd be out of this flat now, if only he could get some money. But Alex was all right, Alex and he got on fine together. 'Ah, well,' said Paul, picking up the cigarettes that had spilled out of the packet and going back to his cane chair and the copy of *Leningradskaya Pravda*. Anna lay down flat on the bed again and resumed her scowling at the sports magazine. She had made her point: Paul was to stay here, if Alex said so, but he was to keep his paws off things that came into her province. The whole thing was damned silly.

Paul tried to read a front-page letter from N. Khrushchev to a Soviet minister called Tovarishch Tsedenbal; he could not tell whether it was a letter of praise or rebuke. He started on a long news item about the fulfilment of some industrial long-term plan or other, full of percentages which all—save for the odd 99 or 98 to make the list look more plausible—spilled over the hundred. The Cyrillic print began to swim; he had to squint to distinguish a *sh* from a *shch*. His Russian was not good enough; he and Robert had wasted a lot of time on that course back during the war; nor had he kept it up since. If only he had foreseen a time when, in summer Leningrad, he would be sitting like this, in a cane chair jolly with fleas in a one-roomed flat in the Kirov district, a dark monoglot bitch from Georgia lying on the bed, he would have spent the long hours when nobody came to the shop in reading *War and Peace* in the original, a crib at the side like a bread-and-butter plate. It would have been good for his French, too. . . .

Comrade Somebody-or-other was jeering loudly at the toothless British lion. 'It is evident,' he told a large committee of heavy-shouldered, heavy-browed men and women, 'that here is the great object-lesson in decadence, the most patent exemplification of the fundamental contradiction of capitalism. Observe the alternation of aimless spasmodic action and sheer paralysis—the craving for exotic sauces thus becoming cognate with a scared huddling into the dusty dark of the past. The same ambiguity is discernible in sex . . .' The voice went harshly on. Paul was now shocked to see projected on a screen as wide and high as the Kremlin a cartoon straight out of *Pravda*: Paul Hussey himself in John Bull hat and waistcoat, but plump with a soft cream-cake plumpness, no solid beef-red flesh, old ormolu clocks tied to his shoulders, simpering along toothlessly, bare hairless legs knock-kneed under a kilt that was no kilt—a drilon skirt rather. 'Highly inflammable,' said somebody; a match was set to it and the image, still simpering, started to burn. There was a noise of splashing water, but that would not put the fire out.

Paul woke to this splashing and a dry mouth. The splashing went on in the real world of the harsh cane chair and the Baltic summer. The splashing, he saw, came from a vision of moving pinkness in the dark farther corner. It was a pink body with a pair of pink arms weaving. It was Anna washing her hair in a basin.

He allowed a sense of outrage to rise. This, then, was

143

what they thought of him, was it? A lump of dough, a piece of old furniture, a discarded boot. That creature over there thought she could switch her breasts on in his presence, did she, without getting electrocuted? Breathing shallowly, pretending to be asleep still, Paul watched her twist and turn blindly, soap in her eyes, doing a sort of little dance in her black-stockinged feet, while she tore away at her scalp with a witch's nails. She was a full-breasted young woman, and her breasts swung in a grave rhythm, minims, say, to the fingers' quavers. Her armpits had black silken beards. The flesh on her well-fleshed upper arms shook and rippled. She was naked down to the navel. The dark-ringed eyes of her breasts ogled him, eyes capable of independent motion, like the eyes of some strabismic Mack Sennett comedian—Ben Turpin, Chester Conklin, somebody like that. Paul was aware of a solid physical response. Which from the neighbouring Hampton takes its name.

He got up from the chair and stole towards her. What a counterpoint of metres—heart, her fingers, her breasts, the flesh on her arms, his stealthy feet. He stumbled against one of his suitcases jutting out from under the bed. She heard that and, still blinded by soap, seemed to sniff in the direction of the noise. She began to grope for the greyish towel that lay on the bed. But Paul was upon her, good strong daring arms about her quite substantial nakedness, the smell of clean soapy hair—tempered by the sharper tang of armpits—a new Russian smell to be prized and hoarded. One would find that particular smell of soapy hair no longer now in the West; there it would be something perfumed, oily, medicated, well advertised on ITV. But this was a smell with no built-in allure: it was honest, harsh and functional. And it was also something from the past. 'God help me,' groaned Paul excitedly to himself; it was his mother washing herself down in the scullery in Bradcaster, himself about ten with an Œdipus limp still: he had been profoundly and unholily stirred by that slapped wet nakedness.

Anna, as was to be expected, knocked at his face and chest as if she wanted desperately to be let in; her eyes were open in shock and outrage, though wincing at the stinging soap; her dripping hair slapped wet at Paul as in some asperges ceremony. And she cried authentic bad Russian words at him, trying to kick with her pathetic black-stockinged feet. The kicking could be checked by Paul's inserting one leg between her two, stopping her mouth with his mouth. He saw himself doing all this and marvelled. The little denture came loose, but he clamped it down with his upper teeth. That was no way to kiss, however; that was the sort of mouth some girls would offer in Postman's Knock, a sort of cushioned boniness. So he opened up moistly, trying to insinuate his tongue in. She, of course, tried to jerk her head away, still fisting strongly at his chest, so he plunged his own fingers into the wet head of hair and held her skull rigid, stopping her mouth with a no-nonsense firmness. It became necessary then to immobilize her completely, for she was using those witch's nails to tear at his cheeks. Gravity; the resourceful man makes use of gravity—bed and the posture of Venus Observed.

He had her flat on that bed in no time. 'Be persistent,' he told himself, 'and every woman must soften; it is in the nature of woman to yield.' Gasping, he released her mouth and swallowed a chestful of Russian air. He and the creaking bed had her sandwiched beautifully. (An image of trying to eat a live frog sandwich, some cruel *Pravda* political cartoon of the French and Algeria.) She yelled at him. In a glorious transport of triumph he raised himself sufficiently to deliver a ringing smack on her left cheek. (Hadn't he done that before, somewhere, to somebody else, here in Leningrad? It seemed too long ago to remember.) Anna looked up at him with a child's eyes and mouth and a doll's red cheek. Then she started to howl like a child. Paul tumbled into a great soft membranous pit of tenderness, saying, 'There, there, I'm sorry, forgive me,' kissing her all over in a punctuation of remorse and a softer sort of desire. And now he was free to crush a dark nipple between his life-line and his heart-line, the milk-blue flesh starting up between his spread fingers. She became all passivity, all waiting. Suddenly the life went out of what he was trying to do; the big proud chord (chordee?) on the electric organ faded to *niente* with the coming of a power-cut, though the player's hands still stayed in position. Once, at nine years old, he had heard an older boy explain in the elementary-school urinal what it was a man did with a woman. Paul had wanted to know why; what was the point, what could they possibly get out of it? It was like that now. Or as in a theatre the actor playing Mellors in a stage version of *Lady Chatterley* would be preoccupied with things quite different from what the love-scene was about. Like that.

She still lay quiet, tears (he had provoked Russian tears: he was really part of the country now) drying under her closed eyes. What image could he lash out of its hole to lash this completely fagged impulse back to something like life? He was astonished at some of the pictures that were drily dealt, like the cards of the Tarot pack—compositions quite as bizarre as the Moon Dripping Blood or the Lightning-struck Tower, though executed in the flesh-tints of cheap Italian religious statuary. Then he heard strange and oddly attractive bell-music—that piece by Opiskin—and smelt wet RAF ground-capes, so he knew it was time to dismount, very quickly. Rolling off, he said, 'Sorry, I can't.'

'*Chto?*' Her eyes opened very wide.

'*Vinovat,*' he translated. '*Ya nye mogu.*' He was standing by the bed now, looking down regretfully. With eyes and mouth equally open she gave him a long astonished stare. Then she snorted and began to laugh, her breasts blancmanging away lazily. The whole episode, far from annoying her, seemed to put her in a good humour.

She got up from the bed, still laughing, and said, '*Muzhchini.*' That meant 'men'.

Paul frowned, then wondered. Why that plural? She towelled her head very vigorously, humming. Was it because Alex was as incompetent as he was? He had not yet found out what Alex was really like; there hadn't been time, somehow. But, lying on his cane chair while Alex and Anna occupied the bed, he had not yet heard anything which sounded like cheerful frotting, the old springs zithering away. He shook his head, taking a Djebel out of the crushed pack, humbly offering one to her. She took it gaily and smoked it, still stripped, while she rubbed away at her scalp with the greyish towel.

Then she dressed her upper half and said brightly to Paul, '*Chai?*' Paul nodded gratefully; he would like nothing better than a nice glass of *chai*. Well, there it was: it didn't matter how you established contact so long as you established it.

Alex came home, excited. He was dressed in his working-clothes—jeans and heavy sports coat—and he carried a bag of food for the evening meal. It was always the same in this week of summer weather: open sandwiches of blood sausage, smoked salmon and ham, a couple of bottles of the very good local citronade. He also carried something flat and square wrapped in newspaper. 'Big ·deal, dad,' he said, waving this latter. 'Jazz, genuine jazz, the real thing. Off of one of the tourists,' he explained. 'Tonight we're having a ball, dig. Boris has this portable record-player and he's bringing it along. A bit of real jazz, dad.'

'Why,' said Paul, examining the clammy sandwiches, 'can't we have something cooked sometime? *Borshch* or something.'

'We'd have to light the stove, dad,' said Alex. 'And we don't do that till the fall.' He seemed to notice Anna for the first time and made a kind of kissing noise at her. 'Jazz,' he said, beaming. 'Did you get any cash today, dad?'

'Thirty,' said Paul honestly. He took out the rouble-notes and laid them on the bed.

'Good good good,' said Alex. '*Khorosho*. We can buy a few bottles round the corner, dad. Make a real night of it.'

'How about the rent?' asked Paul.

'That can wait, dig,' said Alex. 'Nobody will suffer if it waits. The State is the landlord and we, dig, are the State. The State,' he said, 'can wait.' He made a little jazz-riff out of that and clicked his fingers on the off-beat all round the room, swaying his hips ('The State can wait') in rhythm. They were lithe slim hips.

148

Three

THERE were two trombonists on the fourth track of side one, an Indianapolis negro named J. J. Johnson, and a Dane called Kai Winding, and Vladimir claimed to be able to tell which was which. He went further. He said it was possible, on tone alone, to tell a negro jazzman from a white one. This was contested. Vladimir, whom Paul liked because he spoke courteous slow Russian and, so that Paul should completely understand his weightier utterances on jazz, very fair French, grew heated and inadvertently spilt some cheap sticky vodka on to Boris's portable record-player. That caused further heat and some loud threats. Paul's head ached and his lower gum felt painful. This trombone duet had already been played eight times.

But it was like a return to one's youth; or rather it was like experiencing a sample of the youth Paul had missed because of the war—student youth with drinking and arguing going on till all hours. After the war it had seemed too late to think of applying for a university scholarship; well, here was an extra-curricular finger of the life he'd wanted, and he had had to come to the Soviet Union to find it. What he would have liked was for the students to wear caps with shiny peaks and tassels and to smoke big pipes. He would also have liked some nice youthful discussions on religion and the Meaning of Life; but the only dialectic these youngsters wanted was the dialectic of jazz.

The needle pricked at an earlier track and Vladimir said, 'Blackhawk, San Francisco. Miles Davis, Hank Mobley, Wynton Kelly, Paul Chambers, Jimmy Cobb.'

He knew it all, by God: he stayed up late, tuning in to obscure radio stations; he haunted the foreign ships looking for jazz records; he had a map of New Orleans, he said, in his bedroom. He now explained to Paul that Miles Davis was a great trumpet-player and that the ugliness of his tone was deliberate—a subtly cultivated aspect of his art. He was delighted with this American LP: it was an anthology of great jazz.

Paul looked round benevolently from the bed where he was sitting. Alex, Anna, Vladimir, Sergei, Boris, Feodor, Pavel—he, too, was Pavel—Dyadya Pavel or Uncle Paul, because of his age. Next to him was a young man he had not previously met, but he was called sometimes Pierre and sometimes Petruchka and he wore steel-rimmed glasses like Army respirator spectacles: he seemed vaguely familiar, but Paul could not quite place him. Alex and Anna sat together on the floor, his arm absently around her, and occasionally it seemed that Anna sneered up at Paul, her brief friendly tea-making mood quite gone. Paul's head raged; he found that swigs of cognac from the bottle helped a little. There was, in fact, more than one bottle; his thirty roubles seemed to have gone quite a long way.

'Kid Thomas,' said Vladimir, '*i yevo* Algiers Stompers. *Cet Algiers*,' he explained, '*est un faubourg de Nouveau Orleans.*'

'Very interesting,' said Paul. The fact was, not the music. All the music sounded alike to him. Now, a few of the songs of the nineteen-thirties—'These Foolish Things', 'Two Sleepy People', 'Sweet and Lovely'—would, in his boozy mood, be far more acceptable. He said so to Alex and Alex gave a long, rather contemptuous, speech in Russian about what he'd said.

Young Pavel made a comment and this got back to Paul as: 'You like give your age away, dad. Square, that's what it is.' Paul had taught Alex that use of 'square'. 'Or, if you like,' went on Alex, 'it's bourgeois. Real capitalist stuff and the opium of the people.'

'And how about this?' said Paul loudly. 'Isn't this opium, too?'

It was not opium, he was told indignantly. This was proletarian, this was: music of an enslaved race.

'Enslaved race my bottom,' said Paul rudely. 'A lot of dead-beat gin-guzzling reefer-puffing layabouts.' That took some translating. 'And commercial like everything else,' Paul added. He was a bit disappointed in these young Russians; he had expected them to be rebels. But, of course, in a sense they *were* rebelling, like all the young people of the world; the trouble was that the language of rebellion was also, in the USSR, the language of the Establishment. Paul said loudly, 'Look at your own glorious tradition of Russian art—Tchaikovsky and Mussorgsky and Borodin and Opiskin. What about those, eh? Aren't they a lot better than this tripe?'

He shouldn't have mentoned Opiskin; he realized that too late: Opiskin was a dirty word. Alex said, 'What do you know about Opiskin, dad? Opiskin's not talked about much nowadays, dig. They reckon that Opiskin went over to the enemy.'

'What enemy?' said Paul. 'What does anybody here really know about Opiskin? What, for that matter,' he said, warming, over a noisy shipwreck chorus on the record-player, 'does anybody here really get a chance to know? You're only allowed to know what the State wants you to know. The sources of information are polluted. A lot of muzzled bears,' he added, for some reason. A bear—something to do with someone dancing with a bear. He turned to Pierre or Petruchka, puzzling. Meanwhile a lot of noise was going on, provoked mainly by his words. Then he got it. He said, 'Tolstoy.

War and Peace.' Pierre looked bewildered: he knew no English. '*Voina i Mir,*' Paul translated.

'As for *Crime and Punishment,*' Feodor said, 'it was a crime to write it and it is a punishment to read it.' He then shut up; Paul looked at him, open-mouthed: he had not realized that Feodor knew any English.

Alex was translating a pronouncement of Sergei's. 'Western decadence, dig,' he said. 'This is the point, dad—that everybody knows what they need to know. And in the West you still haven't put a man into orbit. So what does it all mean?'

'I don't know,' said Paul, feeling desperate. 'I don't know what anything means. But,' he added, 'don't start telling me about Western decadence. We're not dead yet, not by a long chalk. In Europe, I mean. In Great Britain, that is. As for America, that's just the same as Russia. You're no different. America and Russia would make a very nice marriage.' Saying that, he felt sudden goose-pimples starting. Nobody seemed to be listening to what he was saying; the record-player still blared and thudded. He heard Anna give a loud merry laugh; she seemed to have been whispering something in Alex's ear. Paul reddened. He shouted, 'Don't give me any more of that guff about Western decadence.' Something about a bottle of rum and an open window brought a sudden gust of vertigo. He said to Pierre, 'That's what you're supposed to do. To get on that window-sill there and drink off a whole bottle of rum.' Pierre shook his head good-humouredly, not understanding one word. 'There you are,' cried Paul. 'If you're looking for decadence, here it is. He could do it in *War and Peace,* but he can't do it now.'

'Dad, dad,' said Alex, 'we don't want trouble and we don't want arguments, dig. All we want is to just hear this jazz.'

'But there isn't any rum,' said Paul. 'I see that. I

apologize,' he said, bowing gravely to Pierre. Pierre bowed back. 'No rum,' said Paul. 'So it can't be done.'

'*Dyadya Pavel*,' said Boris kindly, '*zamolchi*.' Johnny St Cyr's Hot Five was at it, very hot.

'I will not *zamolchi*,' said Paul. 'I have as much right to speak as anybody else. More right, really, because I am the eldest here. There's no rum,' Paul said, 'but there's vodka. It could be done as well with vodka as with rum.'

'Listen, dad,' said Alex. 'Tolstoy was a long time ago, dig, and things have changed since then. It was a wilder sort of life they lived then, dig.'

'Less decadent,' said Paul.

'Just as you like, dad.' He hugged Anna to himself with one hand and took a fair draught of cognac with the other. Anna smiled. Johnny St Cyr's Hot Five played a very rough coda; the needle hissed; it was the end of the side.

Sergei said something in Russian; Alex shook his head and said, '*Nyet*.' They all looked at Paul, shyly, grinning a little.

'What's that about?' asked Paul.

'Never mind what it's about, dad,' said Alex. 'You're not doing it, that's what. We're having no *War and Peace* in this flat.'

'Would you mind just explai——'

'Never mind. Peace but no war is what I should have said, dig. Because war is what there'd be if you fell, dad, Jackie Kennedy blowing the whistle and letting the Bomb drop.' Alex mushroomed his left arm into the air and made guttural noises significant of a cracking civilization. 'An international incident, that's what there'd be.'

'Nonsense,' said Paul. His headache was clearing nicely. 'I'll tell you what I'll do. I'll give a free drilon dress to anyone who's got guts enough to sit on the window-sill there with his legs outside the window and drink a bottle of vodka straight off. I can't say fairer than that.' But Alex shook his head and would not translate. To Vladimir Paul said, '*Je donnerai une robe de drilon à celui qui . . .*' He couldn't get any further; his French was not all that good. And now Pierre was putting his arm firmly round him and pulling him up from the bed, smiling. There were cheers. Alex said:

'I'm not having it, dig, I'm really not . . .' He tried to get up from the floor, but Boris and Feodor came over, grinning, and sat on him. They were hefty young men. Alex, now flat down, spoke breathless and angry Russian. Anna giggled; it was Anna who picked up a vodka-bottle nearly three-quarters full and proffered it to Paul. Paul said:

'All right, *khorosho*—we old ones can show you youngsters a few tricks still.' It was a large sash-window, contrived by the State builders probably less to give light than to save bricks. Paul pushed up the lower sash and looked out and down. It had been, as he remembered, the third storey in *War and Peace*; this floor was much much higher. The warm Leningrad summer night, with dawn not far off, was as much below as above. He gazed down into a wide well of shadows, coigns, lights. He felt giddy and sick. He just could not, after all, do it; he was, damn it, a middle-aged man.

From the floor Alex called up in a winded voice, 'Don't do it, dad, don't.'

Paul brought his head back into the room and said, 'All right. It is, after all, just a bit . . .' Then he saw Anna, her lips spread tight in a malicious smile, swaying her hips and shaking the vodka-bottle in both hands, as if it were a cocktail-mixer. She then took the bottle by its neck, turned it upside down, and, with a look of infinite malice, did a coital thrust-and-recoil in

Paul's direction with it, grinning mockingly. 'Right, you bitch,' said Paul. 'Give me that bloody bottle.'

But he didn't like it, he didn't at all, getting up on that window-sill—it was smooth and it sloped—with his head bent as to the guillotine, even though eager hands held him in position. Alex was in the background of the crowd, still shouting, 'Stop, I tell you, dig. This is my apartment and I won't have it——'

Paul sat in terrible fear, his heels feeling for some cranny in the brickwork. The bottle was uncorked for him; the great negro throat, jazzy with lights, gaped below to drink him. Pierre rasped sharp and strong, and the supporting hands, like chocks, left him. He was on his own, launched. He raised the bottle to his lips, but his head was pushed forward by the raised lower window-sash; it could not be tilted back for the act of swigging. '*Ya nye mogu!*' he cried, Russian coming to him clear as a bell. 'It can't be done!' He tried to climb back into the room, thrusting his left leg in first. This leg was at once seized and held strongly. He then found himself squirming, head down, arms desperate, vodka glugging out of the bottle, trying to get his other leg into the room. But he couldn't and, like a Blake Satan, was poised falling and not falling in the immense immense immense. Jeering voices of the heavenly host assailed him. And his literal host cried in distress, 'Oh, dad, dad . . .' Even in this state of nightmare inversion Paul could not bear to think of vodka streaming in the firmament, degging the bluey dew, dewy blue. He inserted the neck into his gob and went glup glup glup glup. This might well be one of the forms of death, or rather the complex Bardo experience of passing in one of its forms. Cheers rocked his left ankle; it was only by his left ankle that he was now being held. A final glup finished the bottle. He shook it neck-down to show it was empty. The cheers were louder. He sent the bottle spinning into the dark emptiness. Afar off it silver-tinklesplintered. He was pulled into the room legwise, cheered, petted, patted. Even Alex had to say, 'Well. dad, if you're the West the West is not decadent, dig.'

Paul's pluck was one raw red burn. The record-player was tromboning black and white again, but this time at 78 r.p.m. so that the dark treacly tones spun mad and high and absurd like some Gothic vision of heaven, bobbed auburn nobs of blasting archangels. 'Shakespeare,' called Paul. 'Sweet William.' There was a jam-jar with a scant bunch of the flower in it, sitting on the cloth-topped soap-box by Anna's side of the bed. 'For that the furtive ties pronounce auriculous,' recited Paul, 'and in fat andirons cross and cowslip lay—then foreshore tits wax loud in holdall brew.' There was applause. Feodor started a sort of frog-dance. They were all old Russia after all, God bless them. 'I suggest now,' cried Paul, 'that we all strip ourselves stark ballock naked.'

Four

'COME on, then, come on, come on, out of it.'

It was incredible that two weak eyelids should be able to shore up all the howling light of the universe. Paul, or whoever he was, opened up a fraction to admit the whole toppling weight of it, right up to infinity's navel; then he shelled his lanced and bitten jellies, crying out as at a gouging. That lad Bob Daring in the *Boy's Magazine* SF serial, 1930 or thereabouts, had been out on the wing of the spaceship mending something or other; he had, in a second's curiosity, opened his space-helmet in that infinite dark and felt the veritable sword of God. Paul had never believed it possible that light could be so vindictive as now. He made a wincing foetus of himself and said:

'Ur ar waririt?'

'You just get off of that floor, dad, though I shouldn't be calling you that any more by rights. I should be calling you rotten drunken bum and filthy bastard, but I'm keeping my temper, dig, and this is more in sorrow than in anger. All I want is just you out of it and that's the end, dig, the end end end end.'

Paul knew who that was. Putting out blind and dithering fingers, he felt all about him. Cancer of the brain, that was what he had, excruciating pincers nipping at the frontal lobes and the medulla oblongata and the pia mater, while the heavy shelled body just sat. He was indeed on a floor; he was fully dressed except for his denture and jacket; his jacket was a sort of pillow; the sharp brittleness under his right ear was the dark glasses he normally kept, this weather of

terrible light, in his breast pocket ready for use.
Getting them out now was like tonging an isotope from
its leaden bower. He spent whole palsied seconds
shifting them to his nose. Then he raised his ruined
head up towards an Alex all twitched up in controlled
disgust. Paul's heart filled the universe with its noise.
There was a great pet dragon crouched somewhere,
metrically thumping the scaly horror of its tail on the
floor and raising dust. He coughed and choked with
this dust. His mouth was Fleet Ditch, filled with
leprous fat, rancid rags, tumbled-in night-soil; it was
that rubbish dump called Hell outside Jerusalem. Like
someone passed on who, at a seance, desperately tries
to send a message through a moronic medium, Paul
asked and asked for a drink of something. But he was
not understood.

'I kicked you and she kicked you,' resumed Alex,
'before we went out to work. Yes, kicked you, dig, like
some big fat drunk snoring animal, that's what. But we
couldn't make you budge. You just lay there and went
honk honk. And do you know what time it is? Eh?
Have you any idea what the time is, lying there in your
filth? Well, I'll tell you. It's three o'clock. It's three
o'clock in the afternoon, dig, that's what it is, you
boozed-up bum.'

'Hrink,' begged Paul. 'Hrink, hrink.' He could see
very dimly a forlorn dull-shining clump of unwashed
glasses on the little table by the cold stove. He began
painfully to crawl towards it.

'That's right,' said Alex. 'On all fours like some sort
of a dirty animal. Go on, then, crawl.' Paul's body was
remembering all sorts of odd acts of violence. He
reached the table, groped up, felt around in a dull
clinking, then brought trembling down a tumbler that
seemed not entirely empty. He squinted at it; the smell
was sickening and raw. But he took his medicine like a

good boy. He gulped whatever it was, panted as if dying, held back his gorge, then climbed up to the seat of the cane chair. 'God,' he whispered, sitting, creaking, 'God God.'

'Yes, dad,' said Alex, 'you do well to call on your square and bourgeois God, dig.'

'Time. Time irrit?'

'Three,' danced Alex. 'I told you three, didn't I? Just one minute ago I said three, so now it's one minute past three, dig? And now you're to get out of it. Come on.' Paul now noticed that his three suitcases —the fourth was with Belinda—were piled on the unmade bed. His heart lunged at his chest, using a hefty shoulder again and again, battering.

'Hofpital.' But he couldn't rise. In the breast pocket of his sports shirt he found his little denture. He inserted it, but his gum was terribly sore. 'My wife,' he said.

'It's you,' said Alex, 'who need that. You need to die on the operating table, dig, you unpleasant drunkard.'

'Please,' said Paul. 'Please. I'm ill. I'm sick. Be kind.' He had a swift Christine image of himself, dying. Vinegar on a sponge. There was vinegar in that cupboard over there. He got up in pain to totter towards it. Alex said:

'What is it you want then, bum?' Paul told him. Alex made a vomiting noise and rummaged among the pathetic cans and packages that made up his stock of provisions. He pulled out a black bottle labelled *Uksus*, a sucking, soothing sort of name. 'Here,' he said, thrusting it at Paul, 'you get sober, dig, so I can say what I think of you, you filthy decadent limey.' Paul drank from the bottle, shuddering. The vinegar carved into his crapula very painfully. He tottered back to the cane chair and fought for breath. Then he said:

'Yes? Yes. What happened? What did I do?' He raked away at his brain, rattling clinker. 'Oh God,' he said. 'That window. I might have died.'

'Better if you had died, dig.' Alex sat on the table's edge, looking down on him, his nose bunched up in distaste. 'It wasn't the vodka, though that was bad enough. It was your filthy sexual habits. How do you think I can ever look them in the face again—my friends, that is, dig? You and your horrible decadent sex.'

'I don't remember. I just do not remember. I cannot recollect a thing.'

'So that's all that goes on in the West, my friends say. Getting drunk and shouting and nasty decadent sex. How do you expect, dig, to get a man into orbit that way?'

'Please,' said Paul, 'tell me,' in pain, 'what happened.'

'I don't dare talk about it even. Anna was disgusted.'

'Anna?' It was coming back. 'So Anna's been telling tales, has she? Well,' said Paul, 'let me tell you that she was as much to blame as me. She was all for it, that she was. There was nothing one-sided about that, let me tell you.'

Alex put on a look of intense shock and horror and turned himself into a film-still. Comets of agony and nausea meanwhile shot all through Paul. Alex said at length, 'What I should really do is to lash you. I should get a steel whip and raise big bruises and weals all over your dirty body. So you tried your sexual lust on that poor girl too, did you? And she wanted no trouble, so she said nothing of it. Well . . . And to think what that poor girl has suffered from her husband. But,' and here he smiled contemptuously, his nose-wings well spread, 'you got nowhere. If you say you got anywhere you're a liar.'

160

'I didn't,' said Paul. 'I couldn't. It's the way I am. What I mean is,' he amended quickly, 'is that, yes, I'm a liar. Just as you said. I was just lying, that was it. I didn't know what I was saying. I never tried anything, not a thing.'

'Yes,' said Alex. 'Of course not. Because you're not made that way. What you like, dig, is your own sex, and that's what's so filthy and disgusting.'

'What precisely . . .' Paul stared, feeling his eyeballs start to crack. 'Go on, let's have more.'

'Oh yes,' said Alex, 'that was your real self coming out, wasn't it? When a man's drunk, dig, he shows himself as he really is. There you were, chasing Vladimir round the room, and then it was Pierre you were after, and you got nowhere with any of them, because they're not decadent like you are, dig.'

'God,' said Paul. 'And did I chase anybody else?'

'Yes, you did. You tried your dirty sexiness on Pavel, and you even tried it on me, but all you got out of that was a big punch in the gut, dig.' That, then, explained a pain which Paul had thought to be a kind of extruded dyspepsia. There were other pains, too, and patches of tenderness; he was not greatly interested in pursuing their origins. 'And then,' said Alex, 'you said you were going to have Opiskin.'

'But Opiskin's dead.'

'Oh, being dead or alive wasn't going to stand in your way,' said disgusted Alex. 'And all I want now is you out of this pad and quick too, because I can't look my friends in the face again, not after telling them that you were a good guy even though you were a sort of a capitalist.'

'Where do you get that capitalist idea from?'

'Coming over here with all those bourgeois clothes to sell, but too much concerned with your sexuality, dig, to really get down to a bit of hard work and sell them. And boasting last night about having a big capitalist shop full of silver and jewels back in England. Everybody was like disgusted.'

'Not everybody would understand what I was saying.'

'Oh, you got down to speaking Russian pretty good by the time you were trying to tear the clothes off of people. So now I'm having you out and now, yes, now now now, because you're horrible and filthy and uncultured.'

'Uncultured, eh? That's a good one, that is.' Paul tried to stand up, but the appropriate departments of his brain were unable to carry out the order. He sat down again. He said, 'You can't just throw me out, not just like that. I'm a sick man. I can hardly move. Besides,' he added, 'I've no money. I gave you my thirty roubles and you spent it all on drink.'

'Drink,' said Alex, 'which you drank, dad. Though I shouldn't call you dad.'

'You're breaking your promise, too,' Paul said. 'How about the people I was going to be introduced to who were going to buy my drilon dresses, eh? You Americans and Russians are all the same. You promise things and you don't keep your promises. You just can't be trusted, that's what it is.'

'Yes,' said Alex, 'I expected that. I expected just those very words from you, dad. Well, history will show that it wasn't me who did any of the letting down. You let us all down by behaving like a decadent pig. But I've kept my promise.' He began digging in the inside pocket of his thick sports coat, bringing out his empty wallet and masses of paper rubbish. 'There was no work this morning,' he said. 'There should have been an English party going round the Hermitage, dig, but they didn't turn up. That was a good thing,' he said, still shuffling through old bills and letters and cryptic squiggles, 'because I would have gotten mad with them all and called them decadent drunken bastards.'

'And it was also a good thing,' Paul suggested, 'because you couldn't have been feeling any too well yourself.' He could see more clearly now, the vinegar doing its work; Alex had a minimal tremor and looked haggard and bloodshot.

'Here it is,' said Alex, frowning at a bit of what looked like toilet-paper. 'This man's name is S. S. Nikolaev. And don't think I'm doing this just to help you, dad, because what I'm really doing it for is the money. I need that money, dig.'

'Which money?'

'The *protsyent*. The percentage. That's what I'm entitled to.'

'I don't see how you're going to get it from me if you're going to throw me out.'

'Oh, I get it from this man Nikolaev. Don't you worry about that, dad—which I should *not* be calling you. I'll get it all right all right. He'll keep it back from you and give it to me.'

'But how much is he willing to pay?'

'That's for you to sort out with him, dig. You know the Dom Knigi?'

'That's the House of Books. That's on Nevsky Prospekt.'

'Well, what he said was for you to meet him outside there and bring the stuff with you. This afternoon, he said. Look, it's afternoon now and you'd have been snoring and honkhonking still if I hadn't come back to the pad. At five o'clock. I said that would be the best time.'

'But that's mad. I mean, that's on a public thoroughfare with all of blasted Leningrad looking on.'

'That's what he said. Perhaps he'll take you some place else then and do the deal nice and private, dig.'

163

'Why couldn't he come here instead? I mean, nobody would have any suspicion that anything was . . . I don't like the sound of this at all,' Paul said.

'There it is,' said Alex indifferently. 'You and him must do things as you think fit. But I'm not having any of this illegal stuff, dig, here in my pad.'

'You've become very conformist all of a sudden,' said Paul. 'Just a good son of the Establishment.'

'It makes you that way,' Alex said, 'when you see what Western decadence looks like. All filth and sexuality.' His tone became savage again. 'Get yourself cleaned up and shaved and try to look like a *man*, dig. I don't want you here by the time Anna gets home. It will just make her sick to look at you, poor chick.'

'I'm ill,' said Paul. 'I can't possibly carry all that baggage as far as the Metro.'

'I'll help you,' said Alex. 'I'll speed you off the premises and only too glad, dig, to see your backside.'

Five

A READING people; more, a book-buying people. And the books they were buying in the bookshop which made up the ground floor of the Dom Knigi were not high-coloured toadstool paperbacks; they were black tomes on, Paul guessed, aerodynamics, afforestation, agronomy . . . The buyers were mostly grim working-men, straight out of the Corresponding Societies of nineteenth-century Britain; but there were many gaunt browsers, in subfusc overcoats despite the sunny late afternoon, who looked like retired clergymen. Paul made a stool of his two dangerous suitcases (the other he had left at the Metro) and sat down near the cash-desk. He was still far from well—giddy and very tired and sick—and out in the street was no place for resting. Besides, it was only ten minutes to five and he did not think this man Nikolaev would come early.

In a little slit of mirror in one of the shops he had passed, he had seen himself, unshaven despite Alex's rough counsel, also bruised below the right eye and with a red cut just by his mouth. Quite a party, then. Alex he could not understand. He still could not understand Alex. Money, he had said: it was commission he was after; and yet he had put Paul quite tenderly on the tube-train, handing him the ticket he'd insisted on buying, shaking his head at him in sorrow and something like pity, as if the earlier show of disgust had been all a pretence, saying farewell with something like regret.

Paul did not think this choice of a crowded street, outside a crowded shop, was at all a prudent one for an illegal transaction. This man Nikolaev would surely want to count the goods, haggle, then tell out his notes with a wet thumb. But, as Alex had said, this rendezvous in public might merely be the prelude to something more satisfyingly furtive. Perhaps they would cross over to the Kazan Cathedral; perhaps Nikolaev knew some empty store-room on one of the floors above (the House of Books was huge: it contained publishers' offices, busy translators of geology textbooks into Mansi, Chukchi, Evenk and Eskimo, thirty-million-copy editions of a zoology primer awaiting forty railway vans). Still, it was all very queer. In the meantime, the best thing to do was to sit, watching the open door for a short man with a cap on (so Alex had, perhaps insufficiently, described Nikolaev), and try to read the titles of the English classics in the Foreign Books section. *Uncle Tom's Cabin*; *Three Men in a Boat* (let Belinda dream or read those; he just couldn't make the hospital today; he might perhaps ring up later; all he wanted was a good sleep in a hotel bed and later some *borshch* and perhaps a nice hot plate of beef Stroganov; she could wait till tomorrow); *Oliver Twist*; *Angel Pavement*; *Martin Eden*; the Complete Works of A. J. Cronin. He watched, too, the people queueing up at counters as patiently as Englishmen had recently queued in English bookshops for those cognate best-sellers *The New English Bible* and *Lady Chatterley's Lover*. The West wanted sex and avatars; Russia the opium of progress. Ah, nonsense. The State was a twisted wire coronal a child would wear on its head. People were people.

Outside the front door a man in a cap stopped, looked round in a burly way, then thrust a *papiros* with a twisted stem into his mouth. He used up five bad Russian matches to get it alight, and Paul watched him cautiously. He was short all right, also neckless. He

.stood there quite patiently, looking into the passing crowds with pale eyes, occasionally stamping his feet as though it were cold. That would undeniably be Nikolaev. Now that the moment had come Paul found himself paralysed; he sat on his two cases huddled up, as before a fire with the knowledge that bone-cutting cold awaits outside. He waited till Nikolaev had finished his cigarette and thrown the crushed-up cardboard stem to the pavement. Then he slowly walked out, a case in each hand.

He and Nikolaev looked at each other in a slack hopeless sort of way. Then Nikolaev said, 'Mr Gussey?'

'Ah, you speak English,' said Paul. He put the cases down. There was no sense, with all these people passing up and down the Prospekt, of naked danger. It was a good idea, after all, to meet here.

'Not match English,' said Nikolaev sadly. 'We do this quick, yes? How much you want?'

'Surely,' said Paul, frowning, 'you want to know how many . . . What I mean is, you haven't even seen——'

'I know, I know,' said Nikolaev crossly. 'Like Mizinchikov. Fifteen rouble for one, yes? Clothes, how many?'

'Let's say,' said Paul, 'nineteen dozen. Nineteen dozen at fifteen roubles each . . .' He should really have worked all this out before. 'Let's call it twenty and then we can subtract. Let me see . . .'

But Nikolaev was impatient. He took a thick envelope from the side-pocket of his old jacket, which was the colour of rather mouldy brown bread. 'Here,' he said, 'is . . .' He shut his eyes tight; his lips computed rapidly; the higher numbers of a foreign language are always the hardest thing to learn. '. . . Is tree tousand, is tree tousand . . .' He cursed; he couldn't manage the other numerals.

It was money. It was well over a thousand nicker.

Paul put his hand out greedily, then he stopped. 'Wait,' he said. 'What's all this about Mizinchikov? How do you know of my connection with . . .' Then he spotted them, across the road in front of the Kazan Cathedral —a parked Zis, two men, his old friends Karamzin and Zverkov. 'Why,' said Paul, 'this is a put-up job, this is bloody treachery . . .'

'Quick, quick, you take.' And Nikolaev tried to thrust the bundle into Paul's hand. Karamzin and Zverkov were just starting to cross the road. Paul cracked, burst, went mad. As lithely as in a PT exercise, he bent to one of his suitcases. He opened it up, disclosing brilliant drilon—gold, crimson, lime, cinnamon. He dipped in, he drew out, he shoved three or four dresses into the arms of a staid and astonished middle-aged couple who were about to enter the Dom Knigi. 'A present,' he said, 'a *podarok*.' The couple would not take: infected, infected, their shooing arms seemed to say. But two plain teenage girls in deplorable summer dresses came up swiftly to examine the offerings. They chattered eagerly to each other. '*Skolko?*' They wanted to know how much. '*Podarok*,' repeated Paul, 'a gift.' Though in the land of Baba Yaga and sputniks, they gaped incredulously. 'It's the truth,' said Paul. '*Pravda*.' Queer that *pravda* should mean the truth, this sort of truth. The girls took daringly, thanked like mad, then went off chattering round the corner towards the canal. Paul dipped in for more. Nikolaev tried, as Paul bent, to thrust the money down the back of his shirt, but Paul was too quick for him. Urgency and excitement were curing his hangover fast. He pushed away Nikolaev's hand, at the same time kicking Nikolaev's foot, which had come down on the unopened suitcase. A crowd was collecting; there were some murmurs against Nikolaev. Here, it seemed, was a mad but good-hearted foreigner giving things away; it was

hardly decent of this native-born one to attempt first
to buy, second to steal. Paul's inspiration boiled up
into the words 'I give to the Russian people . . .'
Translation into Russian was difficult; he flicked
through declension tables as a thumb flicks comb-
teeth, then decided, 'To hell with grammar.' '. . . On
behalf of their comrades the British people.' And then,
dipping, throwing gorgeous colours into still bewildered
faces, he called, *'Angliyskiy narod dayet!'* Nikolaev had
been pushed back by the women and was hitting,
trying to get through, waving his envelope of money,
shouting angry words. An inward tram and an outward
tram seemed to have converged and stopped: Karamzin
and Zverkov were not yet across. 'Gifts, gifts,' called
Paul, 'from the British people to the citizens of
Leningrad.' He had an old image of children's eyes full
of wonder, gaudy balloons in their arms like new-born
babies. He dipped and threw. Men and women were
momentarily turbaned, sashed, cloaked and bibbed in
hurled streaks of primrose and vermilion. One little
old woman tugged at Paul's shirt, saying, *'Moya doch,
moya doch—svadyba zavtra.'* So her daughter was getting
married tomorrow, was she? Paul piled her arms with
gentian, maroon, lemon, midnight blue. Then he threw
daffodil, gold, orange, a lone virginal white at the
crowd—he threw them like benedictions in a ceremony
of aspersion. It was the most satisfying orgasm he had
ever known: spilling this stuff of life in what only
appeared to be an altruistic act, he revelled in and was
ashamed of his total nakedness; he felt a frightful
embryo guilt. But, seeing the dark Slav eyes reflect
brilliance from the colours they drank and the well-
shaped lips move and move in excitement, he thought,
'Why don't we do this more often?' That was an old
song: the tune ran through his head gaily. He tried to
remember the rest of the words and was still trying to

puzzle them (—'Just what we're doing today'—) out when Karamzin and Zverkov at last pushed their way through and confronted him. He did not at first recognize them and said, 'I'm dreadfully sorry, I mean *vinovat*. There aren't any more.' And, as if this were the end of some Russian film, '*Konyets*.' Then he separated their faces out from the rest of the now diminishing crowd and said, 'Ah, gentlemen. Treachery, eh? And now, presumably, dear little Alexei Prutkov doesn't get his cut after all.' He grinned down at the empty cases, much kicked, and at uncomfortable Nikolaev, who now held the envelope of money by one corner, like something dead or dirty.

'Ah,' said Zverkov unexpectedly, 'thou art translated.' He was evidently doing his best to look suave and unruffled.

'I'm not so tidy as I was,' admitted Paul. 'I've become a bit more proletarian-looking.'

'A criminal,' said Karamzin, 'you look like what you are.' He was red, puffed, dangerous. Zverkov nudged him into silence but no show of impassivity.

'I've done nothing wrong,' said Paul. 'In fact, I've done something rather generous. I expect a news-item in *Pravda* tomorrow, if little Yuri will make room, that is. I've done a lot for Anglo-Soviet relations.'

'We know all about your intentions,' said Zverkov. 'It is for your intentions we are taking you in.'

'You know as well as I do,' smiled Paul, 'that you can't do that. Religion is different from law.'

'Here,' said Karamzin darkly, 'we have no religion.'

'We can discuss all that later,' said Zverkov. 'At the moment there are plenty of charges for you to face. First of all, let me see your passport.'

'That's in my jacket,' said Paul, 'and my jacket's in a suitcase at the Metro. I left it in the ticket-office with a very nice man.'

'Well, there you are,' said Zverkov with a little show of happiness. 'A foreigner going around with no papers of identification. And then there is shouting in the street and causing a disturbance. And then—oh, there are many things. There is material for a good long report.' Some people stood around still, gaping, trying to sort out the unshaven wonder that was Paul. Karamzin shooed them away, roughly. 'The car's over there,' said Zverkov, and, in a creditable imitation of a film Highway Patrol chief, 'Let's go.'

'Why don't we do this more often?' Paul hummed as they led him across the road. 'Just what we're . . .'

'Our Zis,' said Zverkov proudly. 'At last we are taking you for a ride.'

As they drove off, Paul said to Karamzin, who was sitting at the back with him, 'I should really have reserved that white dress for the woman whose daughter's getting married. I take it she will be a virgin.'

Karamzin growled and dealt him a little thump in the ribs. 'All our women . . .' he started to say, but thought better of it. There are limits even to patriotism.

Six

PAUL couldn't manage the tough bread of the open sandwiches, his denture being loose (the bit of match he had wedged in hastily had either been swallowed or fallen out) and his gum sore, but he ate the tongues of smoked salmon and rounds of fatty sausage and drank glass after glass of warm neat tea. Zverkov looked on indulgently, Karamzin seemed resentful of such appetite in one who should soon be suffering. The three of them sat round a solid old-fashioned desk in a cosy room that was aromatic of essential Russia (an Edwardian smell, really, to match the furniture: tobacco, spirits, port-type wine, fried butter, leather, metal polish). There was a calendar which announced the month as *Yul*, this having pleasantly Christmassy connotations. The desk was Zverkov's, and it was tidy. Under glass were typed standing orders, a list of personnel and their salaries, and what looked like a printed message of encouragement, full of exclamation marks, from some official very high up. The chairs were comfortable. On the walls were some discouraging views of Soviet prisons and a football group with a much younger Zverkov holding the ball.

'Well,' said Paul, 'that's really saved my life, it has really.' He put down his empty glass, sighing. Zverkov smiled and said:

'You are very optimistic in the West, that must be admitted. You look forward to a future.'

'No,' said Paul, 'not a future. At least not in Europe. America's different, of course, but America's really only a kind of Russia. You've no idea how pleasant it is not to have any future. It's like having a totally efficient contraceptive.'

'Or like being impotent,' said Zverkov. Paul blushed. 'Now,' said Zverkov, 'if you are thoroughly refreshed . . .'

'A cigarette, please,' said Paul. '*Not* a *papiros*, if you don't mind.'

Grumbling quietly like a dog, Karamzin removed from his pockets several battered packets, all nearly empty. He offered Paul, with an ill grace, one with a jockey on, called Derby. Paul thanked, accepted a light from Zverkov, and coughed up smoke bitterly.

'You're not healthy, are you?' said Zverkov sympathetically. 'You don't look at all well.'

'Don't blame that on Leningrad,' said Paul, when the fit was spent. 'I've enjoyed myself here. It's been quite an experience. I mean that sincerely.' Karamzin, ever the sceptic, grunted.

'We are not going to doubt your intelligence,' said Zverkov, sharpening a pencil in a little machine. 'You know what we want. You know that there is no point in wasting each other's time. Tell us what we want to know and we will say no more about your little transgressions.'

'I know nothing,' said Paul. He held out his hands to show they were empty; his sleeves were already rolled up and showed thin forearms. 'We know no more than the Government and the papers tell us. You know as much as we do. The *Daily Worker* is on sale here. It is free to tell everything. It is in no wise muzzled.'

Zverkov sighed. 'Don't pretend,' he said, 'that you don't know what I'm talking about. Espionage, NATO, the Polaris submarines in Holy Loch—we know all about those things. In any case, those are not the concern of this department. What we want to know about is social, not military. You came to the Soviet

Union intending to sell twenty dozen dresses of synthetic fabric. We start from there . . .'

'You got the number right,' said Paul admiringly. 'That would be little Alex, I suppose. Does little Alex give you very much help?'

Zverkov waved him away, along with the Derby tobacco-smoke. 'Prutkov is unreliable,' he said, 'on the whole. He comes with his little piece of information and gets a rouble or two. His bits of information are usually arithmetically right. One can say no more. To revert. You bring in these dresses to sell. It has been done before. It will be done again. But there is something bigger—there is some organization, somebody behind all this. You are little, small, inconsiderable, a mere pawn in a big chess-game. We will win the game,' promised Zverkov. 'Make no mistake about that. We always win at games of chess. But the game has to be played before it is won. There are openings, ploys, sacrifices . . .' Paul could see that the metaphor was about to take over. 'The tournament at your Hastings in England. My brother was champion one year. Did you know that?'

Karamzin growled, 'The English have not the chess mind.'

'Very well,' said Zverkov. 'To put all cards on the table, we have here a matter of more than a few dozen of synthetic chemical dresses for foolish women. There are more weighty things. I will give you an example.' He opened a drawer and rummaged in it. Karamzin was obviously impatient; he looked at Paul hungrily as though anxious to get down to the torture part of the interrogation. 'Here it is,' said Zverkov, and he handed to Paul a very shabbily bound little book with no title on spine or cover. 'Open it,' urged Zverkov. 'Look inside.' Paul looked and saw twenty or so pages of very fair pornography, variations on the Laocoön theme though with more sexes, greater tortuosity and no snake. A snake would have been supererogatory: every man his own. 'Well,' said Zverkov, 'what are your views on that?'

'Too diagrammatic,' said Paul. 'Too sculptural. The essence of good pornography is depth—sumptuous shadows and that sort of thing. I have some very fine examples in my shop. Odd bits of erotica turn up at book sales, you know, in bundles of sermons and other works of piety.'

Karamzin leaned forward hotly. 'So you admit it?' he said. 'You admit you bring such books here?'

Paul ignored that. 'Stick labels on these figures,' he said, 'nun, priest, choirboy, that sort of thing, and you could put them in one of your anti-clerical museums.' He handed the book back.

Zverkov tapped his finger-tips on the desk-top and looked gloomily at Paul. 'There are agencies of corruption at work,' he said. 'I think I have chosen the right phrase. This is nothing, your synthetic dresses are nothing. But when I say that this thing of the synthetic dresses is just part of a big big conspiracy, and that the sea-shore is made of little little bits of sand . . . And also the small corruptions lead to the big ones. Drugs,' he said, 'narcotics. Cocaine and opium. Morphine.'

'Here?' asked Paul. 'Opium for the people of Soviet Russia?'

'They can be hidden in linings and hems,' growled Karamzin. 'Cocaine can be sewed into clothes.'

'Not into those drilon dresses,' said Paul. 'They don't have hems and linings. That's supposed to be one of their great beauties. You can shorten them just by cutting with a pair of scissors.' He turned back to Zverkov. 'I don't see all this about corruption,' he said. 'I thought corruption was only possible in a society like ours.'

Zverkov let out a large unexpected cry of agony which made the school-pens rattle in their glass stand. 'Ah, you don't know, you don't know human nature,' he bawled. Quieter, he added, 'There is a kind of, a kind of . . .' He cast about with his hands for the word.

'Original sin?' suggested Paul.

'That might do,' said Zverkov, mumbling. '*Priro-zhdyonnuiy grekh*,' he translated for puzzled Karamzin.

'Aaaaah,' said Karamzin, nodding. For the first time he gave Paul a scowl of grudging admiration. He turned it off at once, like testing a torch battery.

'Eventually the opposites merge,' said Paul dreamily. 'In different ways our societies move towards the same goal—the creation of a new kind of man who shall be sinless. The free-enterprise society sooner or later goes in for value-judgments. It is wrong, we feel, for a fifteen-year-old singer of popular songs to earn in a week more than many of us can earn in a year. But that's the essence of a free economy. And so the workers go on strike because hard work seems futile.'

'Here,' said Zverkov, 'that would not be possible, any of it.'

'Quite,' said Paul. 'Both systems lead to the same value-judgments.'

Karamzin dinged his fist on the desk-edge. 'This is all talk about nothing,' he shouted. 'He is not here to talk. He is here to tell us who is behind all the smuggling and the narcotics and the dirty books.'

'You are right,' sighed Zverkov. 'All we ask,' he said kindly to Paul, 'is who it is who sent you and sent your friend before you to corrupt our people. Who it is who is in charge of everything. That is all,' he said simply. 'We ask nothing more.'

Paul shook his head sadly. 'I'd like nothing better than to help,' he said. 'I admit that I came here with the intention of selling drilon dresses to your citizens.

176

I saw nothing wrong in that. If I had the goods and people wanted the goods and had the money to buy the goods . . .' He made a Levantine trader's grimace with face, hands, shoulders. 'I just don't see the harm.'

'Would you,' said Zverkov eagerly, 'now like to sign a statement to that effect?'

'To the effect that I proposed doing that thing?' said Paul. 'No. Unfulfilled intentions are God's concern only.' He smiled. 'You're terrible people for God, aren't you? You like to believe that one omnipotent being only is responsible for a multitude of little corruptions. Omnipotent, omniscient, omnipresent. A free society hasn't much time for God. We leave God to Holy Russia. Thou art Lenin, and upon this grad I shall build my——'

There was a knock at the door. Karamzin bellowed '*Da!*', a great cry of affirmation, as though it were God Himself about to enter. But a spotty youth in uniform came in, in Cossack boots that seemed made of cardboard, carrying Paul's harmless Metro-deposited suitcase.

'So,' said Zverkov, taking it.

'You'll find nothing in there,' said Paul.

Karamzin told the youth to take out the food-tray and bring in more tea. The youth parodied a salute, making the tray in the other hand do a kind of sabre-rattle, then went out. Encouraged, Karamzin now reached over, took out Paul's sports jacket and searched the pockets. 'Your passport,' he said, and flicked over the stiff pages. He looked suspiciously at the evidence of travel. 'Rome,' he said. 'France. Western Germany. You ask us to believe that all this was tourism?'

'Oh yes,' said Paul. 'One doesn't try to corrupt the already corrupted.'

'Ah,' said Zverkov, examining a stiff piece of card that Paul couldn't for the life of him remember. 'Angleruss, Angleruss. A dinner at the Evropa Hotel.

Colonel D. Y. Efimov is cordially invited.' Paul remembered: the old Doc, Madox. 'And what,' asked Zverkov, his voice thickening as though blood were being stirred into it, 'are you doing with an invitation cordially extended to Colonel Efimov?'

'It's rather a long story,' sighed Paul, 'but it's all really quite harmless, really.'

'I don't call it harmless,' said Zverkov, 'when you pretend to be Colonel Efimov. I see everything now,' he added. 'You give us a good lunch and say you are leaving Russia and then you go round the city pretending to be Colonel Efimov.'

'Do I look as though I could be taken for Colonel Efimov?' asked Paul; 'whoever Colonel Efimov is.'

'Colonel Efimov,' said Karamzin, and he pointed at Paul. 'Colonel Efimov,' he repeated. His stomach began to throb like an engine with the beginnings of laughter; his whole upper body joined in the dance; finally lights went on in his face and he openly, with a show of back-fillings that Paul hadn't previously seen, let loose curiously high peals of mirth, almost falsetto. 'Colonel Efimov,' he pointed. 'Colonel . . .' It was hard to get the name out. Zverkov smiled; the smile broadened to cracking-point; then he was adding a bourdon of hahaha to his colleague's hehehe. It was a terrible sound, that secret-police laughter.

'Who is this Efimov?' asked Paul crossly. There was a knock on the door; both Karamzin and Zverkov ignored it; it was repeated. 'Shut up, shut up, shut up,' cried Paul.

'Efi . . .' pointed Karamzin, helpless, shaking. The spotty young man came in with a tray of tea. This, for some reason, seemed to be Karamzin's last straw. His neck-arteries looked dangerously distended; he was wine-coloured; he coughlaughchoked. Zverkov's laughter was more controlled but still very loud. The spotty lad Cossack-booted towards the desk with the tea-tray.

As the tray approached Karamzin, Karamzin—shaken, melting, twitching ('Efim . . .')—could not resist a high kick at it. His neat shining boot engaged the tray's flip-side with a rattle of fairy thunder, and the tea-glasses went flying and spattering. The young policeman did not know what to do. He stood helpless, trying to smile, while tilting his tray from side to side to achieve an equilibrium and stop an overflow, the tray being a tepid dark amber lake with foundered glasses. But Paul had a lapful and the breast of his shirt was warmly soaked. He was angry. Stånding up, he shook and wrung tea from his trousers.

'Sheer bloody irresponsibility,' he cried. 'You Russians are nothing but bloody little kids.' He took his wetness over to Karamzin, shouting, 'Shut up, shut up, shut up,' and wrung his shirt on to Karamzin's laughter-ruined mug. The spotty youth took fright and ran to the door, slopping his tray.

Zverkov was mirthful but still controlled. '*Shvabra*,' he called to the lad, meaning a mop. The floor was pooled with tea, though the desk had been more or less spared. The lad nodded and left hurriedly, dripping and splashing.

'*Khorosho*,' said Zverkov, with sudden seriousness. 'We will forget all about that.' He spoke some fast coaxing Russian to Karamzin. Karamzin did his best, shaking his head, wiping his face with a rather dirty handkerchief.

'You still haven't answered my question,' said Paul. 'Who is this man Efimov?'

'He's the head of our department,' said Zverkov, the smile coming back. 'It was rude to laugh, but we Russians are very fond of laughing.' Karamzin illustrated that remark with a brief—but now evidently controllable—burst. 'Colonel Efimov is, you see, an important man and a big man. He is what you would call a very male man.'

'And you imply that I'm not?'

'Oh, it's not that,' said Zverkov, only his eyes smiling now. 'It is that Colonel Efimov is large and strong and could kill a man with one blow of his big fist. He is over six feet in height. He is a very Russian man, you see. Please,' he added hastily, 'I am implying nothing about you. You are perhaps a very brave and clever man and you are certainly a very impudent and bold man to pretend to be Colonel Efimov.'

'I did not,' said Paul, suddenly quite tired. 'It was this man Madox whom I met on the boat, you understand, and he gave me this invitation card when I met him again by chance, and—oh, what's the use?'

'Madox?' said Zverkov to Karamzin, hunched and frowning.

'Madox.' Karamzin, his laughter now totally ebbed, shrugged. Nobody knew anything about Madox.

'Angleruss, Angleruss,' crooned Zverkov. 'It is an organization for good relations between the UK and the USSR. We know nothing against it. It has something to do with an old woman in a wheelchair. An old woman you could describe as eccentric.'

'Or it might be an old man,' said Paul.

'Or it might be an old man,' agreed Zverkov. 'Well,' he said, 'we have wasted much time and learned nothing. Perhaps,' he went on, gloom suddenly curling about him like tobacco smoke, 'you are really telling us the truth after all. But you told us so many lies before —lies about your purpose in coming to Leningrad, lies about your leaving Leningrad, lies about Colonel Efimov. One cannot really tell what is the best thing to do,' he said unhappily. Karamzin, fully recovered from his manic fit, spoke long stern Russian to Zverkov. 'That could be done, that might be possible,' said Zverkov in English.

'What?' asked Paul, who had understood nothing of Karamzin's speech.

'I have to go away for a little now,' said Zverkov. He began to bundle papers together in a way that seemed arbitrary. 'I can leave you to my colleague here. You will be in good hands.'

'Am I going to be beaten up?' asked Paul.

Zverkov was shocked; he tutted. 'We do not use such primitive and barbarous methods,' he said. 'We are a civilized people and we conduct our inquiries in a civilized way.'

Paul felt sorry for himself. 'What's to happen to me?' he said, his lower lip drooped and quivering. 'I've no money, no money at all. All I wanted was just a few roubles and then to go off to a hotel and have a meal and a sleep. And now I've got nothing, nothing.' His eyes dazzled. 'All I have is an open return ticket for my wife and myself. And my poor wife's in hospital.' Zverkov, touched, patted him thrice on the shoulder on his way to the door. He said:

'You mustn't worry, my friend. Everything will be all right. Those things will happen which are destined to happen. One cannot fight against the big historical processes.' And he nodded at Karamzin. 'I shall be back in about twenty minutes,' he said, to Paul, 'and then perhaps we can make an end of all these things.' So he went out and Karamzin, his former truculence fully restored, drank in a good long look at Paul. Paul said:

'Well, what do we do now?'

Karamzin said, 'First, you stand up.' Paul stood up. Karamzin said, 'You remember in the hotel, the night when you came, you struck on the cheek a woman too weak and gentle to strike back. A Soviet worker who was doing her duty. You remember?'

'Oh yes,' said Paul. 'I remember.'

'Well, then,' said Karamzin, and he himself got slowly to his feet and stood looking up at Paul. He was a good three inches shorter. 'This,' he said, 'you will remember also.' And he swung his right arm in a great arc and flapped a great ringing smacker with his flat hand on Paul's ear. The ear played loud electronic *musique concrète*. The pain was great; it was back to childhood with a vengeance.

'You can add to that first alleged act of violence,' said Paul, rubbing away at the loudly hosannaing frostbite, 'two similar ones, perpetrated on yet another fine specimen of Soviet womanhood. One was administered in irritation, the other as part of an erotic assault. You'd better avenge those too, you cowardly bastard.'

Karamzin made a large mottled fist. Paul noticed a cheap but gaudy scarab ring on the ring-finger. 'You cowardly and *dirty* bastard,' he said. Karamzin struck Paul on the mouth and, before that could register, followed it with another fist full in the belly. 'Oh no,' said Paul. 'Hardly that.' He began to double. It brought it all back as though etched out in an elaborate firework setpiece in the nerves, the detail astonishing: a playtime in the playground and that little bastard Evans with his giggling one in the breadbasket followed by crony cheers, the subsequent sensation as of too much Christmas dinner except for the pudding: as for the pudding, that had been somehow fitted into a specially contrived hollow in the belly (open at the front as in some vivisection display) and then brandy-soaked and set blazing. Karamzin said:

'Now you will talk. Or if you will not talk you can have the same thing again.' There was a knock at the door. '*Da!*' called Karamzin. The door opened and the little spotty lad came in, carrying a mop in the shoulder-arms position. He seemed impressed by what he saw.

182

Paul, noticing the mop and re-noticing the mess of tea on the wooden floor, felt a sort of relief that after all he was not going to put anybody to too much trouble. Mopping-up had to be done anyway. Still he said:

'Sorry about this.' Then he was down on his knees, opened his mouth as to pray, and ballooned out an astonishing mess. Karamzin went chaaa with disgust. 'I said I was sorry, blast you,' gargoyled Paul, and he did it again. Blood too, he noticed. *Rvota i krov*: vomit and blood. That would make a good enough title for a new Russian epic of violence. 'I think I've finished,' he said apologetically to the mop-constable. Having got that out of the way he could concentrate on the pain: that was a big job, a big work. The spotty boy did not make too handy a job of mopping: he pushed the mess in instalments towards the open door. 'Look,' said Paul, still on his knees, 'I wouldn't have done that if you hadn't done what you did, so you did that really.' His speech came slurred and wooden out of what seemed to be the mouth of a letter-box. The lad seemed to have a bucket out on the corridor, the mop-head being turned and wrung in it to the faint noise of retching. Karamzin didn't seem too happy, either. He stood above Paul in a stock-still posture of some minor god not sure that it wanted to be prayed to, while Paul, on his knees, prayed out, like Arabic ejaculations, the last coughs and heaves and strings of bloody spittle. Karamzin snapped at the mopping constable to hurry. Soon Paul heard the plash and gurgle of liquid being sluiced down a water-closet, the rattle of the pail-handle and the gong of the pail's body knocking against something. Seeing the floor damply clean, he wondered if he ought to crawl out to that toilet, which seemed to be next door to this office. But then it seemed to him that the trinity of hot pains could now take over: the inner need was spent. He got to his feet, though still doubled, and grotesquely minuetted to the nearest chair. Karamzin did not stop him. Karamzin was weeping. Paul stared. Karamzin was weeping.

'You do well to weep,' Paul said, squaring the wretched phonemes, beating all the deformed words into rough but recognizable shapes. 'You have shown,' he tried to say, 'that modern Russia is really the Western tourist's dream after all.'

'Aaaaaaooooooo,' went Karamzin, now also in a chair, his head in his arms on the desk, like a patient who has heard the doctor's death-sentence. The room had, in fact, the shadowy sepia look of a surgery in some such Edwardian Royal Academy anecdote. '*Nye khotel*—' he seemed to be trying to say, all muffled. 'Aaaaaooooo.' Paul now wondered whether Karamzin had done something unintentionally lethal to him; he felt around his face with trembling fingers, encountering blood and a fat lip, also a gap of a thumb's thickness between canine and canine in his lower jaw. Sore gum, blood, a space. The denture had been knocked out. Paul, doubled up like a racing cyclist, was near enough to the floor to see that it was lurking nowhere coyly, ivory and pink. There was no doubt, no doubt at all, that it had been mopped out of the room and into the bucket and then down the drain. It would now be gnashing its tiny way along deeply submerged pipes towards the Baltic.

'You swine,' said Paul, 'you brutal sod.' He was aware of the subtle coarsening of the sibilants; it seemed to him in an instant's delirium that they had become a special sound which eighteenth-century orthographers represented with an f; a gloomy procession filed by, all with frontal gaps in the lower jaw— Dr Johnson, Garrick, Wilkes, Mrs Williams, Bet Flint, Samuel Foote. 'You beaftly fwinifh fadift,' said Paul.

Karamzin got up from his chair and came blindly

over towards Paul, his hands groping. Paul found it easier to get down than up, so, on all fours, he crawled away from the maudlin penitence, still in great pain. He could think of no specific spot to crawl to, so he just crawled, searching hopelessly for his denture. He heard odd sobs from Karamzin above him, Karamzin speaking English now, saying, 'I did not . . . It was not . . . I did not think.' Paul said to the floor, 'Ah, fhut up.' Then he reached a corner of the room and, as if sheltering from bitter winds, crouched in it, holding his belly. Karamzin now howled:

'Bobrinskoy, Bobrinskoy, Bobrinskoy . . .' He repeated the name until its owner arrived. Its owner was the spotty constable; he opened the door and seemed surprised that that should, after all, be his name. Karamzin gave loud orders. Paul recognized most of the key-words: it seemed that he was to have his wounds attended to and be given cognac to drink. But before the constable could bring what was needed, Zverkov came back. Karamzin cringed and had somehow the fawning look of a dog that knows it has been naughty. He seemed to be trying to hide Paul from Zverkov, as though Paul were a dirty mess he had done in the corner. Which was what Paul really felt he now was. He would have been content to be covered with sawdust and shovelled up and carted off to dung some collective farm or other. Zverkov looked down at Paul in horror. He said:

'Open your mouth.' Paul obediently uncovered blackness in which red flickered, flanked by wolfish infangthief and outfangthief. 'He has knocked them out,' said Zverkov. 'He has gone too far. He often goes too far. This excess is our great Russian fault. It is a matter of swinging from one extreme to the other. That way, to speak confidentially, much of our work is spoiled.' He looked down sadly at Paul.

'Filthy Ruffian fodf,' said Paul's black hole. 'Finifh thingf off. Go on, fend me to fodding Fiberia.'

'Oh, Siberia is nothing to be frightened of any more,' said Zverkov. 'It is all very modern there now.' He shook himself out of what he recognized to be an impertinent didactic phase. 'But,' he said, 'we are not sending you anywhere. Except, yes, out of here. Yes, I think there is really not much more point in keeping you.' Karamzin still cowered a little but was visibly regaining his confidence.

'A pleafant exhibition,' said Paul. 'Me with my teeth knocked out for no reafon. I fhall expofe you, baftardf.' But already the f was being levelled under s. 'Swine,' said Paul.

'Comrade Karamzin is very sorry for going too far,' said Zverkov handsomely. 'But there is no proof of anything. There is nobody to say you did not enter these headquarters in the condition you now enjoy.' He said this without irony.

'You mean,' said Paul, 'all sick and bloody and punched up? That's a good one, that is.' Pain shot through his stomach. He embraced it tight, keening, swaying to and fro in his corner. 'Soviet police methods,' he said at length. 'That will be something for the Sunday papers.'

'Oh, we can remove all traces of violence,' said Zverkov. 'We can shave you and cut your hair and send you out in your good suit. An English gentleman.'

'With no teeth.'

'You have *some* teeth still,' said Zverkov judicially. 'As for the teeth you have not, you came to our country without them already. Who is to say otherwise?'

'What was your pal here crying about, then?'

'He was crying for you. Crying for a lost soul full of original sin. For an English gentleman who came here with some teeth missing and intending to do harm which he was never ultimately able to do.'

'Have you been to the cinema lately?' asked Paul.

'Ah,' said Zverkov, with wide courtly gestures that seemed not necessarily sarcastic. 'We are to sit down comfortably like old friends and discuss the Art of the Cinema.' And he sat behind his desk, made an airy cage out of both thumbs and all fingers, and smiled parsonically. Karamzin, suspicious—some wild creature of the steppes replacing the guilty dog—remained standing. Paul kept to his corner. He said:

'Not really like friends. There was a newsreel, you see. I saw this newsreel. It was at the Barrikada Cinema.' A fresh twinge made him see a screen, a TV screen, with a belly-grasping commercial for STUMS: *Pain can strike any time, any place*—Dear, homely, far Britain. 'What I saw was the return of the Delegation of Soviet Musicians from England. We travelled on the same ship. We disembarked at the same time. What I saw was not only the Soviet musicians but myself as well. Yes, myself, presumably mistaken for one of the musicians. Myself flashing teeth at the camera of Lenfilm or whoever it was. I saw myself, teethed.' Zverkov frowned. 'I know,' said Paul, 'that "toothed" is the correct form, but "toothed" seems to imply one tooth only. "Teethed" is what I was.' He grinned without mirth and knew just how horrible that grin must look. Both Zverkov and Karamzin surveyed him attentively.

'I must have been seen,' Paul said, 'by millions of Soviet citizens. The return of the Delegation of Soviet Musicians must have been an important event. It will still be going the rounds of the provinces. Perhaps now it's being seen in Siberia. An event to be remembered. And soon that film will rest in the archives, testifying that I arrived on your shores with a full set of teeth.'

'A lie,' growled Karamzin, conventionally.

'Ah no,' said Paul, shaking his head slowly and wearily. 'No lie. Check up on it, you sadistic bastard.'

'It will be true,' admitted Zverkov briskly. 'There is every reason to suppose that, this time at least, he is telling no lie. An Englishman,' he explained to Karamzin, 'would not have the imagination to invent such a story. The English are not like the Russians— not any more. They were like the Russians at the time of their Queen Elizabeth I, when they produced their Shakespeare. But not now.' He nodded several times, his chin pressed to his larynx. 'It is the kind of thing, the thing he said, that is bound to be true.' His voice came out very deep. 'Well,' he said, with sudden cheerfulness, 'there is no great harm done. We must get you back to England very quickly, that is all.' His head had come soaring up from his neck, rather tremulous in a coquettish way, as if shaking abundant newly shampooed locks. 'We shall have you out of here on the next available transport.' Karamzin now sat down rather petulantly and began chewing his nails.

'You'll have to get my wife out of hospital first,' said Paul. 'I'm not going without her.'

'We hear all the time about your wife,' said Zverkov. 'Yet we never see her. And you have proved yourself to be such a liar, too. Where do you say she is?'

'In the Pavlovskaya——'

'Yes, yes, yes. We shall telephone. Karamzin will telephone. Or I. It doesn't matter which one. If, as you say, you have a wife here in Leningrad, that will be two people to arrange passages to England for. And yet,' said Zverkov sadly, shuffling through Paul's documents again, 'you have here *two* open return tickets. Perhaps you have been misjudged. Well, we shall see. Perhaps you have not told so many lies as we thought.' He looked tired and worried. 'Who knows? Who knows anything of the depths of man's soul?'

188

Seven

THE cell that Paul was taken to was a cheerful slummy sort of place, already occupied by three happy prisoners who greeted Paul warmly and, when they discovered that he was an Englishman, hugged him simultaneously like three bears. Two of them were young golden giants—brothers, they said, held on a charge of starting a *byesporyadok* or disturbance on a skinful of kvass. It did Paul's heart good to be with them: such muscle, confidence, good-nature, blue-eyed innocence. And their smell was so wholesome, too: it was of work, socks and (the kvass with them not building up to poison but breaking down to its homely elements) rye flour and malt. The third prisoner was a hale old man in pyjamas whose trousers lacked a cord, so that they were held up by a bunchy waist-knot of the striped cotton itself. The trouser-legs thus riding up to the knee, the old man's varicose calves were fully disclosed. It was as if to divert attention from these that he exploited to the full a clinical endowment—a glass eye which stayed still while its live fellow rolled comically. The brothers were kept in shouts and tears of laughter. For Paul's special benefit the old man, who knew that England was still Christian, laid on a gruesome crucifixion scene—gurgling, gagging, the left eye rotating like mad while the glass one stared, the man himself curling bare toes round the wood of the lower bunk, arms stretched on the wood of the upper. There were two of these double bunks; there was also a latrine bucket; there was nothing else.

The brothers wanted to know what Paul was in for.

'*Nye dyengi*,' said Paul, showing his empty pockets. 'No money, so this is my hotel for the night.'

'*I zavtra?*' They evidently thought Paul a fine fellow. 'And tomorrow?' Meanwhile, the old man scratched a varicose patch, his eyes off duty.

Paul shrugged. '*Nichevo*,' he said, but he only meant it in its radical sense of 'nothing'. He would go back to England toothless (partly), penniless (completely), feeling a fool, having slept in the nick for lack of the means to a hotel bed, having previously been bashed, held out of a window by his ankles, proved impotent, interrogated. And other things too, if he had time to think. What he only had time for now was a bit of supper and a lot of sleep. It had been a very wearing day, despite its brevity: three in the afternoon till now, which was about seven of a Baltic summer's evening. His guts ached less, because they had been soothed with cognac. He had been allowed to wash off the blood with warm water. And, as a final gesture of hospitality, Zverkov and Karamzin had offered him a cell. They had, they affirmed, no money for a hotel room. They turned out their pockets and showed miserable kopeks to prove it. High police officials, they pointed out, were still workers; a worker might, said Zverkov, be defined as a man who was wealthy for one hour in a hundred and sixty-eight. This was not the hour.

The brothers noticed the werewolf gap in Paul's lower jaw and asked sympathetically about it. Paul, too weary to work out the Russian, gave a brief mime of a punch-up. The brothers liked that. The old man, resenting theft of his audience, made with the eyes again. But the brothers became song-minded and treated Paul to a counting-ditty of a hundred verses and cumulative knee-slapping. Then Paul was asked to sing something of his own country. He chose 'Land of Hope and Glory' and wondered, la-lahing parts of it (for he remembered few of the words), whether, if Zverkov and Karamzin were to shove him in an oubliette or even make him face the cold dawn squad, England would really care. What he had tried to do he had tried to do in the name of England. Well, of free trade. Well, of Robert.

'Wider still and wider shall thy bounds be set.
God Who made thee mighty make thee mightier
yet——'

The brothers joined in. They liked the tune. Elgar in a Soviet jail. But the old man wavered some sad minor-key cantilena against it, flapping his striped arms.

'God Who made thee mighty, make thee migh—
hightier yet.'

A sort of *militsioner* who was the image of Cullen, the man who'd run the radio repair-shop on Tuesday Street, Bradcaster 14, came in with supper, beaming at the trolled hymn of Edwardian expansion. He brought a tray with tin bowls of blood-coloured soup and very hard bread. The brothers greeted him like a brother. And so, two cach on a lower bunk, the four cell-mates sloshed away at their *borshch*. The elder brother had a pack of White Sea Canal and matches, so all puffed rank smoke at the low cell-ceiling, mellow in the summer evening light, comrades.

The old man took out his glass eye and pretended to munch it, as if he were at some Arab feast. Paul, seated on the bunk-edge, began to nod; then, dreaming that his own eyes were dropping out, he came to, startled. The brothers smiled. They were both really most handsome and wholesome boys, good enough to eat. Paul said, 'I must sleep. *Ya dolzhen spat'*.'

'Tell us a story,' said the elder brother.

'*Da, da*,' said the younger, '*skazka*.'

'Oh, no,' moaned Paul. 'I'm so tired. And I don't know any *skazki*.'

'I know many stories,' said the old man jealously. 'I can tell ten thousand stories.'

'We only want one story,' said the elder brother. 'And we want an Englishman's story.'

'I'm terribly sleepy,' said Paul in English. Seeing they did not understand, he said, '*Po-russkiy—ya nye mogu*. I just don't know enough Russian. Let the old one there tell a story.'

'We want an English story,' said the younger brother. 'We will not let you sleep till you tell an English story.'

Paul sighed. 'Let me lie down, then,' he said. 'I can think better lying down.' And he lay down, closing his eyes. The two brothers sat on the floor to listen. The old man lay on his bunk, offended but pretending to be indifferent.

'Come on,' said the elder brother, shaking Paul. 'The story.'

'Oh,' said Paul, 'once upon a time . . . I mean, *zhil buil kogda-to* . . .' It was strange that he should remember that cosy formula: what it had had to do with a crash course in Ally's Russian in wartime he could not now think. Something connected with crying Robert perhaps, forlorn, lonely, crammed with nightmares? '*Zhil buil kogda-to*,' he repeated, as if that might conjure a story, like spirits, out of the air. 'Ah, no, I just can't.' He heard the old man, supine on the lower bunk behind him, singing his sad song. He opened his eyes to see the brothers waiting with attention. They had such confidence in him, an Englishman. And then, in images, the tale started to come quite unbidden. He tried, though aware of his weak and clumsy Russian, to tell it.

'Once upon a time there were two bolshoi tsars with two bolshoi tsardoms. They were very bolshoi and very strong and they had much land and many clever magicians and sovietniks.' The words were there all right, though the grammar was wretched. 'They were very strong, as I say. Because of that, each tsar had the dream of all strong men. That dream is to be the strongest man in the whole world. And each knew the other had the same desire, so each, each, each——'

'Was afraid?'

'—was afraid of the other. So each had great shows of magic and strength to frighten the other. But each did not wish to fight the other, because each knew the power of the magic of the other, and each knew the power of his own magic. And no tsar wished, in those days, to rule over empty lands, either his own or those of his defeated enemy. And so things stood for a long time.' He began to doze off. He could see the tale quite clearly, a colour cartoon in jerky animation. He was jerked with brotherly roughness. 'What? Eh?'

'The story!'

'The first thing to do tomorrow morning is to go to my wife in the hospital. And then we shall know when we can leave. I think I know who I can borrow a little money from.'

They laughed. 'You're speaking English,' said the elder. 'Let's have the rest of the story.'

'Oh, the story. The *skazka*.' He creaked himself back into his childish Russian. 'Now these two bolshoi tsardoms were next to each other, but there was one little thing between them. Between them was a little piece of land, with a little house and a little man in it. In his house were all the things his father had given him, and also what his grandfather had given to his father, and also what his—his——'

'*Pradyed?*'

193

'Yes, his great-grandfather had given to his grandfather, and so all the way back to the egg. And neither
tsar could say, "You are in my tsardom," for if one
said it both would say it, and then there would be
war. So he was free and had no tsar to rule over
him.'

'*Gdye dyelal pokupki?*'

'Where did he do his shopping? Oh, in both tsardoms.
One tsardom was good for one thing, the other was
good for another. In both he had friends and in both
he had enemies. Sometimes his friends would ask,
"Which way of life is the better way of life?" He would
reply, "There is no better. One is good for one thing,
the other is good for another." His friends then would
say, "What then is the *best* way of life?" He would
reply, "The way of life with everything open: open
tavern, open heart, open mind."' Paul frowned
slightly, looking up at his auditors. The story was
coming through clear to him, but was it a case of the
great sleep-poem which is waking trash, one of those
light-headed hallucinations of omnicompetence? Open
mind—*otkruituiy rassodok*: did that mean anything to
them? Was this all just gibberish really? Their faces
still glowed, looking down on him. The old man was
already snoring. Paul continued:

'And so this little man lived happily with his old
things and his freedom and his dreams. But in both
tsardoms there was more fear than happiness, fear of
war and of great magic weapons that would blow the
whole world sky high. And they said to the little man,
"Are you not afraid?" And he said, "Oh yes, it
is right to have something to fear. Men have
always had something to fear—divine thunder
(*bozhyestvyennuiy grom*) or the end of the world; such
fear is the sauce of life." And then they said, "That is
not real fear; that is not *modern* fear. You must learn

194

modern fear." ' Paul was very weary. He said, 'Enough. You can have the rest tomorrow. I must sleep now.'

The brothers grew angry as cheated burly bears. They clawed clumsily at him as though he had a vest made of honeycombs under his shirt. '*Skazka!*' they cried. 'What happened then?'

'Oh,' lolled Paul, 'they gave him a wife.'

'Who gave him a wife? Which tsardom did she come from? What was her name? Wake up!' They shook him.

'Oh, it doesn't matter where or who. Because one tsardom was the other tsardom seen in a mirror. Seen in a *zyerkalo*,' he repeated. 'And she knew modern fear. And she wished to be back where she could be protected from magic by magic, so she said to her husband that he must join the right tsardom. He would not do this, however, not even for her love. So then she said, "*Khorosho*. You are not a real man, for you will not protect me. You are not a real man, and so you are not a real husband. So I am leaving you." ' Paul was now exhausted.

'And did she leave him?'

'Oh yes.'

'And where did she go?'

'To one or the other tsardom, for both were the same.' Paul blinked and blinked, blinking light back to the world, and felt at the same time a kind of electronic music screaming and thumping in rapid crescendo in his skull. He sat up with a jerk. 'What was that?' he said in English. 'What did I say then?' They laughed; they couldn't understand. He was very wide awake now, even refreshed, as though the tale and its rich jammy language had been the stuff of very deep sleep. Had he even told the story? 'I've got to get out of here,' he said. 'Now.' And then he was over at the cell-door, shouting. The brothers laughed again, as at a born entertainer.

There was a small spyhole in the upper half of the cell-door, big enough for a hand to go through and clutch (as though its owner were vertically drowning in cell-air) at the dim blue lighting of the freedom outside. 'I've changed my mind!' cried Paul in English. 'I've got to see my wife!' The old man in pyjamas grumbled dream-Russian from his bunk. The two brothers came up to the door, courteously pushed Paul aside, then hammered with brawny fists on the metal panel, calling loud words which Paul, story-teller in Russian, did not know. Soon their fists became big mottled kettledrumstick-heads crashing in march-rhythm, and to this bass they added a gloriously loud May Day processional song. After two choruses somebody came. The brothers stood aside to let Paul see a spyhole-framed face that was not a bit like the face of Cullen of Bradcaster 14. Paul said in slow Russian:

'My wife, you see. I must see my wife. This cell is really only a hotel room for the night, really. I'm not charged with anything or anything like that. I'm ready to go now.'

The framed jaws chewed crossly; supper had evidently been interrupted. In growls of international police-speech the voice seemed to say, 'Hotel, eh? That's a good 'un. Any more noise from you, mate, and I'm in there to belt you in the cakehole, got it?'

'I demand to see Comrades Karamzin and Zverkov,' cried Paul. 'They know all about it. They gave me the hospitality of the cells. Come on, don't be a fool. I demand to see your superior officers.'

'You'll have to wait till the morning, got it? In the meantime get your effin head down and no more bleedin' oot.'

'I demand my rights,' Paul tried to say. 'Habeas Corpus. Let me get on the telephone to the British Consul. *Now.*'

It was no good. The face disappeared from the spy-hole. More, the spyhole itself was blocked up from the outside. The brutal feet marched back to supper. Morning, then. Morning would be all right. In the meantime there was no question of getting his effin head down. Thank God or Bog they had let him bring his suitcase in here with him. It was time to put on the English gentleman again.

The brothers watched with close interest, the one leaning with folded arms by the cell-door, the other with his mouth open from his bunk, as Paul shaved (steel mirror, brushless cream, new blue blood-tickling blade). Nail-scissors? There they were; Paul blunted his claws. It was the elder brother's own idea to trim Paul's hair with these scissors, sculpting the nape with the razor: he had done this often, he said, and for money, too: that had been on a collective farm: he had proved useless, though, as a farm-worker. Paul flannelled his visible parts with drinking-water from the jug, put on the white shirt he had drip-dried the day before yesterday, a brown tie with a vertical cream line (bought on the Via Nazionale in Rome), finally his summer-weight fawn suit. 'Ah,' breathed the younger brother. Then he clicked his fingers as in a guessing-game. '*Angliyskiy dzhentlmyen,*' he said. Complete in every detail, thought Paul. Except, of course, for——

The brothers knew, as by instinct. Indeed, every-thing with them seemed instinctual. The old man snored with the profound wicked innocence of the very old; the brothers peered into his open mouth. A whole bottom set was, naturally, out of the question, unless Paul would be willing to have every natural tooth knocked out: that would not take long. But it was highly probable that, after all that trouble had been taken, the old man would prove to have a different shape of lower jaw from Paul. Bits of putty from the window? No, wait . . . The younger brother got down on his knees and began searching among the rubbish that had been roughly swept or even kicked under the bunks. He emerged with a big S of old orange peel. A temporary denture, it was eagerly demonstrated, could easily be cut from that—tooth-white inner skin insoluble in saliva. Paul let them get on with it.

He could not later tell at what point in the night—the elder brother razor-carving orange-peel teeth—he became convinced he would be too late. There was an eventual confused memory of the point being marked almost by some exterior symbol—like the quick minor third of a cuckoo clock striking the half-hour in a room many rooms away. Cuckoo: O word of fear.

Eight

I FELT this morning somehow when they woke me up that you wouldn't be coming in today to see me. I'm not blaming you for that, because there's no compulsion about it, after all, and I know that you've got other things to do, whatever they are—besides this business of selling those dresses for dear sweet deadly Sandra, I mean. I've thought once or twice that you must be perhaps dating some Russian woman or other, perhaps that dark spotty untidy girl we met that night, and even imagined that you might be going to bed with somebody, but that turned out to be a very improbable notion.

I've been less imagining things than remembering. I've gotten quite good at remembering things, even seeing things from the past as though they were bits of movies or something. Perhaps these drugs and things have been helping. Anyway, I've been seeing us, you and me that is, in Richmond, Surrey—that pub (the Cricketers'?) where you knocked over that big pile of pennies they were collecting for cancer or spastics or something, you did that with your elbow and had to pick them all up again, which made you breathless. You were clumsy all right, but I never minded. It always seemed a kind of upper-class clumsiness, as though you'd never had to do anything with your hands or your whole body for that matter. I thought at first you must be some member of an ancient aristocratic British family that was impoverished and so you'd had to take to serving in a shop. It was your hands that looked aristocratic, being very thin and long, and at first I thought your voice was aristocratic too. I guess I didn't really know too much about the British, despite the war and working in Bruton Street after the war and all.

Yes, that pub. And then the river with the swans and the steamers going to Westminster. And the willow trees. And yet it was all a big sham and a show really, like a movie set, and there was nothing underneath or behind. It couldn't have always been like that. There must have been a time when there was something real, but perhaps the war killed all that. I don't know. All I knew about England before coming to War-torn Europe was what was in Dad's books, and that was either very elegant, like in Pope, or very robust and swaggering like in Hogarth or Dickens or somebody. I suppose I was a bit ashamed of Dad with his lectures about Eighteenth-century Background and his maps of Dr Johnson's London. It was like a man giving lectures on Sex Technique without ever having slept with a woman. Anyway, I had to see for myself. And I guess I must have been looking for a mother.

Dear old Mother England, matrix of American Culture, as Dad would say, and the only country in the world where they have to have a Society for Preventing Cruelty to Children. And on her broad bosom shall they ever whatever it is. That was Merry England that was actually staged there by these amateurs in 1940, when everybody in America had gotten very sentimental about England facing the Forces of Evil alone. This performance was for Bundles for Britain or something. When I thought to lay my head on that bosom all the air came out whishhhhhh, and it was just two balloons.

Oh I don't mean it hasn't been sometimes fun and sometimes even magic and poetry, though I had to be very careful and try not to see Hampton Court and Twickenham as places that Dad built himself and the

Tower of London as coming out of his library. But Sussex was pretty free from him, for Kipling and Chesterton and the other man didn't come into his lecturing, and there was the sea and the downs and the pubs and churches. And I've liked it enough to stick it into middle age, despite the silly fat ex-wing-commanders running pubs with tankards on the ceiling and going What What and Old Boy. And the people who sneered about me being a Yank. What right did they have to sneer at anybody or anything, little people with light little voices and absolutely bloodless? And how have you been off for blood while we're on the subject?

You fell for Glamour as much as I did. You fell for the Big American Glamour like you all do and pretend not to. Yap yap yapping about Deadly Transatlantic Influence and hardly able to lap lap lap it up fast enough. Oh you do so much want to be Absorbed. The only way you can go on existing, I guess, is to become an Idea in somebody's mind. A ready-made memory, that's what it is, ready to be bought up by a mind that thinks it's oh so classy to have a long memory and not much trouble in acquiring it. That means you won't have to trouble about the practical side of surviving when you just become the Big American Museum. The men won't have to trouble to breed any more and can just go off with their boy-friends, their dear dead Roberts, without feeling guilty or worrying about Duty any more. And what will the women do then, poor things?

The trouble is, I guess, that you, and I do mean You, don't want to live any more. You want to lay down the burden of having to feel responsible about anything. Wait for the end and meanwhile sell off the furniture bit by bit to buy Sugar-Pops and Caramellos. But don't do anything to provoke the End, oh no.

Wait for Rocking-chair Jack to blow the whistle or Comrade K to kill off with a jumbo-size blast his few thousand Western-type megafolk. Meanwhile moon with your wartime boy-friend and sing the old sad songs you sang when you were in a Tight Corner and keeping a Stiff Upper Lip what what chaps.

Oh, I know I shouldn't be talking. But I've a right to a bit of Love and a bit of security and yes warmth and I've waited a long time for those. What I didn't expect and what I could never even have dreamed of expecting was that I should have to come as far East as this for a bit of peace and a bit of affection and to feel that I'm Wanted. Or perhaps I'm a fool as I was with Sandra but I don't think so somehow. Sandra was very frivolous. Even the special physical things she knew, and my God did she know them, she knew in a very frivolous way, like someone who can play pieces on the piano only through having been shown where to put her fingers. There were one or two others before Sandra, but it won't help any to say who they were. Anyway, I guess that side of it isn't all that important. It's the security that's important. It's the feeling that you're protected from that terrible terrible big howling wind.

And so now there's Sonya—Dr Lazurkina, if that's how you spell it, to you. But it's not just Sonya as a person, as an individual that is, but what lies behind Sonya, and all that's so very solid and real. And I don't mean the Soviet System and the Communist Party, for I feel about Communism much as I was always made to feel, except that I don't see that systems matter much to ordinary little people like me. It's only the boys and girls at the top, I'd say. Everybody I've met seems happy enough. I don't see anybody trembling in Deadly Fear. What I feel about Communism really I guess is that I'm sorry for all the politicians and tycoons and teachers and writers in the West who feel sorry for themselves when they think of themselves having to live in a Communist State. But I'm not clever enough to ever have to worry about that. No, what I mean when I say what lies behind Sonya is something as simple as Love, because Love is about the only thing these people have had to keep them going through all their terrible historical changes, famines and sieges and purges and scorched earth and terrible poverty. And I suppose Love has nearly disappeared in England and the United States of America because there are so many easier substitutes for it.

What has happened is that Sonya is being transferred, which is what she wanted, to this place called Rostov, which is on the Northern Shore of the Sea of Azov, as I've seen from a map. That's more her part of the world, as her mother lives in a place called Simferopol, or near there, which is in the Crimea. I'm still to be under her medical supervision, though really I feel fine now though very very tired, and so we're going down there together, the idea being that she's taking her fortnight's leave which is due to her from last year, so we can get off straight away, which is by the evening plane. I asked about money but she says I'm under the State Medical Service. Then I said I couldn't be under the State Medical Service for everything, but she says that when I've had a Convalescence I can do some lecturing, if I wish. Lecturing in English, that is, on Life in the West. But she says I'm not to think too far ahead into the future but to get well first. I feel quite well, as I say, though very tired, but she knows best, being a doctor. One thing she said I could do was to apply for Political Asylum, but I'm not too sure what that means.

I would like to have some money of my own, though, and you'll be the first to say I'm entitled to it, as it was my little bit of capital that started you in the shop. In the meantime you could let me have some of the money you've gotten out of selling the dresses, say about half the total amount. The way Sandra let me down I guess that's only my rightful due. Sonya suggests you pay any monies into her account, which is quite easy to do. There's the Gosbank in Leningrad and you know Sonya's name and the hospital here, and it will catch up with her and then with me fairly quickly.

I never approved of having both of us on the one passport, so things would be very awkward if I hadn't kept my US passport. This is out of date, as you know, but I guess the US Consulate or whatever it is can put that right for me. Anyway I have Sonya to look after me and there won't be any trouble about documents. When I decide to come back to England I'll let you know. But I'm not giving you any addresses now because I don't want you to have any part of this decision one way or the other.

I'm sorry things have to be left a bit vague, but please remember I am under Medical Supervision and Sonya knows better than either you or me what's best to be done. I guess, to be quite realistic, you'll get along all right without me. But look after Pinky and don't give Pinky *cold* milk, she likes it warmed up with a little sugar in it. And if Pinky wants to sleep on the bed at night don't start pushing her off. There are one or two things I shall want you to send, but it all depends on how long I stay in the CCCP (I've started learning the alphabet already and can write my name in it). Don't worry about me is the important thing, because I'll be fine, I know I will. It may seem a funny sort of thing to say, but I feel as if I'd come home. Not the home I had but the home I should have had. Look after yourself, darling. Love from.

Nine

'ALL right, then,' said Madox, handing the letter back to Paul. 'You let her get on with it, my old mate. But if she was any wife of mine I'd not have her back, not likely. Not that I'm married nor ever would be, not a man in my circumstances.'

Paul was lying dead-beat on Madox's bed, still panting. It had been so hectic a morning, and everything on foot, Paul having no money for a taxi or even a tram. And here in the Evropa Hotel all the lifts said *Nye Rabotayet*; he had had to climb up here to Madox's room. And, coming to the hotel, he had forgotten Madox's name. He had been wretched, striding up and down that vast grubby lounge, from which cruel sunlight thwacked out dust like a carpet-beater, up and down past the bald and scholarly looking man in a dog-collar who was unhappily reading the *Daily Worker*, no other British paper being available; up and down past the three elderly Finns sitting in a conspiracy of misery, as though they too were trying to remember Madox's name. At last it had come as from heaven: 'Paul, thou maddest.' Was that Wyclif's version? He had once sold on commission a polyglot New Testament, all in English.

He folded and then refolded the letter. It was very thick, and it would not take a third folding. He then threw it pettishly into the waste-paper basket. 'Wait, wait,' said Madox, retrieving it from among cigarette-packets and two empty whisky-bottles. 'You want to keep that. For evidence. I'd call that desertion, I would.' He unfolded the letter and began to read it again. He was wearing a shot-silk dressing-gown with blue pyjamas patterned like floral wallpaper; his slippers had fur on them. 'What is a real godsend here,' he said, reading, 'is this business about the double passport.'

'How do you mean?'

Madox came over and sat on the bed. He looked into Paul's face with sincere piss-coloured eyes. 'You said something about wanting money.'

'She's entitled to some money. That's true what she says there, about starting me up in business. Besides, she's still my wife. I have a certain responsibility. I can't bear to think of her left stranded in a strange country.'

'Awwww,' went Madox, gripping Paul's left ankle, 'women can always look after themselves. Better than men in some ways. What I was thinking about was you taking some money home. That was the idea, wasn't it?—to take some money home. Now then.' He inched closer. 'How do you stand with the police?'

'Oh,' sighed Paul, 'all right, I think. Karamzin almost made the sign of the cross this morning when he saw what looked like teeth in my mouth.'

'That must have been a very powerful belt in the grinders,' said Madox, looking into the emptiness between Paul's lower canines. 'But those gums seem to have healed lovely.'

'It's a long story,' said Paul. 'These two lads, you see, good honest artisans, made me a temporary denture out of orange peel. I soon lost it, though. It fell out when I was running.'

'Running from?'

'Running to. The hospital, that is. I knew it, I knew what had happened. When they handed me that letter I knew what was inside.'

'Like intuition,' said Madox thoughtfully. 'It does happen. It's happened time and time again with the

Doc. But not me. It's all thought and working-out-in-the-mind with me. Everybody's made different, the way I see it.'

'Zverkov,' said Paul, 'told me he'd rung up the hospital and been told that there was a Mrs Hussey there. That must have been just before they went off together. God curse that woman.'

'For all you know,' said Madox, 'she may still be there. She may be all cuddled up with this doctor pal of hers still in that hospital there. It seems a bit short notice to me, just buggering off to the Crimea like that. It's very nice down in the Crimea,' he added, 'especially at this time of the year.'

Paul began to get up from the bed, but Madox held him down with a surprisingly tough grip on both his ankles. 'Damn it,' cried Paul. 'I'll go back to the bloody place. Everybody's trying to make a monkey out of me.' But he was exhausted. He sank back again on to the pillow, sighing.

'That's right,' soothed Madox. 'It won't do any good, wherever she is. You just let her have her own way.'

'Brain-washed her, that's what they've done, the bastards.'

'You can't do anything about her now,' said Madox. 'First things first is what I say. Tell me more about what the police said.'

'Oh, they said they'd made provisional bookings for my wife and myself on the *Alexander Radishchev*. That sails tonight. Helsinki, Rostock, Tilbury. It was up to me to confirm the bookings by presenting my open return tickets. They were very nice, I suppose, really. They told me not to be such a silly boy next time.' Paul began to snivel.

'Now, shut that,' said Madox sharply, 'or I'll give you a back-hander.'

'All right,' snivelled Paul. 'You too. It's all bloody violence here. Go on, get on with it.'

'What it is,' said Madox more reasonably, 'is that it's all like a lot of kids. Hitting each other and crying boo hoo hoo. You get into the same way yourself if you don't watch it.' He thought a moment, still gripping Paul's ankles tight as though Paul were a very speedy motor-cycle. 'And of course all that ties up too—this business of giving presents. I should think that business of you giving away all those dresses for free must have touched a fair number of soft Russky hearts high up.'

'How did you know about that?'

'Oh, everybody was talking about it here in the hotel. If this *Pravda* had been more like a real paper and not a lot of bloody Party propaganda there would have been an item about it this morning. Not that I can read much of the language myself. The Doc can, though. Very clever the Doc is. Now then,' said Madox, 'what's the name of that ship again?'

'What ship? Oh, that. The *Alexander Radishchev.*'

'Queer spitting lot of names they have. You get used to them, of course, but now and then it dawns on you that they're a queer old lot of names. Like that music bloke you were shouting the odds for that time on the boat. What was his name now?'

'Opiskin.'

'That ship name sounds like "radishes" and this name sounds just rude. But not to them, of course. And why does this Piss bloke mean so much to you?'

'Look,' said Paul, 'all I came for was a little bit of a loan, that's all. Just to tide me over. And a bit of advice, that's all. Not to talk about Opiskin.'

'Opiskin, Opiskin, Opiskin,' said Madox with his eyes closed. 'I must remember that name. As for a little bit of a loan, as you call it, I think we can do better than that. But first you must tell me all about Opiskin.'

'This other ticket,' said Paul, 'the one for my wife, isn't returnable. Not here, anyway. Back in London, but not here. Just a couple of quid, that's all I need.'

'Opiskin,' said Madox.

'Oh,' said Paul, resigned, turning his face to the wall wearily, 'he was a favourite composer of my greatest friend. This friend of mine thought the world of him. I thought the world of this friend. Selling these dresses was a means of helping his widow. That's all. And it didn't come off. A real bloody mess all round, that's what this trip to Leningrad's been.'

'Don't say that,' said Madox firmly. 'Do not say that. Just let me have a look at that passport of yours.'

'Look,' said Paul, 'if you don't want to help, don't bother. But if you think you're going to get me mixed up in some other shady bloody business . . .'

Madox was rummaging with light fingers, pick-pocket-swift, in the jacket that Paul had removed and hung on a bedpost. 'Ah,' he said, taking out the little book which, between covers solid as walls, affirmed Paul's identity, 'this is it. And very nice, too. A good-looking woman, your missis. A bit of a will of her own, though—you can see that.'

'Look,' repeated Paul, 'what exactly are you trying to . . .'

'Helping.' Madox smiled. 'Helping, helping. Helping the cause and helping you, my old mate. What was that name again—Opis . . . ?'

'. . . kin. Where I'm going now,' said Paul, getting up from the bed, 'is to see the Consul or whoever it is. That's where I should have gone in the first place, damn it. I'm getting out of here, and thank you for nothing.' He was on his feet now, smoothing his wrinkled trousers.

'Where you're going,' said Madox, 'is to see the Doc. The Doc is in bed at the moment, having had a very busy night. The Doc helps people, and helping is very hard work, as you may or may not know. But the Doc, I should think, will be very glad to see you. You just wait here. Five minutes only. Then I will bring you into the Doc's presence. Help yourself,' Madox invited. He opened a chamber-pot cupboard by the bed to disclose shining glasses and bottles. 'No ice, but you can't have everything. Go on, spoil yourself. I'll be back in five minutes. Opiskin,' said Madox and went out.

Drinking a large raw shuddering bourbon, Paul walked round the room, hardly able to think but not really wanting to: his brain played a kind of solitaire with all shiny picture-cards—Hussey as Queen and Knave mainly, holding odd objects of spurious antique interest, but Hussey also as Mr Horsebrass The Curio Man, bowing prettily with an empty shop behind him: empty, empty, empty, ah God. Then a wild Joker with Old Testament Fagin face. Let her get on with it then, my old mate: I never loved her anyway. I hope you'll be happy but I hope you'll wake up suddenly in the night with pains of remorse more terrible than the pains of oncoming menses, and when you think you're going to come back you'll get a bloody shock, my lady. He's moved, he's moved, no we don't know where, oh he sold up the shop lock stock and barrel months ago and never said no manner of word to nobody. Abroad, they say, somewhere overseas to make a new start. His heart was broken.

Broken, eh? That's a good 'un, that is. Paul did not like the taste of the bourbon much; he gave himself a fair slug from a multiface bottle labelled *Old Mortality*. The trembling of the hands was what he did not much care for, either. A tremor of intent. Bottle and glass played a bar from that bell-thing of Opiskin's. Madox came back in. 'Righty-ho,' he said happily. 'The Doc will see you now.' And then, 'You could do with seeing a doc, really, the way you are. But we'll have you fine for tonight. Plenty of rest is what you need. A hero, that's what you're going to be.'

'All I ask,' said Paul, 'is a small loan. I don't want anything else.' Madox led him briskly out on to the corridor. An old *babuchka* was sweeping its long penal-looking stretch very slowly, grumbling, using a yard-brush. The Doc's room was a couple of doors down, not far from the loaded desk (framed family photographs chiefly, including a son in the Navy) of the floor concierge. Madox knocked, inclining slightly to the tough elegant old oak, an imperialist door. A remembered flute of a voice sang loudly that they should enter. This they did.

'Of course, of course—how well I recall the face. But not the mouth. Dear, dear, dear. Our touristic friend. But it was not tourism at all, hm? Ah well, truth is a precious commodity: it is not to be bandied about among strangers. But the stranger phase has passed now, has it not? Very well, then: we can put *some* of our cards on the table.'

Dr Tiresias, in a most fetching brocade jacket, was sitting up in bed. The bed was no better than that in Madox's room, but it had been transformed, transfigured, by what seemed to be a detachable headboard with embossed gilt rococo cherubim, also a lacy bedspread that looked like an altar-cloth. Beside the bed was a silver coffee service, together with a covered toast-dish. The Doctor had let slide to the floor what appeared to be that day's issue of *The Times*: that was not, of course, possible, but the paper certainly had the crisp ironed look of a paper but newly delivered. The Doctor had in his or her long bones of fingers what

211

seemed to be a small devotional book but proved to be Paul's passport. But Paul's eyes were soon drawn back to the magnificent epicene head with its grey mane, an apocalyptical eagle-hawk-lion: Bertrand Russell in Trafalgar Square, Yeats among schoolchildren, Lady Gregory herself, august and sphingine, the bisexual Lilith from which Adam and Eve were, in paltry segmentation, feigned apocryphally to derive.

'A loan,' said Paul. 'The smallest of loans, please.'

The Doctor took no notice. 'A cigarette, Madox; a chair for our fellow-philanthropist. Time is short, time runs out, ah yes, for us all.' Seated by the bed, Paul looked round the room. There was the wheelchair, stripped of its rugs and cushions: in its seat was a snugly fitted lid, as to a commode. In a pang of intuition like earache it was revealed to Paul that this wheelchair had a cryptic function: it was all hollow, its frame, the fellies of its wheels. The Doctor puffed out aromatic smoke of Egypt and said to Madox, 'I think *now*, you know. There are several things to be done.'

'But there's the dinner,' said Madox. 'There's these parcels.' He waved at a neat stack of them in a corner, some very small; others, flat and shallow, were evidently wrapped books.

'All that will be taken care of,' said the Doctor calmly. 'What do we pay these hotel serfs for?'

'Well, then,' said Madox to Paul, 'I'll be seeing you. With the goods for export.' And he winked. Then he went out.

'I see you looking at those parcels,' said the Doctor. 'You are thinking, perhaps, of Santa Claus? That this is the Christmas North, soon enough, God knows, to be frozen, whence the kiddies' presents come? Well, thinking so, you would be almost right.'

'What was all that about goods for export?'

'Madox is facetious,' said the Doctor. 'A useful little

212

man and *loyal*—but facetious. To continue. Those are indeed presents, but not for kiddies—at least, their proposed recipients do not think themselves to be that. Those books in their innocent wrappings—those, God bless us, are not schoolgirl annuals. What are we here for—you, Madox, I? To give people what they want: that, no more. And in return we, naturally, want what *we* want, which is nothing more *recherché* than money. It is not our province to pass judgment on what people want—Blackpool rock, marijuana, stick liquorice, the *Daily Mirror*, plastic mantelpiece ornaments, Mr Priestley's novels, questionable postcards, cocaine—need I go on? What you and I and Madox believe in is the right of choice, is freedom: that is why we are here. We cannot, of course, do very much. We cannot *directly* change régimes or even provide Bentley cars or *bidets* or young elephants. But we *can* supply a reasonable range of consumer goods for people starved of them, ah yes. We can enable a few, a very very few, to exchange what they consider oppression for what they consider liberty.'

'You mean,' said Paul, 'that you're a kind of Scarlet Pimpernel?'

The Doctor smiled. '*Dear* Baroness Orczy. Such a disgraceful prose-style. But her creation, yes yes, has become permanent myth, no small achievement. Now, in *our* case it works somewhat differently. Sir Percy was motivated solely by altruistic idealism, which we are not. Heaven and hell, meat and poison—they interchange: what is one to one is the other for another. And what we do we do for money, than in the making of which—as Dr Johnson remarked—no person can be more innocently employed. Money, yes.'

'A loan,' said Paul again. 'That's all I've come for. You see, it's even so fundamental a matter as getting from here to the port and buying cigarettes and then there's a taxi from Fenchurch Street to Charing Cross. I don't ask much.'

'Your poor teeth,' said the Doctor compassionately. 'You've suffered, I can see that. You have been broken on the wheel. This horrible new sprawling metallic rusty Russia is not for you, ah no. Only people like myself can *ride* it.'

'And how about this Angleruss?' asked Paul, interested in spite of his own growling oppressions. 'This all sounds to me like hypocrisy.'

'Yes,' said the calm Doctor. 'Tonight we're holding our *summer* Angleruss dinner. A pity you cannot come to it. At every place a little parcel, a present. How glad they all are to receive them! Here a book with lovely illustrations, there a very special snuff; for this lady a packet of her favourite tea, for that gentleman some cigarettes of a blend unobtainable any longer in these territories. Ah, the bottom fell out of things when the Tsar and his family were so *brutally* liquidated. That is the *modern* term, you know: "liquidated". Old Rasputin and his dirt . . . Still, there was glamour. A first-class French cuisine in the hotels, a comfortable journey from Petrograd to Moscow—foot-muffs and samovars— and the land under fairy snow: ah, lovely! Sometimes, when Madox collects our dues—our *return* presents, let me call them—from these gift-hungry people, he occasionally finds not money but some residuary treasure—an ikon, say—recalling the days of what was, after all, a *great empire*.'

'Very interesting,' said Paul, 'but . . .'

'I'm glad you find it interesting, you poor toothless boy, you *victim*. And now—for you are obviously impatient to know this—we come to the part you are to play in this harmless, nay beneficial, work we are trying to do. For we may justly call ourselves philanthropists. Is one any less a philanthropist for expecting a reward for

one's philanthropy? To give people what they want—
might one not descry elements of, yes, nobility in a life
devoted to such an aim?'

'Not always,' said Paul.

'Not always,' repeated the Doctor. 'But if, say, a man
called Opiskin wanted one thing only, and that was to
escape from a life of what he termed oppression, and
that one had the opportunity—for a reasonable con-
sideration, of course—of encompassing the means and
occasion of . . . Do I make myself clear?'

'Opiskin is dead,' said Paul.

'Opiskin is dead,' agreed the Doctor. 'Opiskin the
musician died some years ago. Various stories of his
death have circulated. Cancer of the rectum—that was
the official cause of it (ah, dear Claude Debussy died
of that disease, he genuinely did: a life wholly given
up to beauty ending in pain, smell and mess: I knew
him, I knew him in Paris)—the official cause, I say;
but one has every reason in the world, knowing this
régime, to suspect other causes of death. However,
Opiskin is dead, Opiskin *père*—but what of Opiskin
fils?'

'I never knew he had a son,' said Paul. 'I never knew
much about him. It was my poor dead friend, you see,
who was devoted to the music of Opiskin.'

'Ah yes, Madox told me, in his disarming *natural*
way, something of that. You spoke up for Opiskin (I
remember, believe me) because you were devoted to
the memory of your friend. Of course, of course. It does
you credit. *Vicariousness*: that term applies in all our
present contexts. To be brief, the son lives here in
Petersburg with his aunt, in perpetual apprehension of
nocturnal hammering on the door, the waiting car, the
thumps and drunken laughter and agony in the cellar.
It is like Greek tragedy: the whole house of Opiskin
must be destroyed, utterly, utterly. And here you are

215

with a double passport like a double bed—one half crying out to be used. You came with a wife (whom, incidentally, I never had the pleasure of meeting on board that *ghastly* ship: I regret that, for she seems from her photograph here to be a most amiable person) and now you propose going back without one.'

'It's not a question of what I *propose*,' said Paul, catching the Doctor's trick of heavy emphasis, 'and, as far as proposing things is concerned, I don't quite see what you can possibly expect me to do for this young Opiskin. All I came here for was a small loan.'

'Let us not talk of loans,' said the Doctor, 'but of payment for services rendered. Shall we say five hundred pounds? *In cash.* There is a metal box under my bed. You can see the money if you wish.'

'For what?'

'Madox should, by now, though he takes an unconscionable time to dress, already be indicating to young Opiskin—Alexei is the name, I believe, and Petrovich the patronymic——'

'Another Alexei,' said Paul bitterly.

'You can call him what name you wish,' said the Doctor. 'Pet-name, I mean, of course—the sort of corruption of a wife's given name that a husband might contrive. For his official given name must be—however painful for you, and God knows you have suffered pain enough—the name your wife bears on this passport.'

'This,' said Paul, 'is quite fantastic.'

'Oh,' said the Doctor, 'nothing is too fantastic for real life. The tales I could tell you . . . No, Madox will see to all the practical details. It may be that young Opiskin will have to wear clothes of his aunt's: something smarter, more Western, would have been suitable.'

'Madox,' said Paul, remembering a transaction of a couple of days before, 'will see to all that. Not,' he added, 'that I propose, not for one moment——'

'Fortunately, he has been growing his hair long for some time now, with such a golden possibility as this in view. You have no idea, my boy, of the *good* you are doing. He has, naturally, a passport photograph.' The Doctor yawned. 'Madox is very efficient really. The *luxe* suite of the *Alexander Radischchev*. Your joint destination is Helsinki. There he has friends.' The Doctor yawned again. 'And for you there is an excellent air service from Helsinki to London. Five hundred pounds is the fee. You will, naturally, be paid expenses.' The Doctor yawned again.

'I'm not going to do it,' said Paul.

'Russia,' said the Doctor, ruminatively. 'I think we must move on, Madox and I. Towards the East. I am tired of categories, of divisions, of opposites. Good, evil; male, female; positive, negative. That they inter-penetrate is no real palliative, no ointment for the cut. What I seek is the *continuum*, the merging. Europe is all Manichees; Russia has become the most European of them all.'

'No,' said Paul, 'I shan't do it.'

Ten

PAUL and his bride were having a rough wedding feast in Madox's bedroom. It had all been dumped on the table by a vigorous old waiter in pince-nez and tennis-shoes—Moscow *borshch* (a pale frankfurter bobbing among the wrack of cabbage and meat-shreds), black bread, tinned crab, cucumber salad with sour cream. Paul had drunk plenty of Madox's whisky during the day, but he still found it hard to reconcile himself to the ambiguous vision that sat opposite him, slurping and chewing away with bucolic appetite. This the son of a great composer? It was, God knew, all too possible. 'Sweetheart, sweetheart,' went Paul in practice. Young Opiskin looked up. 'You must get used to responding to my endearments,' said Paul. 'Look as though you understand English, blast you.'

'Calm,' said Madox, dressing. 'Take it easy. You two have got to be very much in love.'

Paul sighed and tapped his inner pocket: five hundred nicker, or part of it; the money was distributed all over his summer-weight suit. It was a comfort. He smiled at young Opiskin. That was difficult. They had not really taken to each other at all. Young Opiskin was wearing the drilon dress Paul had sold to Madox, genuine Russian lady's underwear, what looked like surgical stockings, very tight well-worn shoes with Cuban heels. The bosom was a fair construction of cotton waste, though the left pseudo-breast was somewhat larger and (as if because of that) lower than the other. All this would do, despite the burliness, ill-shaven forearms, and massive neck: young Opiskin had

218

inherited none of the delicacy of line that poor Robert had found in old Opiskin's music. But the face, the face: this was, under the heavy wiry ginger hair combed down over the ears, behind the smudged lipstick and floury powder, so leeringly masculine that Paul's heart failed each time he saw it. His passport (and it had to be admitted that the job of substituting the photograph had been superbly done, even down to the simulation of a bit of embossed arc of the Foreign Office chop) now suggested a mean and spiteful revenge on Belinda for her desertion. To give her young Opiskin's leering, chinny, droop-gobbed, staring, insolent face in exchange for her pretty, humorous, alert American one: that hardly seemed British chivalry. But there was a bigger chivalry at work, one that made Paul—watching young Opiskin dunk pebbles of black bread into sour cream—try to be more charitable. A great Russian composer, hated because he composed too well, loved by Robert, had produced this son as his greatest symphony. Moreover, five hundred smackers and travelling expenses . . .

'What I don't understand,' he said to Madox, now clerkly smart in his serge suit, his hair dark, flat, glistening like a grilled steak, 'is where he got the money from. I can see he's travelling towards money, of course—his dad's royalties tied up in capitalist banks —but where would he get it here?'

'They find it,' said Madox. 'You'd be surprised how much money these buggers can get hold of when they try. Sometimes it's not money, though. It's *dachas* and works of art and that. Once we got damn near offered a MiG fighter plane, but that was too risky. When they start wanting to haggle we just say, "And how much does freedom really mean to you, eh?" And that shuts them up.'

'And,' asked Paul, 'does anyone ever get caught?'

'Look here,' said Madox, 'if you two lovebirds have stopped noshing, you'd better be on your way. Sorry there's no wedding cake but you can't have everything. Embarkation at ten. I've ordered what they call the tourist-machine for you. Bribery, bribery, bribery. Ten roubles to make absolutely sure of it. Corruption is going to be the ruin of this country.'

'Come along, sweetheart,' said Paul, giving his rather feminine hand to the worker's paw of young Opiskin. 'Christ,' he added, 'where's the ring?'

'I was never much good as a best man,' sighed Madox. 'Anything on the curtains? Napkin ring? No, too big. Wait, I've got a tin of 555 over there somewhere.' Deftly he picked out the goldfoil from among the cigarettes that lay tinned on the escritoire, then folded and folded and twirled this into a frail glowing round for young Opiskin's thick hairy finger. 'With all my worldly goods I thee and thou,' winked Madox, quoting, clamping it on; the young man giggled. 'And now you'd better say goodbye to the old Doc.'

Paul's bride made untidy use of his compact, then, trying to be helpful, picked up the two suitcases, his and his. 'That will not do,' reproved Paul, glaring up at young Opiskin. He was a well-made lad of about twenty-six, though officially now he wore Belinda's graceful forty, and he looked as though it was possible to thrive on Soviet food-plan failures and apprehension. He thumped out ahead of the other two, a plastic handbag under his arm, fixing, with fresh giggles, a Copenhagen souvenir scarf round his head. Madox turned up his eyes and then made lip-licking money-teller's gestures. 'And,' said Paul, 'there is a certain measure of the heroic about it, I see that now.'

The Doctor, with grey mane blue-rinsed and eyes bright as from dexedrine, was seated in the wheelchair, now cushioned and rugged again. There was a fine

Paisley shawl round the throat and across the breast: the Doctor's sex remained, last as first, a mystery. Paul wondered whether he should be bold and ask now before leaving (and why, incidentally, had that old man in the lock-up worn pyjamas all the time?), but he decided against it. The Doc was right, perhaps: the day of the continuum was approaching: no more division, compartmentalization: the hour of the East. The Doctor said:

'Bless you, bless you, and may the progeny of this act be manifold, beautiful and true.' It was like something from *The Cocktail Party*. 'Both Madox and I regret that we cannot come to the port to wave you off, but we have this big marriage feast of our own. The last, I think. I shall, naturally, not announce the *liquidation* of Angleruss: Madox and I will just go off, quietly, quietly, into the sun. We have done our work here. We may well be remembered.'

'If I may make so bold, Doctor,' said Madox, 'don't pitch into them too hard tonight. Not too much about serfs and peasants and cows rotting in the fields and how they've betrayed their glorious history and all that guff. Some of them get very hurt.'

'Nonsense,' said the Doctor. 'They *like* to be scolded. They *expect* a representative from a *civilized* Western nation to upbraid them for their foolishness. For, believe me, Hussey, this system of theirs is an experiment, nothing more. It will pass, it will die, it will *liquidate* itself. Russia is bigger than its bouncy little shop-stewards would have us believe. You have no conception of its vastness of soul. And something inside the Russians tells them, no matter how pigheaded their orthodoxy may happen to be, that the words of such a one as myself, however barbed and rudely couched, spring from a greater love than the fawning of their Western jackals. Why do they allow the *Daily Worker* in? Only to laugh at. They despise the Western Communists. Their revered English image is an aristocratic one. And another thing——'

'I'd better get these two down to the car,' said Madox. 'There isn't all that much time.'

'Very well,' said the Doctor. 'We will talk again, Hussey, I have no doubt. Somewhere. And now—*proshchaitye!*' That word of goodbye sounded liturgical —bearded and top-hatted—so that young Opiskin looked as though he might, but for the tightness of his skirt, have knelt for a blessing. And so Paul and his charge left the presence.

The hotel was full of guests arriving for the Angleruss dinner. A fat little man in a blue uniform cast a look of desire at young Opiskin. Young Opiskin giggled. He had been told to open his mouth only to giggle: he was supposed to be an English lady. He spoke naturally a deep blurred Russian and nothing else; he was strangely uncultivated for a great musician's son.

Blessed dark out in the street. The clang of rare trams on dear Nevsky Prospekt. 'Here we are, then,' said Madox, taking them to the car. The driver looked sly. 'This bugger's been paid already; don't give him any more.' Madox then shook Paul's hand with great warmth. 'Goodbye, my old mate.' He then breathed a sweetish mixture of vodka and crème-de-menthe on to Paul, saying confidentially, 'Do you know the Ship in Bermondsey? A good booze-up some night when we get back. They know me there—Arnold's the name; they all know Arnold. I'll drop you a postcard.' But Paul knew that that would never be: Madox would shrink and grow grey outside Leningrad; he must be for Paul one of the city's smaller monuments; it was better thus.

On the drive to the port, Paul said in careful Russian to young Opiskin:

'I must say this. I admired your father's work very

much. He was a great man.' Slums, wall-eyed windows
of decaying warehouses, Bradcaster when he'd been a
boy, Byzantine glories, canals slid by. The car was
dirty; its ashtray was jammed full. Paul wanted to cry.
'A very, very great man.' The son of the great man
giggled.

The port gates. The passport. The little official gaped
in. Paul's bride leered phallically. But it was all right.
They were waved on towards the tramlines, bales,
sheds. Paul breathed. At last they came to the huge
terminal, the landward entrance with its great stone
steps, crowds mounting in the dim electric light—
excited as though going into a theatre. And a fine stage
set had been mounted at the far, sea, end: a real
throbbing ship with cyclorama of Baltic summer stars.
The sea-monster siren cried and cried forlornly. Paul,
aware of much money in his pockets, heartened by the
dark bustling, gave the car-driver a rouble for carrying
the bags up the steps.

'*Da svidanya*,' said young Opiskin.

'You bloody fool,' said Paul savagely. 'You're an
English lady, get that? You know no bloody Russian.'

The crowd in the customs-hall was immense, and this
suited Paul well. Moreover, as if this were a wartime
embarkation of troops, formalities were being conducted under the most ghostly of blue lamps. Paul's
bride clomped through the crowds unnoticed. An
English clergyman, oboeing 'Mrs Gunter, where is Mrs
Gunter?', was shooing his flock through to the quay—a
sort of small mothers' union, dishevelled and flushed as
from an outing to hell. There were two Lancashire
workmen, gnarled and bespectacled, jacketless and in
braces, one of them saying, 'T'booggers can't mek tay.'

It was easy, easy. They slid through the customs
formalities; the passport was stamped in a bored trance,
the dangerous page barely glanced at; they were out

under the warm summer sky, in the boarding queue, the *Alexander Radishchev* comforting as some huge docile lighted mother beast, her port flank glowing with teats of portholes. A passenger, drunk but not uncultivated, drank in the plethora of bright Northern stars, his Adam's apple working, saying, 'And that's Pluto up there—Pluto, the arsehole of the solar system.' Safe, safe, safe. They were close to the toiling gangway when a voice called:

'Mr Gussey! Mr Gussey!'

Ah well, they had tried, it had been very nearly a successful venture . . .

'I was looking,' panted Zverkov. 'In the bar, I thought . . . A drink, a last drink . . . So this is Mrs Gussey.' Young Opiskin giggled. Resigned, Paul dragged him out of the queue. It was dark, though; thank God it was dark.

'She's not very well,' said Paul. 'I want to get her into her bunk right away. She's not had much of a holiday.' Young Opiskin giggled.

'She is a fine handsome woman,' said Zverkov gallantly. 'I hope,' he said to Paul, 'there are no hard feelings. We were only doing our duty, Karamzin and I.'

'Where is the good Karamzin tonight?' asked Paul.

'It is the evening for his cultural class. He is studying the History of Choreography. But he sends his kindest regards. And he hopes you do not mind too much about the teeth.'

'Oh, it was only four,' said Paul. 'I've got plenty at the back.'

'It was the result of a little misunderstanding, Mrs Gussey,' explained Zverkov. Here, under the stars, in the warmth of the ship's huge flank, Zverkov seemed very small, very ill-dressed; what hair he had was untidy in the light breeze. 'No real harm was meant.'

Young Opiskin giggled. 'I am sure,' frowned Zverkov, 'we have already met.'

'I don't really think so,' Paul put in quickly. 'My wife's been in hospital all the time.' Young Opiskin giggled again and rolled his large shoulders.

'She has a great sense of humour,' said Zverkov. 'She laughs at your misfortune and at her own. The English-speaking peoples generally have a great sense of humour. I hope,' he said to Paul, 'you enjoyed being in our country. I do not think you will want to come again. There are so many other places in the world to see.' He sank to sudden Russian gloom. 'We are happy here,' he said defiantly. 'We go our own way. We are not always understood.' His eyes seemed suddenly drawn to the muscular forearm of young Opiskin.

'It was fine,' said Paul. 'I enjoyed every minute of it.' He extended his hand. Zverkov ignored it. Instead, he grasped Paul tightly round the body, a real bear-hug, and kissed him heavily on both cheeks. Then he made as to do the same to young Opiskin. 'Don't,' warned Paul. 'She may have something infectious.'

'Goodbye, goodbye,' cried Zverkov as Paul, carrying the suitcases, said politely to young Opiskin, 'After you, sweetheart,' and sent him clomping up the gangway. The taffrail above was lined with cheering men, some cranking football rattles. Soon Paul could look headlong down upon Zverkov, who waved and waved like a bumboat-woman. Then the pretty dark stewardess said, 'Your cabin, please?'

'*Luxe*,' said Paul. 'It's all been arranged by a Mr Madox.'

'*Luxe*, oh yes. It is the suite that Comrade Khrushchev himself once travelled in, by. Which is right: "in", "by"? Perhaps "on"? We try always to improve our English.'

Paul sighed. 'I shall be happy to give you a

lesson . . .' No, no, that would not do at all: not with this hefty clomping bride, already leering at the stewardess in a manner perhaps intended to be sisterly; not with his own Dracula fangs. 'Sometime,' he said vaguely. They were led down a ship-smelling corridor (oil, fried fish, a ghost of sea-sickness) towards the bridal suite. Posters, posters everywhere; wall-newspapers in which the only news was warty roaring goblinesque Khrushchev; finally they approached the bed, beds, in which Khrushchev had slept.

'Who slept with Mr Khrushchev?' asked Paul.

'Oh, somebody else,' said the stewardess vaguely. 'Somebody who is not now much talked of, about.'

It was a roomy Edwardian suite. Paul locked the outer door and inspected every corner and cupboard, sniffing like a cat. Sitting-room with big square lights looking out on a working deck; club chairs, oilcloth-covered table, broken radiogram, a book or two about the achievements of the Party. Bedroom with twin canopied beds and a worn though deep carpet between them. Bathroom strangled with buff-painted pythons of pipes and shiny with flywheels and levers. Bathing would be a muscular job. Safe, safe, safe.

Paul spoke Russian to young Opiskin, piercing him with two guardian eyes. '*Khorosho*. Get into that bed and stay there. You must undress first. No, do not remove *that* garment. A lady's bosom is supposed to be a permanent fixture (*postoyannaya dolzhnost'*). Here is your aunt's night-dress.' He saw those sentences as curiously disjunct—an exercise from *Teach Yourself Russian*. Young Opiskin leered up at him from his bed, horribly male, then giggled. 'All right,' shuddered Paul. 'In here it is permitted to talk—but very, very quietly.'

'Vodka.' Young Opiskin made swigging motions, his arm-muscles rippling. 'Now.'

'You must wait. Wait till we move off and the bar is

226

opened.' Paul sat down on his own bed. 'Tell me,' he said. 'What will you do in Helsinki?'

'Herra Ahonen,' said young Opiskin, doing a mime of steering with arms spread wide enough for a cart-wheel.

'Yes, yes, I know Mr Ahonen's going to meet us in a car, but what then? How will you live? Royalties from your father's works won't last for ever.' Young Opiskin looked as though he had never before heard that word 'royalty' (*gonorar*). He frowned and lighted a Droog cigarette that made Paul cough. 'What I mean is,' said Paul, 'that you must have some trade or pro-fession. What have you been doing in Leningrad?'

Young Opiskin laughed as though that were the biggest joke in the world. It was Paul's turn to frown. And now the ship hooted farewell to the shore. The eager passengers cheered from the port taffrails. Finger-tip contact with the huge bed of a land where, under some mattress, Belinda was lodged like a pea—this was now lost. Inch by inch Leningrad was pushed away towards the past.

'Vodka now,' said young Opiskin.

'I'll ring the bell,' sighed Paul. Bell: *kolokol*. That work by Opiskin *père*. A kind of boiling sweet-smelling jam gushed up at its memory; he gushed jammily at Opiskin *fils*, 'Never mind. Everything will be all right. You shall be looked after, poor boy.' But young Opiskin didn't seem too worried, lying there smoking in his aunt's outsize cotton night-dress. Though he evidently did not trust Paul as a person (the lower-jaw gap did not really invite trust), he seemed to have a sort of sacramental confidence in the power of the money that had been paid out. Having pushed the bell-button in the bedroom, Paul went out to wait by the corridor door. With the promptness of response that, after all, a *luxe* passenger had a right to expect, a knock came. It was a loud knock, cheerful rather than deferential. Paul opened up. 'Oh God, no,' he groaned.

Burton or John Collier evening jacket, baby face, red Stuart nether lip. It was Yegor Ilyich, officer formerly in charge of the first-class dining saloon of the *Isaak Brodsky*, the ship in which Paul and Belinda had made the outward voyage. He recognized Paul right away and began, dancing in nimble pumps, to box him, pushing him with each mock blow farther and farther into the sitting-room. 'Ah,' he went, 'I get name soon soon soon—Dyadya Pavel, yes? And where you missis?' He made loud pouting smacking noises at the air.

'Out,' said Paul. 'Stay out of that bedroom. She's ill —do you hear? Keep away,' he warned.

But Yegor Ilyich danced thither, hair and lower lip ashine under the miniature candelabra. The play-punch he aimed at Paul's gut gently connected. It would not normally have hurt much, but Paul had, the previous day, suffered a blow there which had not been meant in play at all. Yegor Ilyich corantoed and lavoltaed into the bedroom, singing a roguish 'Aaaaah'. Paul was after him, cursing, rubbing his belly. Yegor Ilyich stood agape, staring at the occupied bed. 'This not you missis,' he remarked. 'This not nobody missis.' That summed it up pretty well. Young Opiskin should not have been scratching himself. Not, anyway, in that particular spot.

Eleven

'A joke,' said Paul, with an archaic smile. (Or, at least, he could have scratched that particular spot through the bedclothes. Paul was not pleased with young Opiskin, who seemed to grow progressively less intelligent all the time. He didn't take this matter of life and death with the correct Slav seriousness.)

'Zhok?' said Yegor Ilyich's vivid lip.

'Yes, yes. A *shootka*.' Holding this bright toothless smile was like holding his arms up. 'My wife is not here, she is somewhere else. This man pretends, for a joke, to be my wife. It is funny, yes?'

'*Shootka*,' said Yegor Ilyich, without much mirth. '*Da, da—shootka*.' (On the other hand, thought Paul guiltily, young Opiskin had paid out good money to be transported to safety; he might also reasonably expect, as a decent married woman, to be protected from dancing incursions by over-familiar chief stewards.) 'Now,' said Yegor Ilyich, 'what I bring?' He frowned in a puzzled way at young Opiskin; Paul did not like that frown. 'I bring sturgeon, sour cream, red caviar, yes?'

'Drink,' said Paul. 'We would like to drink. And, oh——' He pulled out from his inner pocket a deck of good English currency and lick-thumbed off a pound— no, make it two. 'This joke,' said Paul, 'is a good joke. You not tell, no?' Make it three. Yegor Ilyich said:

'For five I not say.' Greed showed, corruption. He had been corrupted by the wealth of Tilbury, by the crammed windows of consumer goods round Fen- church Street Station. 'My kids, yes? In London I buy, yes?' Make it five, blast him. ('This is the son of great Opiskin, whose music poor Robert loved.') Yegor Ilyich tucked the money in his breast pocket, behind his five-pointed snowy handkerchief. His sloe-eyes followed the wad back to Paul's pocket. 'Six, yes? Little ting for my wife?'

Paul wondered what was best to do with Yegor Ilyich. He imagined young Opiskin arising, terrible in his aunt's night-dress, to lift clobbering fists at Paul's request. Hide Yegor Ilyich, bound and gagged, in the bathroom, in a roomy wardrobe, till disembarkation time (1200 hours) tomorrow? Throw him into the Baltic? A long sleep, a sufficient silence. He said:

'You and I go together to bar to drink, yes?' He swigged air from his fist. To young Opiskin he said, 'Charlie, old boy, you wait here and I shall bring you something back,' winking, still fist-swigging. Young Opiskin giggled. Yegor Ilyich began box-dancing again. Come on, come on, get him out of here, get him to forget.

'The bar?' said Paul, out in the corridor, the key in his pocket. Yegor Ilyich led him by a sort of crew's way, through knots of dirty card-playing sailors and a sort of still-room where an under-cook drooped cigarette-ash over a tray of open sausage sandwiches he was preparing. They entered the first-class bar through a kind of trap-door and were cheered. There was some heavy drinking going on. It was because of these statutory hundred-gramme measures, sternly served out by a man in a thick undervest. This first-class bar was filthy—a snarl at bourgeois pretensions—and all drinks seemed to be served in beer-glasses. A respectable-looking trembling sort of old woman was handed a crème-de-menthe that looked like a small green light ale. But it was mostly men, singing men, some wearing team-rosettes and cranking rattles. 'Cognac, one bottle,' said Paul, 'and never mind about glasses.' A small wiry man with spectacles said, on a rising intonation, 'Aye aye.'

Paul took a small burning mouthful. '*Za vashe zdorovye.*'

Yegor Ilyich sank a tenth of the bottle. '*Za vashe zdorovye.*'

'This,' said a youngish man with a braying voice, 'is a sure sign of lack of control at the top. My father talked till his dying day of a small hotel in Torquay where the head waiter came into the dining-room smoking a cigarette.'

'*Za vashe zdorovye.*'

'*Za vashe zdorovye.* Peace to bloody world.'

'Right,' said the small wiry man vigorously, 'peace is what we want, right? We don't want any more like the last lot. Not that I didn't enjoy some of it, I'll say that. But if there's going to be any more hanky-panky it'll be you Russky bastards as'll start it.'

'They're the same as what you and me are, the ordinary common people,' said another man who, for some reason, struck Paul as having cancer. 'The man in the street, that is. Tom, Dick and Harry—though they don't have those names there.' He was terribly grey and thin. Paul, for the first time that night, thought of death. The firing squad re-formed in his brain. Death, death, death.

'*Za vashe zdorovye.*'

'*Za vashe zdorovye.*'

He would get Yegor Ilyich drunk if it was the last thing he did. Drunk, incapable, incoherent, snoring till noon tomorrow. Oh, let it be tomorrow, let it be all over. Paul saw himself in some Helsinki bar, young Opiskin waved off to some new free life of his own making; a clean Finnish bar, women's eyes like blue Sibelian lakes, a beer or two till the plane. He instinctively pressed his foot hard on the deck as on an accelerator. Hurry, hurry, hurry, *noctis equi*.

'*Za vashe zdorovye.*'

'*Za vashe zdorovye.*'

'The ordinary worker, the ordinary trade union member, as it might be, doesn't want war,' said the cancerous man.

'I,' sighed the braying young man, 'have specialized in the Early Tudor Voyages. Read Hakluyt. Read the accounts of the Muscovy Company. The Russians haven't changed. 1554. Chancellor reports, "They be naturally given to great deceit, except extreme beating did bridle them." And again, "As for whoredom and drunkenness there be none such living: and for extortion, they be the most abhominable under the sun." What they were then they are now. They can't be trusted.'

'You,' said a fattish man with well-greased pale hair, 'would be a professor, then?'

'A lecturer. Not a professor. Not yet.'

'You're speaking for your own class, mister. That's how it is. The professor class. Now for the rest of us here it might be different.'

'*Za vashe zdorovye.*'

'*Za vashe zdorovye.* English man oh kyeh. English woman oh bloody kyeh. Zhok,' laughed Yegor Ilyich.

'That's right, see. He's a Russian and he's a worker. He's got this fancy evening dress get-up on, but that's like his uniform, see, but he's still a worker.'

'He's not doing much work now.'

A man with a rosette played a loud bar of rattle-music and said, 'They worked all right yesterday afternoon against our lads. Pity there's no buying and selling across the Iron Curtain. That outside-left of theirs, what's his name?'

'Nastikoff or summat.'

'*Za vashe zdorovye.*'

'*Za vashe zdorovye.*' The bottle was nearly empty. Paul
had pretended to drink his share, but Yegor Ilyich had,
so Paul judged, downed a good seven-eighths. His eyes
flamed like Christmas snapdragons, his lower lip was
essential ultimate Creation-day red, Chesterton's God's
colour, but the man himself was sober, upright, ready
to carry on. A little crowd was gathering round.

'Is this a contest, like?'

'—Gave away a penalty for hands and then that shot
went under the bloody bar. Then from their right wing
to What's-his-bloody-name and then on to the other
bugger——'

'Summat ending in insky.'

'Then right into the bloody net.'

' "—And the barbarous Russes asked likewise of our
men whence they were, and what they came for:
whereunto answer was made, that they were Englishmen sent into those coasts, from the most excellent
King Edward the sixt, and seeking nothing else but
amity and friendship and traffic with the people,
whereby they doubted not, but that great commodity
and profit would grow to the subjects of both king-
doms——" '

'Knows it all, he does. Say that for him.'

'*Yeshcho odna butuilka,*' Paul ordered carefully.

'Englishman he is, here, see, but speaks the lingo
like a native.'

'You mustn't call them that. They're not natives.
They're more like you and I.'

Impassively, another bottle of cognac was uncorked.
Paul felt somehow that it should have been sharply
cracked open at the neck. Still, no glasses. Blood and
cognac, each other's blood.

'*Za vashe zdorovye.*'

'*Za vashe zdorovye.*'

'Look,' said a breathy man with a squashed square face, 'if this is to be done on a proper basis they ought to cover the same course. There's one getting more down than the other—you can see that if you look close.'

'Glasses, then.'

'A bottle each.'

' "If any man be taken upon committing of theft, he is imprisoned, and often beaten, but not hanged for the first offence, as the manner is with us: and this they call the law of mercy. He that offendeth the second time hath his nose cut off, and is burnt in the forehead with a hot iron. The third time he is hanged." '

'*Za vashe zdorovye.*'

'*Za vashe zdorovye.*'

'Right,' said the breathy man. 'Here's two glasses. And I'll do the measuring out.'

'No,' said Paul, 'no no no. You don't quite understand. I'm trying to get him drunk, you see. For a special reason. A very special reason. A matter of life and death.'

'He looks all right to me,' said the man with rosette and rattle. 'You look to be the one that's showing the signs.'

'Right,' said Paul. 'You're all sportsmen here. You bet him a quid he can't down the rest of the bottle in one go.'

'Now that,' said the cancerous man, 'is an imposition. That's taking unfair advantage of a man.'

'*Za vashe zdorovye,*' went Yegor Ilyich, his face ardent.

'No,' said Paul. 'You're on your own now.'

'Giving best to a bloody Russky,' said a man who smelt faintly of old frying oil. 'Where's your bulldog breed?'

'All right,' said the fattish man with well-greased pale hair. 'I'll give him five bob if he can do it.'

234

'Oh, five from me, certainly,' said the Tudor Voyages young man, 'for the pleasure of seeing him go down.'

'That's vindictive, that is. And you supposed to be educated. Sheer ignorance, that is.'

'I hate the lot of them,' said the young man. 'I'm glad I went. It's confirmed everything.'

'Ten bob from me,' said Paul. 'Right,' he told Yegor Ilyich. 'You drink all that bottle off. One pound, see? One lovely quid.' He waved the note in front of Yegor Ilyich's nose.

'*Ponimaiu*,' said Yegor Ilyich. 'Understand.' He took the cognac-bottle by its neck and said to the entire company, '*Za vashe zdorovye.*'

'I,' said Paul, 'was *made* to do that, but it was with a bottle of vodka and it was hanging out of the window by one ankle.'

'Let's have him hanging out of a porthole, then,' suggested Tudor Voyages.

'Vindictive.'

Yegor Ilyich drank. His larynx worked away, the level of the bottle went steadily down, the bottle itself rose slowly through an arc whose centre was the fat thirsty clinging lips, from near-horizontal to true vertical. Yegor Ilyich's eyes remained closed, as though against a bright sun—a gardener swigging cold tea.

'By God, he's done it.'

' "Now what might be made of these men if they were trained and broken to order and knowledge of civil wars?" ' murmured the young lecturer out of Richard Chancellor's report. For Yegor Ilyich did not collapse with drooped mouth and upturned eyes; instead he performed an *entre-chat* or two and boxed his audience so that, part-fearful and wholly intrigued, they became the periphery of an *ad hoc* cabaret-floor. Then Yegor Ilyich bowed his legs, thrust out his belly, pouted, frowned, and waddled about in his not very good impression of Comrade Khrushchev. After that he became Khrushchev-with-little-girls. 'All right,' said somebody primly. 'There's still some ladies drinking over there.' Then Yegor Ilyich did a fair Nijinsky leap over to the flight of five wide shallow stairs that led down into the bar, poised on one leg and shot an Eros-shaft from the top step, blew coarse kisses, shouted 'Zhok!' while pointing a finger at Paul, laughed loudly, then marched out trimly.

'Oh God,' said Paul to himself.

'Bar finish now,' said the barman with bitter scorn. There was a rush for one last one. Paul remembered young Opiskin's need and bought a bottle of vodka.

'I should have thought you'd have had enough for one night like,' said the rosette-and-rattle man.

'Oh, the night hasn't really started yet,' groaned Paul. He left the fighting-for-one-last-one and, hugging the vodka like a child, found his way back to the Khrushchev suite past grinning Khrushchev pictures. There was more than grinning, though; there was the wide-nosed cunning triumphant look of one who delivers a good knock-down argument in the form of a peasant proverb: sharpest knives cut the keenest; rain may fall when the sky darkens; a slice of roast goose is better than a stinking fish-flake.

Young Opiskin was snoring, transfixed on his back with his hands joined like an effigy of a knight in a church. Paul shook him roughly awake and said, '*Vot tam vodka*.' Then he went into the sitting-room, sank into a cold leather club chair, lighted a cigarette, and waited. He had a little book of Russian verse in his raincoat pocket, a book he had not really had the opportunity to open since coming to Russia. He turned to the poems of Sergey Esenin, the young man who had been married to Isadora Duncan for a year and, after

236

taking to drink and a kind of madness, had written a
farewell poem in his own blood and then hanged himself. That had been, as far as Paul knew, in the Astoria
Hotel in Leningrad. He now, to the faint accompani-
ment of a glugging vodka-bottle in the bedroom, read
the poem:

'Goodbye, my friend—no word, no clasp of hand.
Do not grieve, do not in sorrow screw
Your brow. In this life it is nothing new to die,
And to live, of course, itself is nothing new.'

There was a knock at the door. 'Come in,' called
Paul. An officer with a young, moustached, knowing
face—but knowing after the Western style—came in.
He wore two rings on each arm. The uniform was good
serge, well-tailored, London perhaps being a suburb of
the *Alexander Radishchev*.

'Mr Gussey?'

'That will do.'

'We do not appear to have your passport in the
office.'

'It's in my pocket. I'm looking after it on behalf of
Her Majesty's Government.'

'Pardon?' It was a thin, genteel English accent, as
though learnt in some school of the LCC.

Paul tapped his inner pocket, smiling. He was not
going to let that passport go.

'If I could see it—for the number, for our records.'

Paul took it out, held it up. The young officer frowned
at the two photographs. He said:

'Perhaps it would be possible to see Mrs Gussey for
a moment.' It was a pity about that Russian G. Paul
said:

'I'm afraid she's sleeping at the moment.' A vodka
belch from the bedroom gave that the lie. 'If,' said Paul,

'Tovarishch Yegor Ilyich has been telling you stories, they're all untrue. The man's drunk.'

'There are many names I do not know,' said the officer. 'There have been transfers from other ships of the Baltic Line. I am only doing my duty.'

'Why do you want to see my wife?'

'There is some rumour that she is really a man. It is very difficult. I was asked to see that everything is all right.'

'Everything's fine.'

The young man looked embarrassed. 'I was ordered to satisfy myself that everything is in order.'

'And aren't you satisfied?'

A rasping cough came from the bedroom.

'I think,' said the young officer carefully, 'I shall come back here in ten minutes and then I shall take both you and Mrs Gussey to the Captain. Believe me, it is for everybody's good,' he added anxiously.

Twelve

'HE WAS right,' said the Captain. 'He performed his duty. It is not for you to talk about treachery.'

'I gave him money,' said Paul. 'I bought him drink. What did this business matter to him, anyway?'

'You cannot be speaking the truth,' said the Captain. 'Members of the ship's company do not take bribes. They are not able to be corrupted. And they regard it as their duty to report what seems suspicious. The State must be protected. This ship is part of the State.'

'Ah, God,' growled Paul. Now that he and young Opiskin were seated in the Captain's cabin—a model of cleanliness and order, clinically lighted, with rows of Russian books on navigation and maritime law—he could see more clearly the forces they were up against. Young Opiskin, though, apparently saw nothing. He had dressed carefully in drilon and Cuban heels, had lipsticked and powdered over the sprouting stubble of the night, and minced giggling along with his protector behind the two-ringed officer. Now he sat, plastic handbag on very visible knees, leering at the Captain. Paul rather liked the look of the Captain: a youngish man, perhaps younger than himself, grown neatly grey, his features sharp and earnest, smoking a *papiros* with a grace that would have better suited a better type of cigarette. Paul saw the Captain's point of view; he felt mean, venal and dirty. But he made dead Robert's image lurch up, the death-mask of a great composer. He said, after his growl:

'You must see all this from another angle. In the West perhaps our minds work too simply, but we regard freedom of movement as a basic human right. Water finds its own level. If you deny that right to your citizens, then you must expect craft, guile, subterfuge.'

'You talk too quickly,' said the Captain. 'I understand English well but not fast.'

'What are you going to do?'

'To do? To do?' He kept his lips in the kissing position, suddenly caught sight of them in the mirror behind Paul and young Opiskin, then spread them wide as though grinning with pain. 'First,' said the Captain, 'we must find out,' and he beetled at young Opiskin, 'who this person is.'

'He's a youngster of no consequence,' said Paul. 'He has no parents, he has no relatives. I'm taking him to some friends in Helsinki. He is handicapped, being unable to speak. He has no education.' Ready tears were brimming in Paul's eyes. 'He has no work, no money. He has nothing.'

'He has the State,' said the Captain.

'The State isn't a person,' said Paul. 'The State has no blood or warmth in it. He needs love.'

'He needs a passport,' said the Captain. 'He needs a travel permit. You have both broken the law. It is terrible. All I can do is to send you back to Leningrad.'

'I'm a British subject,' said Paul. 'I have certain rights.'

'You broke the law,' said the Captain. 'The Soviet law, on Soviet soil. And this ship is Soviet soil. You are still breaking the law. And I think you must be breaking the British law also. You must hand over your passport to me now.'

'Ah, no,' said Paul. The game wasn't finished yet, not by a long chalk. 'I no longer have a passport. I took the precaution of throwing my passport into the sea. You must dredge the Baltic for it.'

'I think you are not telling the truth,' said the

Captain. 'Well, we shall see. We shall leave it all to the police now.'

'In Leningrad?'

'*From* Leningrad. The wireless room will contact the Leningrad police now.'

'Mentioning my name?'

'Mentioning your name. They will pick you up in Helsinki tomorrow. It is not far to fly from Leningrad. They may be even perhaps waiting for us when we arrive.' The Captain's eyes shone at his wall-mirror, as though reflected there, as in trick film-making, was some draped personification of Soviet efficiency.

'I'm prepared to co-operate,' said Paul. 'The officers in charge of my—er—case ought to be the ones to collect us.'

'In charge of your—— You already have a dossier? You admit to previous crimes?' The Captain seemed quietly pleased.

'Comrades Zverkov and Karamzin,' said Paul. 'They will, I think, be pleased to see me.'

'One of them I know,' said the Captain. 'There was a case of suspected contraband. Sometimes it is attempted on the ships of the State Baltic Line. Not,' he added, 'Soviet citizens.'

'Naturally not.'

'Zverkov and Karamzin, then,' said the Captain. 'So you know them well?' He wrote down the names in a fair Cyrillic hand on his memo pad.

'They knocked these four teeth out,' said Paul modestly, showing.

'So.' The Captain was impressed. Then he looked with some distaste at young Opiskin. '*Familiya?*' he asked loudly. '*Imya?*' Young Opiskin giggled.

'It's no good asking his surname or his first name or anything else,' said Paul. 'He can't speak. He can only make noises. Poor, poor boy. Be satisfied that you have discovered the primal fact of his *maleness*. Although, poor lad, he has come, as you see, to think he is female. He is not quite right in the head. Did I say he has nothing? He has less than nothing.'

'Well, we will leave it to the police tomorrow,' said the Captain. 'Tonight where shall I put you to sleep? It is wrong and indecent for you to share the same bedroom. You are not, after all, husband and wife.'

'I paid good money for Khrushchev's suite,' said Paul coarsely. 'I demand a decent night's rest.'

The Captain pressed a buzzer on his desk. 'Second Officer Petrov will take you back to your suite then. I see no harm if the door is locked on you. Also the windows must be wound up and the handles taken away.'

'We're not going to dive overboard,' said Paul. 'In any case, this poor boy can't swim.'

'Officer of the watch can send in reports,' said the Captain. 'My ship must be protected.'

'You flatter us,' said Paul, 'me and that poor boy there. If you would be so good, Captain, perhaps you would not make your proposals too obvious. Do not, for instance, speak Russian to Second Officer Petrov when he comes in. Ensure that we're locked up discreetly. This poor lad is, besides idiotic, much given to quick violence when he thinks his security is threatened. Let him believe that every thing is going according to plan. It is better so, believe me.'

Thus young Opiskin kept to his leer and his giggles. He would do well in the West, perhaps. He had tremendous confidence in the power of money. He took off his woman's clothes for the second time that night, put on his aunt's night-dress in the pathetic conviction that the deception was still going well, that that session with the Captain had been purely social and that the Captain had perhaps even admired this fine figure of an Englishman's wife. Paul now saw that perhaps Opiskin *père* had been, like so many great musicians (from Henry VIII to Adrian Leverkühn), syphilitic and had begotten a son whose brain was deeply mined with spirochaetes. He watched young Opiskin glog off two hearty slugs of vodka in a tooth-glass, then settle down to confident sleep. He didn't say good night. Paul was a mere instrument, like the money.

Paul slept fitfully. It wasn't really young Opiskin's snores that nudged into his rest—he could accept their rhythm, like the softer one of the sea as they moved towards Finland. What made him toss and thump his pillow was his wonder (insomniacal as dexedrine) that his excitement should be so completely unmixed with apprehension. He was, he supposed, exhibiting the Englishman's finest attribute, that of hopeless optimism. Young Opiskin snored in confidence; Paul watched in it. When he slept he dreamt of crowds cheering. As in one of those montages that form a background to a TV sports-news title, he saw cricket, football, a boat race, the high jump in heraldic quarters. The brass band tore off a red-hot march. Cheers and cheers and cheers. Belinda had never really understood sport, fair play, that sort of thing.

By grey dawn, in his drowsiness, he scented landfall: firs, lakes, Tapiola—Finland sidling up to starboard. He slept. He woke again to see young Opiskin's bed empty. His heart pounded away at him as though he were a punchbag, it a heavyweight in training. Too late, a failed mission. But in the sitting-room he found young Opiskin eating with such appetite that, to blurred morning eyes, it looked as if his entire body was involved in the act: prehensile feet reaching for the coffee-pot, arms twining out for more bread as if they had extra mouths instead of hands at the end of them. '*Zavtrak,*' munched young Opiskin in greeting. He was dressed in very old-fashioned female underwear. 'I know it's breakfast,' said Paul crossly. There was cold rice porridge, apricot jam, very fatty sausage slices, smoked salmon, *black* caviar, hard-boiled eggs, oranges, pumpernickel, butter. It was a breakfast for condemned men. Blinking, Paul looked out on deck. It was full summer northern morning. Green landfall, a distant prospect of conifers. There were men taking queasy exercise, recognized from the night before. Paul saw, swaying all alone, the young Russophobe lecturer, hands in sports-coat pockets, reading the sky as though the sky were a page of Hakluyt. Paul went over to the square wound-up window ('light' was the correct term) and knocked on it. The Tudor Voyages man recognized him, nodded. Paul mouthed urgent words. Soundproof. The young man shrugged. Behind Paul, young Opiskin munched away. 'Wait,' mouthed Paul. 'Wait, wait, wait.' He picked up his little book of Russian verse, tore out the fly-leaf, found his ball-point in a jacket pocket, then wrote, small and clear, 'The following is *true*. Please take action when time comes.' Then came the thriller clichés: 'Political asylum. Secret Police. Disguised as woman. Help.' He took the bit of paper over to the window or light and stuck it on, inscription outward, with spit at the four corners. And we shall shock them. Naught shall make us rue. The young lecturer read. He believed on the first reading. He brought others, football supporters, to read: the fattish man with plastered pale hair, the man with cancer, the man who had worn a rosette and cranked a rattle. All looked ill and read very slowly. The Tudor Voyages lecturer made tearing-down gestures: somebody Russian coming. Paul crunched his plea into a ball. Young Opiskin made himself an open sandwich of sausage and caviar. Paul gulped coffee, jumping with excitement, and went to shave. Timing was everything, timing.

244

Nobody came to clear away the breakfast dishes. Young Opiskin took a bath, his body-hair floating like fronds on the water. He shaved blind in the bath, using Paul's razor, gashing himself crimson on chin and neck. He dressed carefully in his woman's clothes, plastered powder over his blood-clots, painted a clown's mouth. In the sharp sea-light he looked horrible. Bravely Paul said again, 'I want you to know that I admire your father's achievement. You shall be safe. Trust me, trust me. Everything will be all right.'

Finland came nearer, cautiously, sniffing at the ship like a dog. Paul sat on the cold leather settle under one of the lights, smoking endlessly, his mouth foul. Men came by, thumbing up when they saw him, each one heartening as a shot of brandy. The young lecturer kept close by, a sentinel, distrusting the Russians as far back as Bloody Mary. Young Opiskin hummed dreamily, one fat knee over a club-chair arm, watching the copulation of flies on the ceiling. The suitcases stood packed and ready. They waited for Helsinki as if Helsinki were a taxi.

It came on time. Before the noon eight bells Helsinki was there, the ship easing in to it, a modest harbour for a modest capital. The ship's loudspeakers played intimidating Soviet music. Paul could see nothing of the quay's activity, only roofs of sheds, Lutheran churches beyond, low rain-clouds. He could barely, over the noise of his blood, hear the dropping of the gangway. The air roared in his throat. Young Opiskin was infected by Paul's tremors and began to sweat. It was an ample rolling sweat that caked his face-powder. 'Now?' he said to Paul.

'We must wait,' said Paul. 'We must wait till somebody comes to tell us what to do.'

'Herra Ahonen?' asked young Opiskin.

'No. Mr Ahonen will be waiting below. With

245

transport. The men coming now will seem hard and cruel (*zhestokiy*), but that is nothing. Trust me.' Young Opiskin looked puzzled. Both watched the door. They smoked two more cigarettes apiece.

Feet, voices, the turn of a key. Second Officer Petrov appeared first, saying apologetically, 'I am sorry it could not have been an ordinary, pleasant voyage. There are two policemen here to take you back to Leningrad.' And so there were. Paul had not seen them before. They were monoglot and had humourless Tartar faces. Their plain clothes bagged and were of the same sick brownish colour. They came in, looked at Paul, then at young Opiskin. They nodded at him. Young Opiskin seemed to know one of them. He gave Paul a look of great malevolence and thought to run to the bedroom, poor boy. The two policemen were on to him, an arm each. They lifted him on to his toes, marching him back towards the corridor door. Young Opiskin opened up a flood of Russian which Paul did not at all understand, though it was all for him.

'Trust me!' called Paul.

Young Opiskin strained his head round from the corridor to yell, spit, revile. He was strongly, expertly held. He was easily marched away. 'Well,' said Second Officer Petrov to Paul, 'it is very regrettable. It is not nice to see a *luxe* passenger carried away by the police.'

'How about me?' said Paul.

'I am afraid you must wait a while. But I am sure that you will be called for with the miminum of delay.' He spoke like a dentist's receptionist. That, Paul told himself, must be the first job back in England. His case could legitimately be held to be an urgent one; that way one could jump over the National Health waiting lists. He could almost taste the warm wax in his mouth. 'So,' said Second Officer Petrov, 'I will lock you in here again till they come for you.' He went out with a troubled smile, his eyes glowing genuine regret: life could be so simple, so beautiful really. Paul waited. He smoked a cigarette, then another. He was half-way through his third when his own turn came. Second Officer Petrov opened up and showed in two gentlemen it was almost a joy to see: they belonged to the safe past of things enacted, familiar Bradcasterian smells, the Leningrad that Paul now knew he loved and regretted he would never see again.

His first words had been well prepared. 'Well, Comrade Karamzin, and how is the History of Choreography going?' Karamzin and Zverkov were both very smartly dressed today, as for a Sunday occasion: those suits were the work of no Soviet tailors. Karamzin grunted but did not look dangerous; Zverkov said:

'Somehow I knew. Somehow I had a premonition.' Hadn't those been Belinda's words? 'We were destined to meet again, all three of us. Strangely, I had a dream of some foreign sea-port—bigger than this and much hotter: I could not tell where. Things are going to end satisfactorily after all.'

'The whole business has been most unfortunate,' said Paul. 'What do you think will happen to me?'

'In a way,' said Zverkov, 'you have done us a great service. This man has been looked for everywhere and for a long time. I do not think very much can really happen to you personally. There may be some high-level talks, of course. This kind of thing does not help Anglo-Soviet relations.'

'This poor lad,' said Paul angrily. 'His only crime is to be the son of a great man you hate because of his greatness, because of his large free spirit.'

'Oh, let us get on with it,' growled Karamzin, ever the impatient one. 'There will be time for talking later.'

'I'll go quietly,' said Paul. 'I hate vulgar scenes. Shall I carry the luggage?'

'Oh, Karamzin will do that,' said Zverkov. 'A prisoner is a privileged person.'

'I am not a common porter,' rumbled Karamzin. Paul opened up his mouth. Karamzin said, 'Oh, very well, this time I will do it.' And he bent to pick up the cases. His hair seemed freshly barbered.

They marched down the corridor. In the vestibule, into which fresh Finnish air blew, young Opiskin stood, roughly gripped by his guards. He had a bruised, dishevelled look and seemed to be giving his entire attention to the problem of breathing. Each intake made him visibly wince. 'Swine,' said Paul. 'You're an uncivilized people.'

'Some are uncivilized,' said Zverkov gravely. 'That is our trouble. The caterpillars of the commonwealth.'

Grey rainy light. Paul could now willingly throw over all action, all decision. He filled his lungs, taking in enough for young Opiskin. They passed the final poster of roaring Khrushchev. Paul prayed.

Thank God they were there. To left and right of the gangway's head, held back formally by junior ship's officers, there were men who had sailed to Leningrad to see a football match and, having seen it, were now sailing back again. The specialist in Tudor Voyages was to the front of the left-hand group, very alert. There was no noise. Paul reckoned there must be nearly two dozen there, waiting. He recognized very few of the faces. Really, there was only one face—the great humane face of the British working-man in two dozen scarcely distinguishable allotropes. 'Quickly, now, quickly,' said Zverkov. Young Opiskin was given a shove. A sailor guarded the way down to Helsinki.

'God for England etcetera,' said the Tudor Voyages man in a normal lecturer's voice. Then, with the cries appropriate to football-queue jostling, the two little phalanges made for each other, almost casually crushing and hugging Zverkov, Karamzin and their two bullies in the middle, driving the cordoning ship's officers to the rails. It was easy, it was unviolent, there was nothing in it. Young Opiskin gaped: he couldn't believe it. 'Right,' cried Paul, pushing him, 'you deal with that bugger there,' and, the press courteously making way, he threw him on to the bewildered sailor who guarded the gangway. He seemed a decent boy, very pale-eyed, but young Opiskin delivered a dirty left and a filthy right to the groin. He was ready to do more, but Paul shouted, 'Down, down, down!' over the throaty noises of the jostlers. Zverkov and Karamzin fought with mouths open and soundless as drinking-fountain gargoyles. 'Thanks, lads!' called Paul. The Tudor Voyages lecturer was laying into Karamzin lithely. Young Opiskin began to stumble down the ramp. 'I said you could trust me,' panted Paul.

Thirteen

PAUL sat in the beer garden near the town centre. It had gone smoothly, butter-smoothly. Young Opiskin, with no backward look, had been carried off to a future which was no concern of Paul's. Paul had booked a seat on the Caravelle leaving Helsinki Airport at 19.55 and arriving in London (or Lontoo, as it was called here) at 01.45. He must report at the terminal—Töölönkatu 4—about ninety minutes before flight time. Luggage? Hard to explain the lack of it: he had humped four heavy bags up the steps of Fenchurch Street Station, that he remembered well. Now he had nothing. The bag left on the boat? The Russians might well worry that to death, as a dog will worry a bit of trouser-leg torn off its escaped quarry. Or it might come suavely back to Sussex through Intourist's British agents. It didn't matter.

He was near the end of his third glass of mild Finnish beer. He had changed five pounds into finn-marks: he must get through those before leaving Helsinki. Soon he would have a Finnish meal some-where. It was always exciting to be alone in a foreign country: remember that time in Leningrad? He liked the look of this town, homely and miniature, with its drab buildings, its Lutheran earnestness, its tinned pineapple in the shop windows, its cool breath of lakes and forests blowing in—ozone and chlorophyll. He thought the women charming. They were Nordic and Parisian at the same time: astringently fair-haired, eyes of blue ice, but also animated, their wrists and ankles most delicate. The boys were charming too—very clean and glowing, as if they had all had one of those steam-baths, then birch-twig flagellation (delicious), then a cold dip, all bare together. A loudspeaker in a nearby radio shop was playing popular music—American and new: that made one feel safe. A tram occasionally went by. A mature-looking student with medical-looking books under his arm and a peaked and tasselled cap on called in for a quick beer. Paul had an impression of health and order. Also freedom. But what in God's name was freedom?

As if expressly conjured to answer that question, Karamzin and Zverkov walked into the beer garden, under chestnut-trees, Karamzin limping a little. Paul hesitated. But, after all, they were all dead now: they had moved to a cool limbo where causes rang hollow. These were people he knew, old friends you could say. He waved at them. Karamzin jerked at once like a puppet; Zverkov held him with a strong hand. Zverkov switched on a smile and brought trembling Karamzin over.

'We shall join you, then,' smiled Zverkov. Karamzin seemed to have a sort of cat-scratch, nearly two inches long, by his nose. That would be the Tudor Voyages man.

'Sit down,' said Paul. 'Did you miss your plane?'

Karamzin began a string of bad Russian words but sat down as far away from Paul as he could. 'Temper temper temper,' said Paul. 'You're not at home now.'

'So,' said Zverkov, 'we are not at home, either you or us. But the Finnish police are very co-operative. We have just come from them. There is no question of missing any plane. It is a pleasant train journey back. But we shall find him yet.' A handsome plump blonde waitress, about thirty-eight, her fine large breasts efficiently supported, came over for the order. '*Kolme olut*,' said Zverkov. She went off to get it.

'I don't see,' said Paul, 'how you can expect the co-operation of the police of a free state in a matter of this kind. It isn't as though he'd done anything criminal.'

Karamzin's trembling modulated swiftly and horribly into a kind of mirthless baying. People, decent Finnish bourgeois drinkers, looked round with curiosity. Zverkov laid a soothing hand once more on his colleague's arm. Zverkov said, 'Why it is so hard to take you seriously as a man who likes the bad better than the good is because you are very innocent. You are as Tolstoy thought all men were or should be. I cannot remember what. I have no time to read books. But who did you think this man was?'

'The son,' said Paul, 'of your great composer Opiskin. And that's not a question of thinking but of fact. And it's one of the things about your régime I just can't stomach—vindictive persecution for its own sake. Kill the son because of the father; not that the father did anything wrong.'

'What proof have you,' asked Zverkov patiently, 'that he is who you say he is?'

'You,' said Karamzin, 'are a fool.'

'They should have knocked some of your teeth out,' said Paul. The waitress had arrived with three beers. 'Look,' said Paul, in English and pantomime, opening his mouth to the waitress. 'The bloody Russkies did that. A vicious brutal people. Don't let them swallow you up.' The waitress looked puzzled and then saw that a response of pity and horror was demanded of her. She gave this and took Zverkov's money—finnmarks and a kopek tip.

'One beer is for you,' said Zverkov to Paul. 'It will restore the colour to your cheeks.' He smiled up at the waitress and said, '*Sepä hauskaa!*' He said to Paul, 'I speak a little of their language, you see. It is sometimes helpful.'

'Fool,' said Karamzin, shaking.

'Look,' said Paul, 'tell this plug-ugly here not to call me a fool.'

'It is, in fact, foolish to believe what is untrue,' said Zverkov. 'This young man who travelled as your wife and who you think to be the son of the discredited musician Opiskin—he is the real plug-ugly. A very ugly customer. A criminal by any standard. In a way you have brought him out into the open. He was last heard of in Kiev. Then nobody could find him anywhere. There is a great deal you can tell us. Who paid you to do this thing?'

'All this is just one of your stories,' said Paul.

'Believe it or do not believe it,' said Zverkov, sighing. 'His name is not Opiskin but Obnoskin—Stepan V. Obnoskin. He is still young but he has done everything. He is idiotic in himself. You can see in him the influence of environment, the lack of a settled background when he was a child. You can blame capitalism for that. Capitalism, the Fascist aggressor. His father was killed by the Germans, his mother died of a chest disease. I forget where now. Also he was hit on the head very hard when he was a young boy. I forget who did this. He has been very brutal, you must understand. He has worked as a sort of brutal man for others. Smugglers of narcotics. Circulators of forged notes. Like the so-called hero of Dostoevsky, he is suspected of battering an old woman to death for her few roubles. A vicious criminal type.'

'No,' said Paul.

'The disgraced pseudo-musician Opiskin,' said Karamzin. 'He did not have a son. *Fool*,' he added.

'I don't believe all this,' said Paul. 'I *won't* believe it. Where would he get the money from?'

'No,' said Zverkov, 'you do not wish to believe it. You wish to believe you are doing some big noble

Western deed, like your Don Quixote and Sancho Panza. But you have let a murderer loose in the Western world.'

'He will be caught,' promised Karamzin. 'Here. Today.' He suddenly and most artificially leered amicably at Paul. 'Let us go together to the W.C.' he offered.

'Ah no,' said Paul, 'I'm not such a fool. Knock me unconscious and take me home as one of your drunken friends. Nothing doing.'

'The money,' said Zverkov, 'would come from the people who have used him. He is a link perhaps. There is much we could find out from him. He knows many names. He is stupid but cunning.' He swigged some beer. 'Some crimes are hard to prove. It is not always possible to find witnesses. But he has certainly,' he said, with a sort of gloomy pride, 'gone through most of the really vicious crimes, living on his wits, as you would say. And there was a suspected case of rape also.'

'I just can't,' said Paul. 'What I mean is——'

'What you mean is,' said Zverkov, 'that you thought you were being a hero. You thought you were rescuing some persecuted innocent person from a cruel tyranny.' He shook his head. 'Believe me, there are very few cases of really innocent people wanting to leave the Soviet Union. What can they want outside it that they cannot find inside?'

'Freedom,' said Paul.

'Freedom,' sneered Karamzin. 'Freedom for stupid football people to interfere with the law. *Vol'nost*,' he repeated, with a heavier sneer.

'What happened when we left?' asked Paul.

'What *could* happen?' said Zverkov. 'They said it was all a game. Besides, we did not want anything to happen. There is the question of *face*.'

'Ah, the Oriental coming out,' said Paul.

'They were lucky,' growled Karamzin, 'we were not armed.'

'So,' mused Zverkov, 'we still have not met your wife. We still do not know where she is.'

'You can take it,' said Paul, 'that I haven't got one. It's easier that way.' His ear had been intrigued for some minutes now by a new kind of music singing from the shop near by. It sounded familiar. But it was not Opiskin; it was certainly not Opiskin.

Zverkov was squinting at the shop-signs in Finnish and Swedish. The Roman alphabet reigned here; it seemed to make Zverkov uneasy, an outsider, one whose family had never belonged to the greatest club of all time, the Roman Empire, and it was too late now. 'A strange language,' he said. 'Finnish. A sentence has always stayed in my mind, and I do not know who taught it me or why I should wish to remember it. *Talvi on tullut pitkine öinensä*. That means, "The winter has come with its long nights."'

Paul shivered. 'The winter's a long way off.'

'For your little countries,' said Zverkov, 'no. Finland and Sweden and Denmark and this gambling country where a film actress is queen and your own country too. Dark dark dark. You will have to seek the sun and you will find only with us or with the other people across the Atlantic the heat and light you need to go on living. The big countries, the modern states. Soon it will just be one state.'

Paul recognized the music. It was the last movement of the Fifth Symphony of Sibelius. He suddenly felt drunkenly confident: the Finnish bottled ale was not so mild after all. 'You've sent me away nearly naked,' he said. 'Toothless, wifeless—ah, never mind. I don't even know what I am any more—sexually, I mean. Still, Shakespeare's sexual orientation is far from clear. And then there was Socrates. I'm going back to an

255

antique-shop, but somebody's got to conserve the good of the past, before your Americanism and America's Russianism make plastic of the world. There's a lot of summer in front of me yet. Listen to that music of a little country.' The movement had arrived at the re-capitulation of the swinging heavy horn-figure in thirds, a noble tune singing over it. 'You'll learn about freedom from us yet,' he said, and felt a doubt as soon as he'd said it.

'Freedom,' sneered Karamzin.

'Freedom,' mused Zverkov. 'Whatever it is.'

The movement came to an end: sharp chords for the entire orchestra set in wide spaces of silence. 'Whatever it is,' agreed Paul.